PRAISE FOR *FIEBRE TROPICAL*

"Inventive and heady mixture of Spanish and English."
—*WHITE REVIEW*

"*Fiebre Tropical* is a story of migration, queerness, brokenness, and love. Juliana Delgado Lopera has written a novel across borders that buzzes with verve, fierceness, and raw emotion. She forks her tongue for this book, weaving English and Spanish in inspired and irreverent prose. This book is absolute music to my ears."
—INGRID ROJAS CONTRERAS, author of
Fruit of the Drunken Tree: A Novel

"¡Ay Dios mío! This book's got tumbao. With energetic prose and a sharp sense of humor, Delgado Lopera brings us a queer coming-of-age tale that explores diasporic identity from Bogotá to Miami, and the complicated ways that religious fervor impacts same-sex desire and one's relationship to community. Delgado Lopera's eye for detail is fierce, and this novel is easy to devour."
—JOSEPH CASSARA, author of
The House of Impossible Beauties: A Novel

"Lit by neon Miami sunsets and the hot glow of the Christian apocalypse, *Fiebre Tropical* is a literary explosion filled with sweaty Jesus-crazed teens, fainting church-goers, powerful melodramatic mothers, and drunken grandmothers. In a rollicking, multilingual prose both wise and irreverent, brimming with snark and queer humor, Juliana Delgado Lopera crafts a coming-of-age tale, a coming-out tale, a migration tale we've never read and badly need."

—MICHELLE TEA, author of
Against Memoir: Complaints, Confessions & Criticisms

"When you drive around town, when you stare out the window, when you wake up in the middle of the night, whether you know it or not, you are waiting for a book like this. *Fiebre Tropical* is a triumph, and we're all triumphant in its presence."

—DANIEL HANDLER, author of
Bottle Grove: A Novel

"Delgado Lopera's riveting new book is propelled as much by its hurricane-force language as by its unforgettable characters: storm-tossed women making the best of their new lives in a new country. This queer coming-of-age novel explores first love, but it also looks at the myriad ways humans find solace and connection."

—CAROLINE PAUL, author of
You Are Mighty: A Guide to Changing the World

"*Fiebre Tropical* is a magnificent novel, by turns electric, hilarious, sexy, thrilling, wrenching, and profound. Pa' decirlo clarito: Juliana Delgado Lopera is a writer of explosive talent, and this book is a fierce and radiant contribution to queer literature, Latinx literature, and immigrant literature, yes, but also to literature, punto."

> —CAROLINA DE ROBERTIS, author of
> *Cantoras: A Novel*

"Breathless, hungry, funny, fun—the new immigrant novel in a knowing, see-all Colombian lesbian voice. Juliana Delgado Lopera does for American literature what Philip Roth did a half century ago: wakes it up! Sacrilegious in the best way, loving, this novel is much needed and alive."

> —SARAH SCHULMAN, author of
> *Conflict Is Not Abuse: Overstating Harm,*
> *Community Responsibility, and the Duty of Repair*

"Gorgeously written, tragic and hilarious by turns, *Fiebre Tropical* is the tale of a teenager from Bogotá coming to the United States and coming of age. But more than that, it's about a crumbling family of matriarchs gone crazy for religion, and the soul-saving, soul-crushing power of first love. Delgado Lopera's voice prickles with tears, outrage, and sharp details that make us believe in her characters, and more importantly, to believe in their survival."

> —ANNALEE NEWITZ, author of
> *Autonomous: A Novel*

FIEBRE TROPICAL

A NOVEL BY
JULIANA DELGADO LOPERA

THE FEMINIST PRESS
AT THE CITY UNIVERSITY OF NEW YORK
NEW YORK CITY

Published in 2020 by the Feminist Press
at the City University of New York
The Graduate Center
365 Fifth Avenue, Suite 5406
New York, NY 10016

feministpress.org

First Feminist Press edition 2020

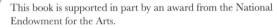 This book is supported in part by an award from the National
ART WORKS. Endowment for the Arts.

 Council on
the Arts
This book was made possible thanks to a grant from
the New York State Council on the Arts with the
support of Governor Andrew M. Cuomo and the
New York State Legislature.

First printing March 2020

Cover and text design by Drew Stevens

Library of Congress Cataloging-in-Publication Data
Names: Delgado Lopera, Juliana, author.
Title: Fiebre tropical / Juliana Delgado Lopera.
Description: First Feminist Press edition. | New York, NY : Feminist Press,
    2020. | Novel in Spanglish.
Identifiers: LCCN 2019018314 (print) | LCCN 2019019024 (ebook) | ISBN
    9781936932764 (E-book) | ISBN 9781936932757 (pbk.)
Subjects: | GSAFD: Love stories.
Classification: LCC PS3604.E44395 (ebook) | LCC PS3604.E44395 F54 2020
    (print) | DDC 813/.6--dc23
LC record available at https://lccn.loc.gov/2019018314

PRINTED IN THE UNITED STATES OF AMERICA

For my mom

CHAPTER UNO

Buenos días, mi reina. Immigrant criolla here reporting desde los Mayamis from our ant-infested townhouse. The broken air conditioner above the TV, the flowery couch, La Tata half-drunk directing me in this holy radionovela brought to you by Female Sadness Incorporated. That morning as we unpacked the last of our bags, we'd found Tata's old radio. So the two of us practiced our latest melodrama in the living room while on the TV Don Francisco saluted *el pueblo de Miami ¡damas y caballeros!* and Tata—at her age!—to Mami's exasperation and my delight, went girl crazy over his manly voice.

Y como quien no quiere la cosa, Mami angrily turned off the stove, where La Tata had left the bacalao frying unattended, then Lysol-sprayed the countertops, smashing the dark trail of ants hustling some pancito for their colony behind the fridge. Girlfriend was pissed. She hadn't come to the U S of A to kill ants and smell like puto pescado, and how lovely would it have been if the housekeeper could have joined us on the plane? Then Mami could leave her to the household duties and concentrate on the execution of this Migration Project. Pero, ¿aló? Is she the only person awake en esta berraca casa?

On the TV, another commercial for *Inglés sin Barreras* and Lucía, La Tata, and I chuckled at the white people teaching brown people how to say, Hello My Name Is. Hello, I am going to the store. Hello, what is this swamp please come rescue us. It was April and hot. Not that the heat dissipated in June or July or August or September or even November, for that matter. The heat, I would come to learn the hard way, is a constant in Miami. El calorcito didn't get the impermanence memo, didn't understand how change works. The heat is a stubborn bitch breathing its humid mouth on your every pore, reminding you this hell is inescapable, and in another language.

We'd been here for a month, newly arrived, still saladitas, and I already wanted to go back home to Colombia, return to my panela land, its mountains, and that constant anxiety that comes just from living in Bogotá. That anxiety that I nonetheless understood better than this new terrifying one. But Mami explained to me over and over again with a smirk that, look around you, Francisca, *this* is your home now.

Our to-do list that doomed Saturday of the ants and the bacalao included helping Mami with the preparations for the celebration of the death, or the baptism or the rebirth or the something, of her miscarried dead baby, Sebastián. It has been argued—by the only people who care to argue: La Tata and her hermanas—that my dead brother's baptism was the most exciting event in the Martínez Juan family that year. This mainly because La Tata drank half a bottle of rum a day, couldn't tell Monday from Friday, so obviously a fake baby's baptism at a pastor's pool was more important to her than, say, the fact that by the end of that month my younger sister, Lucía, was regularly waking in the middle of the night to pray over me. Or the fact that I would eventually remember this time, the first months after our arrival, as Mami's most sane, grounded moment.

Pero we're getting ahead of ourselves, cachaco. Primero la primaria.

We'd been prepping for the baptism celebration even before departing from our apartment on the third floor down in Bogotá. Inside the six Samsonite bags that Mami, Lucía, and Yours Truly were allowed to bring into this new! exciting! think-of-it-as-moving-up-the-social-ladder! life were black-and-gold tablecloths, handcrafted invitations, and other various baptism paraphernalia. There wasn't enough space for the box of letters from my friends or our photo albums, but we nonetheless packed two jars of holy water (instead of my collection of CDs—The Cure, The Velvet Underground, The Ramones, Salserín) blessed three days before by our neighborhood priest, water that was confiscated for hours by customs (*You don't think we got water in the States?*) then quickly flushed down the toilet by Tía Milagros, who now, soaking in Jesús's Evangelical Christian blessing, believed, like the rest of the Miami matriarchy, that Catholic priests were a bunch of degenerados, buenos para nada. Catholicism is a fake *and* boring religion. Christianity is the true exciting path to a blessed life in the name of Jesucristo nuestro Señor, ¿okey?

Now Mami hustled her bare butt around the dining room, head tilted hugging the telephone, wearing only shorts and a push-up bra, fanning herself with a thick envelope from the stack of unopened bills. Anxiously phoning the Pastores, the incompetent flower people (*Colombianos tenían que ser*), the two lloronas in black—Tía Milagros's idea—who would professionally mourn Sebastián while charging Mami fifteen dollars an hour.

Miami wanted a dead baby's baptism, motherfucker, and Mami was gonna *give it*.

Homegirl didn't see anything wrong with chipping away—I would find out later—at our life savings by buying tears and feeding the congregation.

Pero—óyeme—you couldn't fight her.

Esa plática ya se había perdido. Esta costeña estaba montada en el bus already. Mami never got a break. Never stopped to smell the flowers. Cómo se te ocurre. From the moment we arrived, Myriam del Socorro Juan was on her crazed trip to *get shit done*. We were handed to-do lists; we were yelled at, directed; we were told what to do every single step of the way.

We were obedient. What else could we do? Where else could we go?

The outskirts of Miami are dead land. It is lago sucio after dirty lake with highways and billboards advertising diet pills and breast implants. With almost nonexistent public transportation, no sidewalks, but a glorious Walmart and a Publix Sabor where a herd of colombianos, who came all the way from their land, buy frozen arepas and microwavable Goya plantains. Lucía wasn't complaining. La Tata barely had strength to fight Mami. The surrounding swamp collaborated with Mami to make every single day excruciating.

Pero, mi reina, siéntate pa'trás—we're only getting started.

For the last month, we'd been pushed around from this church service to that church dinner to that church barbecue. Meeting this hermano, that hermana, and that very important youth leader. We'd listened to our tías spill all the church tea over and over again during lunch and dinner. Even during onces they wouldn't shut up. Everyone arguing over who was a true Christian and who was just calentando silla. I quickly figured out that there's a lot to being an aleluya daughter of Jesucristo and that attending church on Sundays was just the tiniest tip of the faith iceberg.

My dead brother's baptism was part of the iceberg. Dead babies need to be baptized, mourned, and named so their souls don't linger, so they too join the fiesta celestial. This was part of La Pastora's explanation, and Mami just nodded with her hand on her chest saying, Ay sí, el dolor es tan grande.

Now La Tata and I eyed each other as we watched Mami's frenzied torbellino around the living room. Mami going on and on about all the items on the to-do list that we still hadn't done or didn't do the way she wanted. Tata and I wanted to hold Mami's hand, tell her, *Ya ya, Mami. Come on now, Myriam, carajo, deja el berrinche.* We wanted to slap her a little because we still believed that underneath this new layer of holiness there was the pious Catholic neurotic we'd known so well. Tata and I had some serious eye-to-eye magical power going on. I knew she needed a rum refill when her left eye went *Give me a break*, and she knew I was this close to slapping Mami when my eyes went *Buddha shut*. After signing the divorce papers, Mami had rolled around for three days with the same crazed energy she had now, painting our entire apartment in Bogotá a tacky red then crying because her house resembled a traqueto's wife's. And when that wasn't sufficient to kill her mojo, this cartagenera costeñita de Dios bleached Lucía's and my hair with hydrogen peroxide because na-ah! no hombre is going to ruin Mami's life, not even your father. In those moments she was too gone inside herself, too deep in her darkness. Glassy-eyed, pale, making endless to-do lists, and yet her hair was always blow-dried, impeccable.

Y ahora there was no man but a dead baby who needed to be baptized inmediatamente. Y ahora Lucía helping Mami with the final touches on the cake: the black-and-gold icing underneath the Jesús in the plastic cradle retrieved from the pesebre box. Tata frying the bacalao in the kitchen, yelling at no one (but of course at Mami) that pero claro, Myriam doesn't have any birthing hips no wonder she lost a baby. If she heard her, Mami se hizo la loca. If she heard her, Mami did her usual deep breathing, deep sighing, did not bother with Tata.

Then Lucía sat next to me on the couch. Her tiny legs next to mine. The TV still on, but we paid no attention. We sat staring at the ceiling fan, drooling, captivated by its speed; the hum of the blades both terrifying and quieting, drowning out the sound of Mami and La Tata, giving us a break. The possibility of it breaking and cutting us all to shreds. Lucía and I did this often. We never had a ceiling fan in our house in Bogotá, we never needed one. But here we sat side by side in silence staring at it, mesmerized by its movement. I concentrated on the sound, a little motor promising wind. A short relief from the heat. Lucía smiled at me and I felt a sudden rush, wanting to hold her tight, kiss her curls, place my head on her shoulder. Instead I just turned around, closed my eyes, pretended I was somewhere else.

~

Between phone calls Mami gave us The Eye: the ultimate authoritative wide-open flickering of lashes with an almost imperceptible tilt of the head that had us on our feet and running. She did the same thing whenever the nuns sent home a disciplinary letter back in Bogotá, searching for my guilt, and I tried to resist, daring myself to withstand The Eye for as long as I could but always failing. This time, we were too exhausted to resist. We were exhausted from moving our shit around. Exhausted from meeting this youth leader, that former-junkie church woman (*¡La drogadicta encontró al Señor!*); every señora de Dios fixing our hair, squeezing our cheeks, commenting that we were either too skinny, too fat, too pale, or—my very favorite—too Colombian (*Cómo se les nota que acaban de llegar, tan colombianas*).

The "too Colombian" comment offended Mami. Being too Colombian meant it was evident that her hair wasn't blow-dried every other day; our rough edges were showing, o sea, criollas, o sea, Mami didn't even understand ni pío of English and that threw her in the bottomest of the bottoms of the hierarchy. All she could say was, Yes yes cómo no. But I was fifteen, coño, qué carajo too Colombian. I didn't care if I was too Colombian. To me, everyone was too Colombian and that in itself was part of the problem. All I wanted were my girlfriends back home, cigarettes, and a good black eyeliner. None of which Miami was giving me. Instead it gifted you with an infierno that crawled deep into your bones and burned its own fogata there. A surreal heat that veiled everything, like looking through gas, all of it a mirage that never dissipated. A stove burning from within. I didn't want to admit it to myself or anyone but I was pure Soledad Realness, pure loneliness eating at my core. Dándome duro. Did living with La Tata help? Did living close to Milagros and my other tías and primos and the freaking Pastores and that señora from the congregation who always brought us arepas and called me La Viuda (*Toda negro siempre, Francisquita, como La Viuda*) on Sundays? Did this aid the transition in any way?

Falso.

It made it worse. Their enthusiasm was unbearable.

Because this wasn't a Choose Your Own Migration multiple-choice adventure with (a), (b), and (c) laid out at the end of each page and you could simply choose (b) Stay in Bogotá, you idiot. Cachaco, please. This was militant Mamá Colombiana popping Zoloft, begging your daddy to sign papers, then finger-waving at you to pack your bags while she sold your remaining books, CDs, the porcelain dolls nobody wanted; as she donated your Catholic school uniform (that you hated, but still), locked herself for hours inside the bathroom with the phone and a calculator and then emerged puffy eyed informing Lucía and your sorry ass that ni por el chiras, you were not leaving in six months but next week because Milagros got Mami a job (that never materialized), and then *boom boom boom* some Cuban guy speaking condescending English stamped your passport, shot Mami a smirk-smirk for those boobs—he literally said *boobs*—and when she asked you to translate you simply said, Ay Mami, pero you didn't know people speak English in the U S of A?

Óyeme, la cosa no termina ahí.

Porque what did we really know about migration, mi reina?

I knew nada before forever jumping across the Caribbean charco. You kidding? This homegirl lived in the same apartment on 135th Street, next to the same tiny green patch that passed for a park, next to the chapel where I got fingered by two boyfriends; the same Cafam supermarket, the same corner store where Doña Marta sold me cigarettes religiously under the same excruciating smoggy Bogotá clouds. Complaining about traffic every single day for the entirety of my fifteen years. We were so anchored in Bogotá, so used to our homogeneity, that the girl in school from Barranquilla—the only girl in school from outside the city—was an exotic commodity. The girls at school made fun of her ñera ways, the way her mouth ate all the vowels as if only for our amusement. And although Mami is originally from Cartagena, she moved to La Capital when she was sixteen, losing her costeña accent. We only traveled to the Cartagena coast on vacation once a year, which in itself was the Event of the Year (planned for months) and caused enough commotion to last until our next visit: ¡Las maletas! ¡El pancito for your tía from that special panadería! ¡El sunblock! etc. New haircut, blow-dried hair, and new (awful, hated forever) sunflower dress with matching gold communion studs worn to impress the epicenter of the matriarchy.

Every trip felt so painful because Mami didn't (and still doesn't) like change. She likes to stay put and, if possible, very still so nothing moves. Anything new sends her on a roller coaster of anxiety that she, por supuesto, denies and hides very well. She's obsessed with routines and systems, lists and crossing things out with a red pen when they get done. The day we left Bogotá the stress casi se la comió, a rash of tiny red bumps grew on her back and she didn't stop scratching until the señorita flight attendant said, Welcome to Miami.

~

A few days before the baptism, Mami arrived with a huge yellow dress for me. Yellow is such an ugly color. Plus I hated dresses. Mami knew I hated yellow—and red and orange and all warm colors. You know what was yellow? My Catholic school uniform. Freaking pollito yellow with orange stripes and a green sweater embroidered with the initials of the school and a tiny brown cross. The nuns made sure there wasn't the slightest possibility of prov-ocation or desire that could awaken the evils of boy temptation, which only existed outside of school, while we respectable teenagers—an endangered species—were protected by the tackiest most unfashionable pieces of clothing ever invented. As if someone's barf had become the color palette of choice. Men didn't piss on us to mark territory, we had the nuns to thank for that. And now here it was, that dreaded color popping up in my life again in the form of a baptism dress inside a Ross bag coming to me via Mami's exhausted joy.

Le dije, Mami ni muerta am I wearing that dress—

She stopped me halfway and said, You haven't even looked at it closely. It is so bello, ¿verdad, Lucía? Look how bello y en descuento. You haven't tried it on, nena. Try it on, ven pa' acá.

Ay Mami. In my heart I knew the dissonance my body felt every time I wore a dress, a kind of stickiness. But Mami's face is Mami's face, so I nonetheless removed my black shirt, my shorts, and right there in the living room, surrounded by all the porcelain bailarinas and their broken pinkies, I became once more a sad yellowing sunshine. I looked like a lost kid at a parade. Yellow dress, dirty white Converse.

Mami first said, Francisca, why aren't you wearing a bra? Horrible se ve eso. Followed by, Who taught you not to wear a bra? And then, Ay pero mírala, how pretty. Your grandma can fix the sides but it fits you perfectly.

Tata and Mami discussed the alterations on the dresses. Mami bought a pink one for Lucía and a black mermaid one for herself, a gorgeous piece, but with tiny holes around the neck pointing at its 50 percent discount. It is true that Tata and Mami shared an unimaginable love for Jesucristo, but it is *also* true that their deepest connection was the sale racks at Ross, the coupons at Walmart, and the impossible variety of pendejadas para el hogar at the dollar store. And, reinita, don't even get me started on

Sedano's. The discounted world of chain stores a sudden miraculous revelation. The world may be coming to an end but at least there was nada nadita nada you couldn't get for under five dollars *if* you looked hard enough, *if* you knew where to go, on what dates, and what coupons to bring. Mami and Tata memorized the entire sales calendars of all their favorite stores, and once a week out they went in Milagros's borrowed van to do the family's shopping, which brought us stale bread, rice with tiny squirmy friends, and pompous dresses from Ross with holes around the armpits.

Tata will fix those was Mami's answer as I stared into my dotted armpits. She dismissed my concerns, treating the needle-and-thread process as her own personal designer moment; as if the holes were not there because part of the dress had literally been eaten by moths but because it was an unfinished masterpiece waiting to be completed by Mami's unique fashion vision.

Parezco un cake, I said.

She chuckled. You look bella, like you used to when Tata sewed your dresses, remember?

I didn't say anything because it was *pointless* to fight her over this, plus as much as Mami angered me back then, there was also that face of hers suddenly brightened by the baptism. Still, I stood in the living room—as Tata took measurements, placed pins in the dress—staring at the horizonte in front of me with the martyr look I'd learned from my tías: my eyes looking to the side slightly, as if about to cry but holding it all inside; it was Virgen María's suffering meets Daniela Romo's anger meets a Zoloft commercial. A pose that I will use over and over again

throughout my life. A pose passed down through the generations of Female Sadness stacked inside my bones, all
the way back to Tata's mother's mother. A pose that says:
I'm here suffering pero no no no I do not want your help;
I want you to stand there and watch me suffer—witness
what you have done—and let me suffer silently, with my
discount glam.

~

Outside, the sky in all its fury released buckets of water
that swayed with the palm trees. El cielo gris, oscuro. Talk
about goth. Right at noon the sky transformed itself from
orange light to chunky black clouds that gave zero fucks
about your beach plans or the three hours you spent
ironing that hair, splaying all its sadness right in front
of you. Washing you with its darkness. Right before the
rain the humidity intensified, the soil-smell mixed with
garbage-smell almost unbearable. Sweat a constant, all
the way to my butthole. Dampened skin, fishlike. Water
came from all places: the ocean, the sky, the puddles,
our armpits, our hands, our asses. Our eyes. Lluvia tropical is nature's violence. And here it was a lluvia tropical on acid, a fiebre tropical. Tropical fever for days.
Nature soltándose las trenzas, drowning the ground so
that by the evening, when the rain subsided, the land had
turned into a puzzle of tiny rivers, small ponds where
worms and frogs alike built homes and where Mami's
feet and pantyhose sadly met their demise several times.
More than once she arrived at the door mojadita de
arriba abajo, not wanting any help but just yelling at

me, por favor por favor, to look at her feet and remove any animalitos.

¡Tengo bichos por todas partes! she'd say, disgusted. And I would try to help even though she said she didn't need any, but of course I'd remove the worms and beetles stuck to her pantyhose; I'd bring a towel, dry her hair, comb and braid it. All the while she kept saying she didn't need anything.

What I need right now is for you to look at this sorpresa I found, said Mami toda happy, all the attention on the larger-than-life Ross bag.

Out of the bag she pulled a naked baby doll with blue eyes and a swirl of plastic black hair. A beat-up Cabbage Patch Kid like the ones I begged for when I was younger, but this baby had seen some truly rough days: the cheeks shadowed with dirt, the left eye missing part of its blue, the skin a worn light brown.

Pero this was only the beginning, cachaco.

Then came the tiny set of little boys' clothes: pants, shirt, even a black tie.

Why ask her? Why ask her when you already knew the answer? Nevertheless there was an urgency inside me to have this crazy Jesucristo roller-coaster ride echoed back at me so that I knew I wasn't losing my shit. So that I didn't doubt my own reality. *This is happening, right? Mami* is *laying out a doll's outfit on the couch, she* is *tying her hair back with a scrunchie, she* is *fanning herself with the receipts, she* is *ignoring me when I ask the following question:* Mami, what is all of this?

Either homegirl didn't hear me or she was too enveloped by the muñeco now trying on his new baptismal couture. She placed the doll on her lap and, with great care, dressed the piece of plastic with the tiny pants, the tiny shirt, and the tiny black tie. The gender of the doll was questionable—equal amounts of blue and pink—and my insides chuckled thinking Mami was dressing a girl doll in boy drag. So much for that beloved son! I questioned his gender out loud, but she didn't care. She could have been dressing a giraffe—it was her lost baby and she loved him.

¡Encontré a Sebastián! she announced with such enthusiasm.

Who would have thought my dead baby brother would come back to us via discarded toys in the sale section at Ross. Who would have thought he would come back at all.

Doesn't he look like he belongs to the family? She laughed. Then, sensing the silence, continued, A little rough, yo sé, but nothing a few damp pañitos can't fix.

She had a point. The only big difference was most people in the family had a heartbeat.

It was then my turn to nurse the fake baby, carry him in my arms. You know, I used to love my dolls when I was a peladita. In my own way. I chopped their hair, drew trees and clouds on their bodies. I searched incessantly for their genitals. My Barbies would sit around drinking cafecito waiting for the one Ken Man to show up and whisk them away, but Ken Man would take so long the girls would inevitably get bored, get hungry, and eat each other's hair, sometimes their limbs; sometimes they drew tattoos on their bodies, other times the Barbies fucked their golden retrievers. My Barbies' children consisted of Legos, pencils, and a little squirmy hamster by the name of Maurito. No human children allowed for my girls.

Take the baby! Mami handed it to me. Take it, carajo, que no muerde.

I grabbed the doll by its head, a little disgusted by the thing. But Mami wasn't having it.

¿Es mucho pedir? she said. Too much to ask that you not handle him like he's trash?

I wanted to say, *But he is trash.*

Instead, I angrily hugged him tight while Mami continued explaining that of course he's not a real baby, Francisca, ¿sabes? He is a symbolic bebé, ¿sí? Like Jesús is not *really* in our hearts? It is a *metaphor.*

She kept talking about the flesh-and-bone baby. Said something about his soul, his eyes, something about the dress for the baptism, but I wasn't listening. I heard the Venecos blasting music outside, Lucía blasting Salvation upstairs, and the rumbling of the air conditioner trying as hard as it could to not let us die in the heat. Then I remembered Mami's white scar. The squiggly milky river dividing her lower belly that I traced with my finger when I was a kid. The one exposed right now cause she's heated, almost en cuera; the one she pointed to every time we needed a reminder of all she'd done for us. They chopped me up, she'd say, this one is *you.*

Standing below the ceiling fan, I locked eyes with Tata, who winked at me and mouthed, Tenle paciencia a tu mami, then patted my hand so I would refill her rum.

Before I could say anything Mami turned to me.

Are you listening?

(I wasn't.)

Obvio que sí, Mami. I'm right here, I told her, holding Tata's hand.

Women in my family possessed a sixth sense, not necessarily from being mothers, but from the close policing of our sadness: your tristeza wasn't yours, it was part of the larger collective Female Sadness jar to which we all contributed. Your tías could sense your tristeza even before you sensed your tristeza. As if the arrival of sadness shed a specific smell only detectable by the leonas; the older the leona the more masterful, the quicker she detected your soul stinking up the place. They pointed at your sadness to make theirs more secretive and therefore grander. Epic. Yes yes, you're sad, Francisca, but how about your tía Milagros working twelve hours under the sun? How about your mami losing a baby? Losing your father? How about that? I have countless teenage memories in which my sad emo adolescent body didn't even get a chance to relish in its tears, to soak in the obliqueness of a dark life, because there was always a tía yelling from the couch as I stepped into the living room: Ay pero here she comes with that face. Ay pero si acá no ha pasado nada.

Rapidito. Faster than they could sense their hairs curling up before the rain.

Inevitably now, Mami turned to me and said, Ay pero what's with the face? Cualquiera diría that you're having a bad time. But you're not, nena, so brighten up. Deja la pendejada.

CHAPTER DOS

La Tata was obsessed with Don Francisco.

Sábado gigante was Jesús before Jesús was Jesús. Even before moving to Miami, homegirl watched him religiously every Saturday, mumbling amorcitos from her rocking chair to the television. Back in Colombia, Tata had visions where she stepped onto Don Francisco's set in a glorious dress, spun the magic wheel, and won a car. Or a kitchen set. Or a vacation for two. She'd hold my hand and say, Ay mimi, ¿te imaginas? You and I en el Disney World. Once in Miami, she called the 1-800 number several times leaving detailed messages: Sí, niña, Alba. That is A-L-B-A, sí, *Alba*. Can you tell him to call me back? It's important. In Miami the galán dream was close; so close was Tata to having that Chilean-born papi read her name tag, call her from the audience holding out his arm for her, *Alba is la ganadora!* Above everything she wanted to be the winner. Of what? Of that moment of recognition, of that spotlight. Of Don Francisco landing a faint kiss on her cheek. Tata would sit in the first row with the rest of the Cuban señoras, but she'd be his favorite. The one with the special juju. She would have hung the photograph of Don Francisco with his arm around her next to her Blessed Woman of the Year certificate from church. If the never-aging papi called, she would wear the dark green dress and the only gold earrings she still owned; she'd walk down the steps like she once did at the Club Unión in Cartagena, sending kisses this way, kisses that way, but this time she would mean it. Pero niña, did Mr. Tumbalocas call?

Y ahí estábamos: on the couch watching some señora hold Don Francisco's hand and win Tata's kitchen set.

Mírala, Tata said, she doesn't even know how to spin the wheel.

Mami didn't understand how Tata praised Jesucristo all day then watched that low-class crap where fake Cuban blonds with huge cleavage danced around El Chacal (now, damas y caballeros, if you don't know who El Chacal is, I dare you to google it) and gifted people slimy kisses, kitchen knives, and trips to Kissimmee, and wasn't Tata supposed to be working on the arroz con coco? Didn't Tata under-stand that the baptism was happening soon and Mami's hair needed two days of work and nobody—and I mean nobody—was helping her? And WHY HASN'T ANYONE CHECKED THEIR TO-DO LIST?

Take it in: there are three baptism to-do lists. Tata used hers as a coaster. The other two were posted on the fridge, each of our names double underlined, LUCÍA and FRANCISCA. Not even Lucía finished her endless list, which included stuff like Baptism Playlist, Baby Crosses from the dollar store, and Cleaning Sebastián's Face con el Lysol. All with a huge ¡OJO! scribbled on each side, little eyes with eyelashes filling in both of the Os.

We let Mami rant. I sat on the couch behind Tata popping blackheads on her back. She paid me twenty-five cents a pop, money that never materialized, but I nonetheless sat every time she asked because I loved squishing her back fat. I was the special chosen kid who got to squish my tata's skin and liberate her from the horrors of blackheads and pus. If she was tipsy enough, she'd let me draw on her back with a black pen. And I always did. Once, back in Colombia, as she undressed for a medical checkup, the doctor gasped in horror at the drawings of headless zombie women eating their babies that I had meticulously traced on Tata's back. Nurses were instructed to clean her immediately before the traumatized doctor could continue checking Tata's heart.

Mami was still on the phone negotiating something or other.

La Tata moved around, pulling at her dress, getting her round and wide costeña ass comfortable on the sofa.

Pájaros tirándoles a las escopetas, Tata finally said. Habrase visto tanta huevonada. Those people, she continued to Mami, are Jesús's hijos too, ¿okey? And the arroz con coco will get done whenever the arroz con coco gets done.

A una ni la dejan—she wouldn't drop it—I can't even watch Don Francisco in peace, no joda.

Of course Mami wouldn't let it alone.

Pero Mamá, Mami continued, this is blasphemy. Do you think this is proper Christian behavior? Don't you remember what the Pastora said last week about those who deviate from the Savior's path? And where in the Biblia is that passage? Show it to me porque Jesús did not die on the cross so half-naked women could dance around that man. Ese show es tan vulgar.

What Mami really meant was that she was anxious, she was tired, and here we were watching girls in glittery short dresses hold balloons and yell on TV.

Tata responded the best way she knew how: a sigh so loud it sent waves around all of South Florida. A shutting of the eyes so intense and precise. Then homegirl rearranged her ass against the couch so that it creaked and shrieked, let the couch embody all her emotion. Then she sighed again. Louder.

Señoras y señores, you do not know sighing until you've experienced the masterful, polished, revered Colombian Female Sighing. In this family, sighing deeply, sighing loudly, is the biggest and most annoying form of protest. Because it inevitably begs the question: *¿Qué pasó?* Because it comes with the inevitable answer: *Ay nada*. A form of protest that continues questioning itself to eternity for the sole purpose of soaking up all the energy in the room until someone breaks down and tells you their secret.

Tata truly was pissed. She broke the circle of silent protest way too soon.

Yes, Tata finally said, slashing the silence with cuchillo. Jesús died for all of that and more. He was crucified so Sebastián could die and my Francisca could be born.

Por el amor de Dios.

Do I really have to narrate Mami's annoyance at this? Can't you already visualize her peeking at Tata through her glasses, the weight of that disappointed look landing on all of us?

¿Y yo? I turned down the volume, didn't look at either

of them, and just relished the shade that was sure to come. I both hated and loved their fights. They were el pan de cada día, the viscous river of blood that kept that house pumping with life, Jesucristo, and the endless pursuit of a 50 percent discount.

The ceiling fan on high flipped the pages of Mami's color-coded notebook, where the budget, the visa, the church, the baptism were all detailed in bullet points and perfect handwriting. In Mami's hand, also, a yellow high-lighter was used to differentiate between IMPORTANTE and DEMASIADO IMPORTANTE. Whenever she finished her long lists and the bullets did not perfectly align, Mami ripped out the page and started all over again. I've never seen more meticulous, polished, straight-lined, organized handwriting in the history of my life. Mami's handwriting said to the world: *I got my shit together, what do you have?* It was all condescension. I tried to replicate her handwriting many times but mine always said: *I'll never be enough.*

Mami eyed Tata while Tata gathered herself. Mami eyed Tata as Tata walked into the kitchen. Mami eyed Tata as she turned on the stove. Mami eyed Tata, took off her glasses, and then proceeded to compete with Tata's sigh—ay Papi Dios—a perfected sigh that culminated in a somber *ayyyyy*, but this time—this time, mi reina—she left no space for anyone to reply. This sigh ended all other sighs. Right then the phone rang again, Mami picked it up and in her most joyous voice told Tía Milagros that of course she could bring two more guests. Cómo no, Mila-gros, claro que sí, ni más faltaba.

Tata banged pots and pans. She threw the coconut against the floor, then asked me to pick it up. Homegirl continued to mumble as she usually did, and if you asked her what she was mumbling about she'd say, Acá no más asking my husband Jesucristo to give me fuerza.

Mami knew the joy Don Francisco brought to Tata. But if stubborn has a name, if stubborn has a face, it is Myriam del Socorro Juan with a notebook and an array of Davivienda pens. Plus this was Mami's house: Mami earned head-bitch status and thus demanded that everyone sacrifice their lives for the cause. The migration cause. The baptism cause.

The story? Sebastián was Mami's first baby, the one and only boy, never born to bloom into a muchacho. Whenever she retells the Horrible Miscarriage Story, thick lines appear on her forehead, she stops every other sentence to catch her breath. Her voice recedes.

Back then our cartagenera was only twenty-one years old with a three-month criollito growing eyes and legs inside her belly. That's what she says now (*Ay mi bebé*). The criollito didn't last. El pobre. A pool of blood in Mami's underwear and a trip to the hospital all because she tried to lift a kid at Unicentro. The irony (she doesn't see it). Before she was Born Again in the Name of Cristo Jesús, the Horrible Miscarriage Story ended there with a painful look and a light chuckle when she remembered she didn't wait to be pregnant again. Your father went to work right away (*Lo puse a trabajar*). *After* receiving Cristo Jesús in her heart, the story elaborated on the hospital, the horrible nights of crying, the longing, the speaking with God about her child's soul. The pain. The pain. The pain. Eventually in the story I am born. I was joy, but I wasn't Sebastián. What to do with all the baby-blue clothes?

Now Tata's mumble turned into singing as one of her favorite alabanza songs came on. Súbele mimi, she said, and I turned up the chorus of the Espíritu Santo flying in and out of a blessed mountain. This was Tata's jam. She sipped on her pretend Sprite, banged and chopped the coconut. Every now and then she stopped to take in the entirety of the lyrics and, with eyes closed, yelled, ¡Amén! or ¡Cristo Jesús!

When Tata's aleluya popstar moment came to an abrupt end, Mami retold the Horrible Miscarriage Story so we didn't forget what was really happening here, what was really at stake here. Focus, people! Chop-chop.

Because, Mami informed us, you two don't know el dolor, all the pain I'm going through.

Tata whispered to me, It's been seventeen years! To Mami she said, A ver what else needs to be done?

~

At the Heather Glen Apartment Complex there was no gate, no lights, no tall buildings, not many people on the streets. There was a moldy Jacuzzi and a small pool where dead insects, used condoms, and mutant ducks with red lumps on their beaks congregated and left trails of green poop. The cool colombianos y venezolanos and some of the emo boys also hung out there. Blasting salsa over aguardiente. The loner kids included the weird sad maricón from Argentina and they hung by the lake with all the mosquitoes and frogs. The apartment complex was ten blocks away from Iglesia Cristiana Jesucristo Redentor and six blocks from the Pastores' house. Our townhouse sat facing the dumpster and, beyond it, the lake surrounded by dying palm trees, framed by the crisscrossing highway. From the third floor we witnessed the stunning orange sunsets eating at the sky while families of possums violently dug up their dinner. Sometimes por la mañana I'd wake up to Mami's screams, Dios mío, one or two possums killed that night in a gang fight over scraps of avocado. En Colombia: truchas. En Miami: el animalejo ese. They particularly enjoyed Tata's fried plantains, would crucify each other with their pointy teeth for them. Possums were giant rats that we pretended were not giant rats because this was the U S of A, the Promised Land, where friendly giant Coca-Colas handed you a green card to shop inside a luxurious McDonald's until the end of your days. There were no disgusting animals here. Cómo se te ocurre. Estamos en los Mayamis donde todo es luz, todo brilla, todo tiene descuento. Pa' balancear la cosa, air fresheners suddenly appeared in every outlet of every room in our townhouse, meant to do exactly what Mami loved: conceal the true smell of our lives. Instead, we smelled like an out-of-business candy store. Rotting amid the strawberry vanillas and the Fabuloso. Every time people came to our house Mami asked us to shut our doors so they couldn't look out the south windows into the dumpster or see Tata's room, where letters, notes, and pictures with no frames populated the walls with their clear tape and terrible handwriting. Tata taped up every note that every person at church sent her, and Mami thought it was, ay, so low-class; they fought about it constantly. Por lo menos, Mami argued, at least use a frame, Mamá. Tata didn't care.

Este, Tata said, este es el museo de mi vida.

Mami so impatient con Tata, so impatient con el mundo that wouldn't give her a real house, a real job. So what if Milagros promised her an accounting job at a Colombian newspaper that didn't need any accounting but instead sent Mami to distribute flyers in the suburbs, to rich people's houses at night, where she was thereafter chased by the neighborhood police. The first night, Mami returned giggling like a fifteen-year-old running from home with her machuque, but after a week of this degradación, she wanted nothing to do with the flyer pendejada. Soy una mujer educada, carajo, she'd say with watery eyes. Did the neighborhood police care about Mami's wall-to-wall windowed office in Bogotá? Did they care about the secretary who watered the plants and delivered tintico in the mornings? Cachaco, *please.*

Where was the Miami life we all dreamed about from those Marc Anthony music videos? Where was our South Beach and our Versace and our long shiny hair unbothered by the humidity and our larger-than-life apartment overlooking the playa? Where was that feeling of grandiosity and fullness? Where was that sense of superiority that we'd briefly felt the moment we told everyone in Bogotá we were moving to the United States—uyyy a los Mayamis—and amid the tears, the feeling of reverence? Cachaco, perdío. Nowhere to be seen. Instead, we jammed our life into Tata's townhouse—Tata had sashayed to Miami a year before, joining the Exodus of the Juan Family out of the País de Mierda. She joined my tías when Grandpa was found dead on the toilet. We joined Tata when Mami's heart died one too many times.

La vida es dura, Tata always said. Life is hard, girlfriend.

CHAPTER TRES

Category is: my first time at the evangelical Colombian church inside the Hyatt Hotel. Only the holiest, most respectable panela people walk this category.

It was hot, it was humid, it was time to praise Jesús for the first time.

And there it was—the Holy Trinity at the center of the room snapping fingers and aleluyas a lo que da: El Pastor, La Pastora, and their adopted daughter, Carmen. Women in navy-blue suits showered in fake gold jewelry hurrying up and down the center aisle, directing people to their seats, pulling me to them with their infomercial voices and a *Dios te bendiga, mi niña*. Ujieres—I learned their official title when Mami joined them a few weeks later, ironing her navy suit every Sunday and snapping her fingers at people for not following the seating chart.

There were the men reeking of patchouli, showcasing manly gold necklaces with Jesús fish dangling from them, or their *Got Jesús?* T-shirts. Showcasing chest hair in the name of Cristo Jesús. Exhibiting their new jobs at 7-Eleven, at Walmart, exhibiting their new English words: *Hello! Bye! How are you!* So much enthusiasm for every word in the English language. Every word pronounced in English seemed to lift you in some invisible hierarchy where only the holiest and most versed in this Germanic tongue existed while patronizing the herd of colombianos who were still stuck down there in their *Buenos días sumercé*. English, I would learn, could be a powerful condescending tool.

This was the real church of Jesús, hermana. Straight from Miami, Florida: Iglesia Cristiana Jesucristo Redentor. A stinky room in the Hyatt Hotel nobody cared to vacuum. Because who needs Gothic churches; who needs divine architecture, angels dropping from the sky, a crucified Chuchito bleeding over His decayed muscular six-pack? Who needs a statue of the crying Madonna and Child when God is everywhere, including the windowless back room with the stained mustard carpet that a herd of pious colombianos got weekly—and for a discount— because Fulanito's son worked as a hotel assistant manager there?

THIS IS A REAL CHURCH! GOD IS EVERYWHERE, SISTER!

Back in Colombia during the weekly school mass, whenever I searched for spiritual or moral guidance, the image of the bloody, bearded, and—let's not forget—*hot* Son of God shook me back to my senses: stop kissing the Salserín posters, Francisca, He died for you. And although my religious skepticism started at the age of eleven when I began falling asleep during mass, stealing my tías' cigarettes, and rubbing myself on the edge of the bed, the crown of thorns created a fear so deep I found myself praying unconsciously after each sin.

Ten fear points for the Catholic Church, zero points for the room at the Hyatt.

This would soon change. No creas, mi reina. Acá la cosa se pone brava.

Before I could say, *Uy mamita esta la veo grave*, before I could understand the magnitude of its reach and retrace my steps to forever hide underneath Tía Milagros's van, Mami informed me in a whisper that in an hour Lucía and I would split off from the main congregation to join the youth group. People your age, nena, learning about Dios. Increíble, ¿no? She said this with such enthusiasm, like joining the youth group was an invitation to the best underground club in the world where only the chosen could rave with Jesus. This was exactly how the church saw itself: VIP exclusive and the only true access to the One Above (*¡y ahora en español!*). I should be grateful to witness and partake in such a thriving holy subculture.

Because I'm such a considerate narrator and we're about to enter the peso pesado butthole of Christianity—the forgotten corner where culty blind devotion to Jesucristo meets merengue, bachata, and arroz con pollo—Imma walk you through that first day.

Primero: Like good colombianos, we don't start the day until we've said *Buenos días* and *Que Dios te bendiga, hermano* to *every* motherfucker in the room. You thought the *hola hola* kissing at the Saturday family onces with your tías was already pushing it, but here everyone acts like your tía and they all get shades of lipstick on your cheek to prove it. If said person is part of the Holy Trinity or is a Youth Leader, shekina (more on this later), Lead Ujier, Lead Músico de Dios, lead *anything*, there's a lingering reverence and you should add something like, I felt the power of the Holy Ghost last night and today—¡milagro!—my headache is gone. *Or*, Ay hermana, I keep praying for El Señor to grant me misericordia with this man. To which La Pastora will reply, He is your husband. He works forty hours a week. He is a good man.

Or you can just say, Look at this ugly day. El de Rojo must be lurking around.

Tata called Satanás "El de Rojo" (*Mimi, shut your mouth, no le hagas caso al de Rojo*).

That's points for *you*, hermana, and hopefully down the line those points will add up and you too could grow up to be a leading holy sirvienta de Dios.

The goal here, as I understood that day, is to be the most Christian, the most Chosen, the most Holy. And to be honest, it was a hard call. Everything counts. Everyone has eyes and ears, everyone is watching and hearing. Even the children with their perfectly gelled hair, ironed shirts, and crayons, even *they* will judge you. The next youth leader, the next pastor could be you! The competition is always on and any slight gesture can send you speaking in tongues, eating with the Pastores, or cleaning the bathroom. You decide, hermana.

Segundo, tercero, y cuarto: Let nobody say there ain't no party here. Let nobody say Christians don't know lo que es bueno. Acá se goza. Jesus is in the house, and the Holy Spirit is our DJ supported by an arch of blue balloons framing a rainbow sign in the back reading ARCO IRIS DE AMOR with Juanito on the drums. Give it up for Juanito! I'd never seen Tata shake her wide-ass booty the way she did that sad Sunday morning to the song "Nadie como tú, Señor." Beating the floor with her cane. Raising those arms like I didn't know she could. Osteoporosis be damned. *Tata*, I thought of saying, *¿qué carajo estás haciendo?* But she was so into it. All the songs memorized. Deeply felt. I just sank to the bottom of my chair. I mostly sank to the bottom of whatever container contained me until the moment came to move to another container, and then the process would start itself back up.

But I'm telling you about that first day. About the one-hour-long alabanza in which the church turned into a sea of swaying arms. Of loud prayer and too much amén. Of drums and keyboard and the shekinas bursting into dance, pirouetting for God with tattooed smiles, gold ribbons, and white dresses. Tambourines jangling. Hypnotic music creeping into every part of the service, sending the hardcore devotees fainting and crying. Singing to praise Jesus. Adore Him. Singing to thank Him for all His blessings. Louder, hermana. Bien duro so He hears how much you're willing to live your entire life in His name. Soft Spanish Christian rock. Holy bachata sin tumbao. Nada de moverme la cadera too much.

Music is at the very center of the service. It announces each transition. It sets the mood for the next segment. It is always and forever a Hallmark card spelled out in beats. Predetermined. Nostalgic. Tragic. Poking at that very thing inside your rib cage. When the praying gets intense, the music turns to a slow ballad, the Pastor commands the microphone again, and in a voice that reminds me of an antidepressant commercial, he whispers:

Are you hurting, hermana?
Tell God why you're hurting.
God is here to forgive you.
God is here to take the pain away.
But only if you follow in His footsteps.
If you don't give in to temptation.
Papi Dios doesn't want pieces of your life! He wants your entire
heart, your soul, your mind, and all your strength, hermano.
ARE YOU LISTENING!
(¡Amén!)
ARE YOU LISTENING!
(¡Amén!)
God doesn't want partial commitment, partial obedience, and
crumbs of your time.
He wants your entire devotion. He wants your entire life to serve
and adore Him.
ARE YOU LISTENING!
(¡Amén!)
Do not give God crumbs!
(¡Amén!)
¡El pueblo de Cristo dice!
(¡Amén!)

I sat next to Tata the entire time, overcome by a mix of shame and boredom. Someone had given me a Bible and I held it awkwardly on my lap, leafing through its golden pages, not sure what to do with it. That morning Mami complained about my outfit, sending me back to wash my hair and wear jeans that don't make you look like you don't have a mother, Francisca. Because I do have one and she's reaching for the ceiling, chanting a lo que da.

A woman in front of us held her face in her hands for the entirety of the alabanza, coming up for air from time to time, red-faced, barely able to open her eyes. A man sat with his hand on her back, whispering prayers. She nodded. Her crying came in spurts, soft at first, then following the intensity of the music. Crying, fainting, and screaming was apparently so commonplace, I didn't understand why she, specifically, had personalized prayers. What was so special about her. What happened to her. I tried searching for any evidence of her wrongdoing but only found a small tattoo on her lower back: *EMILIO*. A lover? A dead kid? Tattoos were considered markings of the devil and yet here she was among the repented criollos. Eventually she fainted. Eventually three men carried her out to the améns of the congregation as the Pastor whispered in the microphone that the Lord was with her, in her, cleansing her dirty soul.

The power of God is with us! For those Santo Tomases in here that need proof. You need proof? Here's your proof!

Tata pulled my arm and clapped her hands, trying to get me to join her dance. Mami was already full entregada, arms stretched out like she was waiting for a hug that wouldn't come. How did Mami know all the songs already? I remembered hearing her speak about the church back in Bogotá. I remembered she went to a few church services, leaving us with my father at a McDonald's for hours. Was this what she'd been doing? She may have bought a few Christian CDs. She may have invited a pastor to our house. I can't remember. The last few months in Bogotá were a total blur.

I stood up to watch the men carry out the crying

woman. The woman's head hung to the side like a water balloon, as if it didn't belong to the rest of her body. They laid her on the floor in the back, and then I noticed one of the ujieres, a short woman I later learned was Xiomara, rushing over with bottled alcohol. Ujieres always had fainting kits at their disposal. The women carried the kits, the men stood back to receive and carry any fainting souls. These were their assigned jobs. I know this because as soon as she fainted and I freaked out, the praying man called another one with his finger, called another one with a wink, mouthing a Venga, hermano, ayúdeme. Immediately they got to work. They all knew what to do. The Fainting Team.

The rest of the congregation kept at their singing. Stronger now that someone was winning at the art of being possessed by Jesús. The singing louder, the wailing deeply felt. *¡Aleluya!* here and there for no good reason. Wormy fingers out to get the ceiling fans. Everyone wanted to be noticed by the Pastor, to be called by him and prayed over, but our fainting girl's act was hard to follow.

I felt an awkward embarrassment, an urge to tell everyone to please turn it down a notch. Amazed at the lack of shame in blasting and singing Christian rock while normal gringos peeked in from time to time, entertained by the free Spanish spectacle happening right here at the hotel.

Shame on those who give in to temptation!
Shame on those following Satanás and his dark angels!
¡Arriba Cristo!

People are watching you, I wanted to say. But at that moment, all everyone cared about was proving who was Jesús's Number One Fan.

A part of me knew this couldn't go on forever. The part that had known Mami in her Catholic ways, Mami in her cumbia ways. Mami back in Bogotá vibrating her shoulders in the hallway mirror calling me to dance with her. Calling my father a good-for-nothing. Kicking my father out of the house. Sipping tinto in her large office, delegating like a boss bitch. I'd known a matriarchy rooted in that cultural Colombian Catholicism that said no to Satanás but yes to sin. *El peca y reza empata* or *La puntica no más*. But here we didn't walk on solid ground. This swamp overheated everyone's common sense and now our life goals included durational aleluya singing, fainting, and baptism planning.

What will you say to God when you knock on San Peter's door?
How will you face God, hermana?

Dear God, I started. Come collect your ridiculous children. And bring me a black eyeliner.

Tata pulled my arm so I'd stop staring at the fainted woman and pay attention to the Pastor. No seas grosera, she said, and blew me a kiss.

That's when I noticed the sheer gowns and gold ribbons making their way to the front. Tambourines ringing against thighs, hands. The girl dancers (those were the shekinas) entering through the back. An army of angelic hippies led by one girl waving a gold flag with an enormous gold fish necklace dangling from her neck. Most of them around my age, beaming with a light I couldn't trust. A repulsive shiny aura. Smiling as if they'd just been given a puppy. Each smile the same as the next, as if someone had drawn, cut, and pasted it on each girl before sending them to twirl for Cristo. I felt nauseous watching them dance with such ease. Worse than seeing women faint was witnessing girls my age enjoy themselves in this circo de mala muerte. As the invisible shady bitch perched on my shoulder, I read every single one of them in my head as an airhead—simple, basic, pendeja. Estas pobres estúpidas. As I went through the motions of cutthroat sisterhood, as I spiraled into an abyss of feminine shade, an incredible sadness rigged my stomach, and this time I really felt like puking. I went to the bathroom and delivered my entire breakfast into the toilet. When I came back, they were still at it. The diligence of their faces, their connection to the ceiling above—which I later witnessed at their rehears-als—so solid. They were dead serious about their dance, their love for Jesus. They knew this to be true, you could see it in their faces. I had none of this. What were they feeling that I couldn't feel?

Above us, the ceiling fans whirling with not enough force. Struggling to keep the air circulating. I imagined myself pulled by them. Lifted into the humid air, out of the church, out of the townhouse, and into the glittery sea.

~

The first thing La Pastora said to me was that just by gaz-ing at a passing colombiano she could instantly tell if Jesús resided in that heart or if the colombiano played on the other team, Satanás's team.

And I can tell you want Him in your life, she said to me, kissing my cheek. Cristo te ama, nena, she continued. Your mami here only wants the best for you.

I looked at Mami, who just looked at the Pastora like she was in love with her.

La Pastora was from Barranquilla, as evidenced by her long black hair, tacky yellow highlights, and that toothy grin forever carved on her oval face. A tiny skeletal woman, always perfectly manicured with her makeup on point and an ironed office suit. *Girl*, I wanted to say, *you're running an overheated hole-in-the-wall operation with a bunch of lost people, stop pretending.* Homegirl was not a kind, warm, hospitable costeña but a sharp dictatorial female whose smile was less an invitation than a mandatory law. The most devoted mujer in the entirety of Miami-Dade County (if you asked her, in the world, this one and the next), a real chosen servidora de Cristo whom I disliked from day one. She had this force with Mami and all the women in the family, a hypnotic pull hidden behind that stupid small smile, and a condescending way of saying *Dios te bendiga, Dios te bendiga* every other sentence. Her response to anything was always *Hay que orar en Cristo* and *The Beast is a false prophet waiting at the corner to jump you.*

But I didn't know all of that yet.

What I *did* know was that when the music ended, La Pastora specifically searched for me, grabbed my arms, and demanded I go with her.

You're a special girl, she whispered. Cristo is very happy you're in His house now.

I wondered what Mami had told the Pastora about me and why I was special when I didn't want to be special— not right now in here with her walking me to the back where people jumped up to touch me, introduce themselves, and ask all sorts of questions. My wet hair plastered to my head, my eyes all black eyeliner, my shoes beat-up black Converse. On my hand I'd drawn stars with a blue pen so that I could carry a small cosmos with me. The people I met stared at me like it was evident I hadn't found Cristo yet. My hand with its stars especially got insane attention. Everyone's eyes landed there, then my shoes, then my face. Pointy stars are a thing of the devil, I'd soon learn. Writing on your hands is for criminals and lowlifes. Jesús cleans you inside out. Loving Him comes with a new wardrobe, new hair, new hygiene. More on that later.

Finally I was passed on to Xiomara in her ujier uniform, enormous cleavage and a hand over her mouth in awe because she could not believe I was Myriam's daughter.

¡Mi cielo! I held you when you were *this* big. Look at you now! So skinny and pale. ¿Sí estás comiendo? With all the McDonald's in this country and you looking like that, por Dios.

She proceeded to tell me—like many women in my life had before her—that she'd wiped my butt when I was a baby. And like all of them she asked, You don't remember?

From the back I saw the ocean of black heads sit in unison as the Pastora began the second part of the service. I spotted Mami in the first row, next to the Pastor and his terrible mustache, while Xiomara and her gelled curls escorted me out of the room. I got a glimpse of Lucía already in the adjacent room teaching little kids how to properly color Jesucristo.

You come with me to the youth group, mi cielo, Xiomara continued. Vas a ver que es de lo más fun.

We passed two tables stacked with books, CDs, T-shirts,

etc. All advertising doves, fish, light breaking from the sky. *Jesucristo es mi parcero* and *Jesús's Team*. Another table sold all sorts of Colombian goodies from arepas to Bon Bon Bums to panela to achiras, and at the end I saw flyers with pictures of ajiaco, flyers for Colombian restaurants in the area: La Pequeña Colombia, El Rincón Colombiano, La Tiendita de Sumercé. Christian restaurants, because food tastes better when it's cooked under the blessing of Cristo Jesús. Gente de bien, tú sabe.

Here's a little something for you, mi reina: all these colombianos migrated out of our País de Mierda to the Land of Freedom—in this case, Miami—to better themselves, to flee the Violence or whatever, to seek Peace, or, really, to brag that they're living in the freaking U S of A, and hello credit card, hello car you can't afford, hello hanging out in a room at the Hyatt with the same motherfuckers you ran from. Like they couldn't have done that in Bogotá? Barranquilla? Or Valledupar?

And there it was, all in gold, the Promised Land in full color with a sign duct-taped to the door that read: *Jóvenes en Cristo*. Inside, a group of kids my age stood in a circle, bowed heads, a string of hands. We'd disturbed a moment, clearly. Xiomara whispered something to the lead youth, and I was left there in the middle of the room as ten pairs of eyes landed on me. Nobody did anything. I wanted to disappear, but then an arm pulled me inside the group and everyone launched into prayer. I held a sweaty palm that didn't want to be held by me, but when I tried to break loose it tightened its grip. I looked down at the circle of shoes: all shiny pristine church shoes against a navy-blue carpet. My shoes el patito feo del gang with scribbles from Colombia: *T.Q.M.*, *P.U.T.A.*, tears drawn in black Sharpie. The room stank of mold and coffee. We prayed for what seemed like an eternity. We prayed to be soldiers of Christ, to be brave so we wouldn't fall into the temptations of experimentation. We prayed to rid the world of Satan and evangelize all those poor souls who could not see the Truth. Satan, apparently, was also everywhere in hiding, waiting for the right time to jump your ass with booty calls, loud music, and marijuana.

I didn't understand what we were supposed to be experimenting with in this secluded dump. Each other?

The world offers temporary pleasures, someone continued, that leave us unfulfilled and disappointed, but Jesús gives meaning to our lives. He loves us, fulfills us, and takes special care of the children who follow His word.

When we were done, I introduced myself. Everyone knew the women of my family; I was another addition to the Female Juan list. My family already ranked high among the church devotos, with Tata serving as the assistant lead ujier and Tía Milagros hosting Bible study in her house.

A few of the shekinas were there with their tambourines, wearing flip-flops and glaring at me, annoyed that I was there. Up and down they studied my body as if I had just dropped from the moon. They asked the youth leader in English to let me know I couldn't be wearing the sign of the devil on my hands. Everyone turned to catch the blue pointy stars exploding on my left hand. I had sat that morning on the kitchen counter meticulously tracing line after line, admiring the way my arm quickly morphed into a canvas, a different ecosystem. Decorating my body like I used to back home.

I covered my hand.

But I don't even want to be here, I wanted to say.

Wilson, the youth leader, didn't pay attention to them and asked everyone to give me a warm welcome. The Jesucristo militia proceeded to sing a short, embarrassing song where Jesús hugs and kisses all of His sheep, even those that have veered off from the herd. The black sheep always return, said the song, because in Jesús we find a home.

I was hugged, given high fives, kissed on the cheek more times than I could count. *Dios te bendiga* was the official/unofficial background murmur everywhere I went. We sat on colorful pillows listening to Wilson describe new youth-group outreach efforts in South Beach, at Walmart. Everyone was instructed to bring a friend and share their Life Changing Testimony. One of the bitchy shekinas raised her hand and said—in English again so that I couldn't understand—that probably not everyone knows what a Life Changing Testimony is. And wouldn't Wilson explain to the new people that in order to have a testimony you must have a life in Jesús first?

Don't pay attention to them, the kid next to me whispered. You'll find Jesús soon.

Wilson broke down the next week's activities for everyone. They covered soccer games, Bible study, bowling, rehearsals for the church play, rehearsals for the second church play, snacks to attract people during outreach—

Y aquí se pone buena la cosa.

The door hit the wall with a bang, and then she clumsily proceeded to close it with another bang. When she entered, everyone fell silent. Wilson's face lit up in a shy smile. He stepped back slowly, opening his palms as a way of saying *The stage is all yours.* The lead angelic hippie in that sheer gown with the huge golden fish around her neck like an advertisement for a sad aquarium. She looked different up close, smaller, pimply. With a terrifying energy and a command of the space like she could pull a string and any of these sheep would bow and move. I felt everyone's reverence including the two shady bitches behind me, who transformed into smiley, kind girls the moment Carmen saluted the eleven-person crowd with a *¡DIOS LOS BENDIGA MUCHACHOS!* Barranquillera, morena, waving off Wilson with a flirtatious smile, passing out flyers depicting light exploding from gray clouds and, in bold letters: *CRISTO VENDRÁ, ¿ESTÁ USTED LISTO?*

I wondered when Christ was coming and what was taking Him so long. And if this were all true, would He know that I at least tried?

Okay pelaos, she began, this is how it's going down. I want all you lazy dizque followers of Jesús to get that colita moving or else our Papi Dios is left with nada. ¿Me están oyendo? Tonight, go home and think of that friend in school, that kid with those awful black satanic shirts next to you in English, math, Spanish class. You know who. The kid in desperate need of saving. Bring that godless kid here. Bring that kid before Jesús so that he may feel His power, so he may feel the Espíritu Santo and repent. Are you listening?

¡Amén!

We're bringing the power of the Word to every destitute heart! We're bringing soldiers to our Lord Jesus—are we full clear, pelaos? ¡El pueblo de Cristo dice!

¡Amén!

They all went wild. Cheering, praising the ceiling, speaking in tongues. Girl's a preacher. A hypnotic one. Demanding with no berraco respect that we—that *I*, without knowing her—do exactly as she say. *Okay reinita*, I thought, *you have my attention.*

CHAPTER CUATRO

Hola hola, welcome to Sebastián's baptism. This is immigrant criolla reportando from the depths of Jesús's favorite holiest house: the Pastores' pool in Miami. We got holy signs on the front lawn so you don't get lost: *Those Who Look For Him Shall Find His Glory*, and farther down, *Sebastián Found His Glory*, and lastly, *Will You Find His Glory?*

Entra, mi reina, sin compromiso.

Our car is a borrowed beat-up baby-blue Honda that smells of burned cigarettes and stale milk, but we nonetheless ride in it even though the Pastores' house is six blocks away. Because cómo se te ocurre that your mother is gonna walk in this heat and mess up the hair that took two hours to blow-dry and curl. Because cómo se te ocurre that this family is going to show up like nobodies caminando bajo el sol como desplazados.

I admired the piles of trash on the street from the back seat of the car. Just to mess with Mami, I pointed at every homeless person, every ripped bag of trash, every carcass of what was once a car or a motorcycle where boys in threadbare wifebeaters leaned back smoking. Every heap of broken palm tree lining the way like yellowing corpses.

Mira, Mami, even the palm trees here are dying for Sebastián.

Chistocita, she said, not really listening to me but biting her tongue and looking to both sides, searching for the Pastores' house. Everything here looked the same. By then we'd been in yanquilandia for over two months. And even though Mami had been to the Pastores' house over eight times already, Florida is not like Bogotá. You can't just say, When you get to the bakery with the flaming *Calentico* sign and the sleeping señor con el bigotico, take a left. No, mi reina. Acá la cosa es un espejo. La cosa is an endless repetition of the same image: pastel townhouses, highways, palm trees, trash. A labyrinth of sameness.

Baby Sebastián lay on my lap staring at me with those glassy blue eyes, brown plastic skin. I felt anxious looking at the damn baby, swimming in that *stunning* yellow dress from Ross that took up half of the back seat and had me scratching my butt the entire six blocks. Lucía on the other side with a matching pink dress rehearsing her baptism psalms in whispers. She turned, searching for me, but I just sighed and looked away. I'd stopped asking out loud *Why are we even doing this*, but it remained the background music blaring in my head. *Why are we even doing this. Why are we even doing this.* From the moment we stepped into this Jesucristo swamp: *Why are we even doing this.* Sebastián with the same content expression. Like he didn't create all this commotion. Like his soul wasn't about to enter the heavens. I wished my soul had some direction. Wished for some of that calmness and easiness that this doll seemed to have just taking up space on my lap without any awareness of the Carnaval shitshow he had spearheaded. *Are you happy now, asshole?* I wanted to say. *Contentico now that you have all us bitches throwing you a fiestica so your poor struggling seventeen-year-old soul may leave purgatory?* May I remind you, querido reader, that Sebastián's death was the beginning of my life. That his birth would have meant Yours Truly would not have materialized. Pero pobrecito, imagínate, el único hombrecito de la casa perdío en el cielo sin encontrar a Papi Dios. I knew he was a doll but I was angry at him. Our house was a mess, Mami was a mess, Tata was a mess, but all of our energy those first two months was spent organizing this baptism and dealing with la neurótica de mi madre.

I really hope you're jumping on one leg up there, I whispered to Sebastián before gently slapping him on the face. Because you're still dead, pendejo.

The Pastores plus Carmen waited outside the house, Bibles in hand. Everyone took this baptism extremely seriously. A couple weeks ago we even had an obligatory baptism meeting at their house during which they explained, using a diagram and irrelevant Bible quotes, why it was essential that all dead babies be baptized. Sensing my silent disbelief, the Pastora hurried to explain: Porque what if it was *you* running in circles como loca inside purgatory?

Y yo queriéndole decir: *This, querida Pastora, this right here is purgatory.*

Standing on the lawn, they were all dressed up: tie, dress, pantyhose (in Miami). Black balloons galore. Carmen the only one wearing some basic black pants and her *Jóvenes en Cristo* T-shirt with that know-it-all smile stamped on her face.

Inside the car, Mami reached for her notebooks, rehearsed our duties and all we could and could not do—obviously directed at me. No swearing, no asking about Carmen's real parents, no disclosing too much about our "situation." Read: *Ay de que you tell anyone I'm unemployed and Milagros has been stacking up the pantry.* No making fun of people, Francisca. No smoking, Francisca. To Tata she sighed, put her hand on Tata's pashmina. Mamá, let's have a good baptism, ¿sí?

Pero claro, responded Tata, although I myself had filled her water bottle with rum.

Before stepping out, Mami outlined her lips in the car one last time and asked if I wanted any lipstick. I didn't. Pero Francisca, red lipstick goes exceptionally well with that stunning yellow dress. *Coño, Mami, dele con el cuento del dress carajo.*

A ver, I said, give it to me.

Without a mirror, I smeared the red lipstick on my lips. Full chapped lips and the bozo I had been growing since twelve, which I now refused to wax to the *ay ay ay* disappointed melody of the matriarchy. Careless about the outline. My entire face was my lips. A sad clown in a pollito dress. My face was mine to do with as I wished; my face and only my face still belonged to me. Everything else we left to rot in the Andes. At least I thought so. I looked like I'd eaten red paint. Tata saw me, made a face. Mami, reacting to Tata's face, turned around, angered beyond reason but calmed because the show must go on—because no berrinche is gonna ruin this precious moment for your mami—she whispered an Arreglamos esto en la casa, and slammed the door behind her.

La Tata speaking to the air but clearly to me saying over and over again, Pero Señor mío, who raised these stubborn hijasdeputa?

I didn't want to say it so I just chuckled, looked at her, muttered, I am very happy he died.

Once out of the car, I repeated the same thing to Carmen just to get a reaction from her. I'm very happy he died. Carmen laughed, No you're not! and pulled me into the house. It was impossible not to be pulled by Carmen, and I, so bored and aimless, couldn't care less where she took me. Even when I didn't want to go, her determination and adrenalina killed all my resistance. Most things those first few months in Miami felt the same way: passing through me, like a trencito that was leaving me behind. Chu-chu. Bai-bai.

Homegirl had more energy than a sirirí, more bum bum que un cohete.

That day she needed my help picking her shekina dress. Midway through the hallway the Pastora stopped us.

Where are you taking Francisquita? I need her at the entrance with the guest book. As part of this life-changing event, Mami brought a Recuerdos de Tu Bautismo notebook from Bogotá that she now expected every attendee to sign.

But what are people going to write? I asked Mami when she unbeknownst to me pulled the cuadernillo out of our bags the day we arrived. She wasn't listening, of course. Ay pero mira la portada, Francisca, she'd said. Don't you think this cover is just exquisite?

And cover yourself with something, Francisca, said the Pastora, still staring at me in the hallway with an annoyed face. What on Diosito's earth happened to your mouth? Ven pa' acá. Clearly your mother is incapable of raising you right, Dios mío.

If Mami only knew how the Pastora talked about her sometimes.

Y right there and then she pulled out a pañuelito. Y right there and then in the hallway with Carmen anxiously waiting for her to finish, as is custom for women to do, La Pastora licked the pañuelito, uno dos three times, and reached for my face. Before I could stop her, the holiest woman's saliva cleaned the sides of my mouth. Ahí está, un poquito mejor. She smiled.

Everything passing through me, cachaco.

I can take it from here, I said, feeling the sadness swelling like a balloon.

Why do you always have that amargada face? Carmen asked me. From the very first day, Francisca, even at church that cara de pan doesn't change. If only you smiled.

I caught a glimpse of my long pale face, the huge ears, the dress so odd, ill fitted for my body.

It's the one God gave me, I said. I don't have another one.

~

There we are: Mami's mourning entourage in pompous dresses and enough sweat to fill a pool. Enough sadness to drown your heart. Enough empanadas, quibbes, niño envuelto, platanitos to feed South Florida, mi reina, and then some. Mami doing what she knows best: clipboard in hand, pointing to missing decorations on the tables, the pool, the speakers hooked up to the iPod; pointing to Lucía, to the baby, to the gray sky. Pointing to the professional mourning ladies in black crying for Sebastián. Mami La Doña del Pointing. With the finger, with the mouth. All the sons and daughters of Papi Dios como ovejitas following her commands, her voice. Que la comida, que las bombas, que no me ensucie la entrada, carajo, que acabo de barrer.

Did I mention she paid more attention to the arrangement of the food, the gold bows on the shekinas' dresses, than the actual baptism of the baby?

Bitch, was she thriving or what. Look at Mami in her salsa mandando, serving True Jefa Realness just like God intended. A bombastic energy swirling around her. Look at her, unmoved by the ducks outside tugging at her dress, unmoved by Tata's disapproving slightly drunk face, winning at this baptism spectacle. Because nothing was going to ruin this moment for Mami.

I hadn't seen her like that since her days back in Bogotá when she pointed at the hairdresser, at her secretary. Swirling in that finger power.

I tried staying inside Carmen's room for as long as I could. Carmen was annoying and weird, but there was just one of her instead of dealing with the Jesús army outside.

What do you think, pela'a? she said, holding two sheer shekina dresses, one baby blue, one gold. She was in charge of leading the young shekinas in a warrior dance around the pool, right before the fake baby was submerged in water. I'd seen them rehearse a few times already. More times than I wished was true. After I popped my youth-group cherry that first day at church, Carmen called me *every single day* until I agreed to join her and the chicos buena onda que aman a Cristo in an outing to the mall. We'd spent one sad Saturday afternoon at the Dolphin Mall bowling and distributing *Jesucristo Salvador* flyers. I mean, they bowled. I sat in the back staring at them blessing each other, high-fiving in the name of Cristo Jesús. Gloria a Dios, batiendo palma ahí no más en el mall sin ningún tipo de vergüenza. On my right Team Jóvenes en Cristo, on my left Team Jóvenes Llenos del Espíritu Santo. Everyone kept a polite distance from my The Cure T-shirt and black eyeliner that day. All of them welcoming me with distrust and condescending smiles—they all knew Jesús had yet to colonize my heart. That I hadn't officially blurted out The Prayer That Will Save You and thus my soul still played on the other team, the one closer to Satanás, and when the Rapture came I would still disappear in flames—Puff puff! said Carmen—while they all drifted upward, swaying al delicioso ritmo salvador, to Papi Dios's arms. Wilson tried to get me to join them in prayer, tried to encourage me to join the winning team, but I'd put my hoodie up, Discman on. Pero then Carmen tenía un volador por el culo and was dele que dele trying to get me to play at least once, sharing her fries with me, buying me a strawberry milkshake when I told her I didn't have money for anything other than the stupid rental shoes, which I wasn't using anyway. She sat next to me the entire time, telling me things like, You won't be lonely when you let Chuchito into your heart, and when she didn't score, Jesús knows what's best for me, and then, Did you know Wilson thinks I'm the most beautiful shekina in the congregation? and then, Come help outreach at Sedano's this Sunday? Carmen had been wearing the same sweater (without a bra) that she was now removing (without a bra), the one with the candle lit inside a rainbow. It's the light of the Holy Ghost, she'd explained, licking greasy french-fry fingers at the mall. Her nipples pointing at me.

The rainbow connects the heavens with the earth, and the Espíritu Santo is the energy between them. Ajá. I nodded staring right at her heart.

She didn't ask, but I turned around overwhelmed when, in her room, she removed her sweater. I was used to all the women in my family parading themselves naked in front of each other, it was part of our family dynamic. In a five-to-one female-to-male ratio familia, everyone knew the size of each other's nipples, commented on each other's cellulite and stretch marks like they were another set of accessories (*Ay mire cómo le han servido los masajes a Milagros en esa cola*). But I was embarrassed for Carmen. *Girl, I just met you,* I wanted to say. *Don't be getting all naked up in my face.* I was embarrassed by her skin now exposed, her belly now suddenly revealed, the black trail on it not unlike my own—her lack of shame around her body.

Pero Francisca, she complained, how you gonna help me if you don't look at me?

Trágame tierra.

I heard Mami yelling, looking for me. Relieved, I ran out to meet her.

~

The dark gray sky crocheted with patches of blue, like a giant Diosa, scooped up pieces of rain cloud. It was four p.m. No mountains. No wind. Just a congregation of thirty colombianos winning at the holy life, sudando la gota gorda. The air a surreal thickness, a humidity so absurd that by the end of the baptism I swear we'd developed gills. The holy baptismal pool in the center, lined with the few rays of sun peeking from behind the black-and-gray cumulus clouds. Piscina mayamense turned Jordan River, así no más. A crown of half-dead palm trees creating a depressing arc of yellows and greens where black and gold balloons swayed, birds chirped and discharged poop onto the black tablecloth Lucía was arranging. Pero cachaco, in Mami's head this was the freaking Hilton en Cartagena papá, this was the Plaza Hotel; this view of a gray lake with a growing pile of trash was the extravagant! luxurious! sueño Americano we'd all been waiting for.

She left her life back in that País de Mierda to come win in the U S of A, and motherfucker look at her *ganando*.

A constant female murmullo mixed with Christian merengue, Christian bachata. Women of God sat around the tables complaining about hair. Hairs thickening, rising like bread. Hair spray pa'quí, hair spray pa' allá. From hand to hand to hand to hand. And then: a drizzle. Panic.

Aquí va a llover, someone muttered.

Aquí lo que viene es un palo de agua, someone echoed.

Will the fiebre tropical ruin Mami's spectacular moment?

Acá ni va a llover, ni aceptamos ese tipo de actitud, Mami barked back.

Do not ruin her show. Do not bring your low-class bad attitude to the spectacle Myriam del Socorro Juan had dreamed up for months. Can't you see she got no job, she got no house, she got no man, but motherfucker she has a clipboard and a dead baby waiting to be baptized. And not even the rain could ruin Mami's show; this time, only this time, *she* was the ultimate power. Let Diosito know that He can run every show but Mami runs *this* house.

Ay juepúchica.

Our guests arrived. I was their doorman. The Pastora dragged me to the door with her long brown impeccable skeletal hands—the hands of a woman who has never worked or suffered, hands that have known manicures since they could point. And point she did, to my face. To the notebook. To the spot next to the entrance where for two hours I fake-smiled *Buenas tardes, welcome to Sebastián's bautismo, please sign here and share a message of love with the mourning family* and pretended to be the daughter of a woman I didn't recognize baptizing her dead baby. Who was Mami? Confusion doesn't even come close to how I felt about Mami; she left me by the entrance with the Pastora policing my every move. Was Mami really into this or was she just tripping? It was La Tata who relieved me of my doorman duties when I had to help her down the hallway as she stumbled to the bathroom. La pobre, so tipsy I had to help with her calzones. Mimi, she said chuckling, tu abuela used to be called La Muñeca. Tu abuela was going to be a star. Everyone in Cartagena bowed to me, ¿sabías?

I know, Tata, I said arranging her frizzy white hair.

You heard it here first, reinita. All the unfiltered tea. The baptism about to begin. The fake baby in a gold robe. You heard the Pastor snap his fingers into the microphone—yes, they brought an hijuemadre microphone for the twenty pelagatos—mic check, soooooonido. ¡Dios los bendiga, hermanos! You heard him point to someone to start the iPod's holy music, and you heard the Christian salsa beats reverberate around the pool and the señoras slightly moving their shoulders and the hermanos slightly moving their hips—the body memory of a life once lived in sin. A life that once used that salsita for sexy entertainment purposes, but now the salsita, the merengue, the siseo corporal were followed by swaying hands, by aleluyas, by rhythmical prayers sent to the humid sky. It's not like we didn't pray back in Bogotá. Not like we didn't wake up early every single Sunday to kneel in front of a bleeding Christ, eat the body of Christ, and smell of incense all day. Not like we didn't all get baptized as babies by a dude in a robe drizzling some agua bendita. But this agua reeked of chlorine. The robe in this baptism was worn by a baby now dead, now submerged in the pool by the Pastor, now glimmering with drops of water, now lifted to the heavens like this was some Criollo Lion King remake. Mami's feet barely touching the water. A happiness on her face I didn't recognize. Clapping when the baby rose again to the cheers of the congregation. I stood on the other side, far away, by the entrance, picking my cuticles until they bled, keeping Tata hydrated, trying as hard as I could not to watch Mami. Ignore Lucía. Keep my eyes on my fingers, my grandmother's hands. Something tangible, legible, something I understood. Later that night I would lock myself in the bathroom figuring out an escape plan. I would call my dad, but as usual, he wouldn't answer. I'd consider calling my friends back in Bogotá but couldn't deal with the sadness, the embarrassment of this new life. How would I explain this to them? Coming to the USA is the dream! And I should be happy happy happy! I considered walking out, taking a bus. Where? With what money? I didn't know anyone. Spoke basic English. I sat on the toilet, phone in my hand for twenty, thirty, sixty minutes until I understood there was no one outside Miami, nobody who would come for me. As Mami said, Esta es our new vida, Francisca. Look around, this is your home now.

CHAPTER CINCO

For the next few weeks nobody knew what to do with the plastic piece of baby in the house. La Tata thought it was a pendejada to keep it. Lucía and I refused to let Mami place it among our books and CDs, and Mami, even though she wouldn't admit to it, was slightly embarrassed to have a muñeco a esta altura del partido on her bed. After being the center of attention, Sebastián now served no purpose. The Pastores did not specify what to do with the metaphorical baby after the baptism, once the real baby rose from limbo to Papi Dios's arms (where eventually he'd meet Mami and the rest of the family in what I imagine is a little pachanga celestial).

The night after the baptism Mami left Sebastián on the dining table, and the next few days you could see her startled every time she entered the dining room, as if expecting the doll to walk out or disappear or find a life purpose or, better, hustle it down and bring Mami some much-needed G.

It was a strange time for Mami. What was she going to do now that the baptism was over? She was having her own postbaptism depression, roaming around aimlessly.

She'd pace the house trying to find a nook for the fake baby, holding it by its head, which I took to mean she was *finally* coming to her senses about the piece of plastic. Nunca es tarde. But as with everything with Mami, it's all a sorpresa. She'd go out with Milagros two or three times a week to distribute more flyers, work on some Colombian dude's Christian magazine about finance, make some billullo here and there, but when she came home, ay de que you'd touched or moved the berraco baby!

Pero Mamá, I said, I thought we were done with this?

Done? Mi reina, she wasn't even close to done. At the time I thought the hot humid infernal weather was messing with Mami's brain cells and I moved the baby on purpose just to get a reaction from her, just to watch La Tata close her hazel eyes in frustration and finally tell her: Myriam, grow unos putos cojones and I'm throwing out this pedazo de mierda. Sebastián gone to the dumpster, leaving the smell of chlorine and a small void in the house. I knew Mami to be obsessive, but Miami was sending her into another level loca obsesiva that I hadn't known was possible. Was it the heat? Was it the air-conditioning? Was it the intense soledad that had her crying solita at night thinking nobody heard but of course I did because Soledad Eterna was my middle name and obviamente I wasn't sleeping either? Obviamente I was smoking by the tiny terrace having my own pity party, all of a sudden over-hearing Mami's own tristeza.

Dios mío.

Mami wasn't having it with Tata throwing away the muñeco. This baby is gone when I say it's gone, ¿estamos?

Mami, I wanted to say, *let it go*.

Pero this is Myriam del Socorro Juan we're talking about. Homegirl would fight you because she is right and you are wrong. And she got that killer stare to prove it. Myriam who began losing her estrato embarrassment and started fighting the cashiers at Sedano's in Spanish because she just *knew* the bag of rice was buy one get one free. Yo de aquí no me voy, she said to the poor latinita at the register. Llámeme al manager. Fought the manager until the man caved in and handed her the bag of free rice. ¡Es que le quieren ver a uno la cara! And then at the dollar store. And then at Walmart when the coupons wouldn't scan. ¡Llámeme al manager!

Was it really about the rice, you ask? Was it really about the coupons? Cachaco, it's never about the bag of rice. Homegirl spent her days licking envelopes, crying, hustling in a van with no AC with Milagros, so the poor señorita at the register took all the *indignation* with this vida that Mami couldn't admit was turning kinda cray.

But Sebastián was Mami's project. The baby she supposedly—not really, but okay—mourned for seventeen years. The baby that gave her a goal-oriented project those first months. Was she about to drop the fake baby forever?

Out of the dumpster she retrieved the muñeco. Wearing pantyhose and a skirt, she looked for it and brought it back all smeared with ketchup and reeking of butt. Lucía and I stared in amazement. I was dividing the space of our bedroom (again) with Lucía, who taped Jesús paraphernalia after Holy Spirit paraphernalia on the walls and demanded I wear a color other than black in her presence. Right down the middle of the room, I drew a line with my black eyeliner and she whispered, annoyed, Mami is gonna *kill you* for ruining the carpet.

¿Y qué?

Then we heard a crash out the window and what do you know there's Mami limping back to the townhouse.

Even Lucía thought it was demasiado. What. Is. She. Doing. In the traaaaash.

Lucía, who dared not challenge Mami in anything. When Mami said jump, Lucía threw herself off a cliff.

Our eyes meeting in a shared recognition, a brief moment of connection over our mother's cucú locura. We used to bond over Mami's tornadoes, as we called them, the swirling of energy that got her running after something without paying attention to what she was doing. Stomping on her own path. Didn't matter. Mami's turbulence was our connection. Lucía and I sat time and again in our room back in Bogotá, watching Mami fuming over disorganized socks, throwing everything out of the closet and making us fold T-shirt after T-shirt until the entire house was color coded and arranged by size. But here. Girl, here we didn't get no piles of clothes to fold. The food ran low. All we had to organize were these three chiros we were allowed to bring. I had decided to wear black and only black as my mourning veil for all that was lost. My closet smaller than everyone's.

I just can't understand, Lucía continued, if there's so many colors that Diosito created, why you, Francisca, choose the darkest one. Lucía and I were like María Magdalena and la Virgen María. The sinner and the holy. Although I was hardly sinning, sadly. We used to get along. We used to chase each other around our apartment and create choreographies for every telenovela theme song. We used to pretend we were rich: Lucía in Mami's heels, fake pearls. Me in my dad's tie, Sharpied mustache. We would stand in front of the hallway mirror sending kisses to the imaginary proletariat who had traveled for miles just to catch a glimpse of our fabulosity. Pero ahora Lucía was another Lucía; she'd slipped into the Jóvenes en Cristo so easily, born again so quickly—her conversion like a Cinderella lost slipper had transformed the girl without any rough marks, as if she'd been waiting to pray with Jesús's Colombian guerrilla mayamense for the entirety of her twelve-year-old existence and, niña, did this sister succeed. I mean, there she was volunteering in youth outreach on South Beach, plastering Sedano's with flyers, recording herself reading Bible verses for the children, calling out La Tata for cursing? To the point that even Mami— óyeme, even Mami—as Lucía lectured La Tata over her use of *hijueputas*, told the culicagada to calm down. Bájate del bus, niña. Cálmate, Lucía, cálmate, carajo. But there was no calming her. Jesús was with her, in her, all around her. This was her calling. She had been, as La Pastora constantly reminded us, touched by God. And those touched by Him are forever changed. A whole month it took for this cachaquita to transform into a full-blown hija de Dios and, motherfucker, was she proud of this. Lecturing you like bitch got some degree in Jesus Studies. Recently, she'd been promoted to Assistant Youth Leader and there was nadie que se la aguantara. The prouder Lucía grew, the more time I spent staring at the ceiling fan, fighting with her over my Smiths posters, sneaking out to smoke. I picked up the Greyhound schedules and stared at the list of mystery places where I could go for only fifty bucks. Atlanta. Jacksonville. West Palm Beach. New York?

And there he is, our blessed hijo. Back from the depths of the nearby dumpster. On the chair next to Mami like the príncipe that he is.

Maldito.

Pero claro, Lucía did not have an opinion about this. Ahí sí tenía el opiniadero dañado, ¿no? Pero I did. I had many opinions. Many opinions that I didn't know how to articulate, how to get out. It was all inside me snowballing with the heat and the air conditioner and the daily ale-luyas and the and the and the. It wasn't until Mami dared to wipe some remaining filth from the muñeco's face that my gut went na-*ah.*

Es ridículo, I started. Don't you think, Tata? Wasn't the baptism enough? Where you gonna put that piece of plastic now?

Underneath the table La Tata patted my leg. Her way of saying, *Just leave it alone, mija.*

A short silence. It looked like Mami wasn't saying anything. Like she would continue drinking that juguito de lulo like it was nothing. Historically Mami had been a tremenda Connoisseur of Silence, a Reina del Silencio, which meant she knew when to drop silence like a stink bomb and manipulate its emptiness, closed on its edges, to get a certain outcome. Silence, reina mía, is a powerful tool in this family.

Ay ya, Mami said.

Then nada.

It was better when she actually fought, you know? At least I had something to grab on to and return to her with my own malparida spin. At least I could climb those words or pile them inside me. Turn them on my tongue to make some vague sense of this new realidad. But now she just stared at her arroz con pollo, chewing a little too slow, which just meant there was something building inside, something we weren't gonna know right now and when we did it was going to be a blowup. That's Mami for you. She lays the prelude, then shies away so you yearn for more.

And I fell for it over and over and over.

Mami? I said.

It was in moments like this when I could either go all Gloria Trevi on her ass—I imagine myself Herculean, pushing the dining table with such force there'd be no rastros of pollito—or swallow the shade and let it beat against my rib cage. ¡Pao! Like a mad pajarito wearing itself down.

Maldito muñeco, I said to no one but of course to Mami.

Ay no, said Tata.

Las palabras tienen poder, said Lucía.

Putting her fork down, Mami stared at me. Francisca, in this house no maldecimos, ¿okey? Then she whispered some blessing to herself.

Could she kill you with that shit or what? We couldn't say *maldito* because words have power and we should be sending blessings into the world, so instead the muñeco should be a *bendito* muñeco. Every Sunday we learned "new ways" of expressing our feelings. New ways that followed our Savior's selective wording. I imagined Jesucristo walking up to La Calavera with that big-ass cross getting whipped, punched in the face, yelled at by some non-believers pero ay, you don't think homeboy muttered an *hijueputa* under that breath? Cachaco, please.

Plus *bendito* wasn't close to what I was feeling. The damn baby was a freaking maldición. A sign that we, that I, that this new life was cursed and we should swim immediately to the other side of the charco.

Mami kept Sebastián, and I avoided her room at all costs. Every time I passed by it to go to the living room se me paraban los pelitos, a ball of anger and defeat in my throat.

My fifteen years wasted.

What I'm saying is: I sat in my room and inhaled the little AC allowed in the house. We couldn't lower it past seventy-eight degrees cause *freak-out*, the electric bill. I carried a bag of ice to put on my feet every time I sat on my bed and stared out the window. We couldn't open the windows because there was no vientecito para orear la casa. I stared at the dumpster, at Roberto, the old Cuban borrachito in a wheelchair who flirted with Tata every chance he got, y más allá, at the square houses, one after the other, pastel houses glaring in the sun. Somewhere on the other side of those dry palm trees was my home, beyond the lake, beyond the venezolanas in bikinis wrapped around flashy boys in the moldy pool, beyond the crisscrossing highways. Beyond the flowery bedspread under which I unsuccessfully tried licking my two dry fingers and putting them inside my shorts before going blank in my head. And now Pablito interrupting it all with his acne scars and his Star Trek shirt, knocking on our door asking in that Argentinian singing accent if one of the niñas would accompany him to the mall.

¿El mall? I said looking him up and down. ¿Tú quieres que yo vaya contigo al mall?

This pendejo asking *me* to go with *him*—of course nobody else outside of church had asked me to join them in nada.

That is correcto, he said shyly. To the arcade.

I sighed.

Yo no voy a salir contigo, maricón, I said.

This was Pablito's fourth try. He'd knocked on our door a few times, introducing himself, selling his drawings, but I always left him standing at the door. Mami, annoyed at my rudeness, invited him inside sometimes for tintico. Invited Pablito to church. He wasn't Christian, but his politeness caressed something deep in Mami. The "loser" sign stamped on his forehead ignited a wave of pity in Mami and Tata.

Mami yelled from the kitchen that maybe it'd do me good. Pablito mumbling, With all due respect I'm not a maricón, I swear. Hands clasped behind him. I saw myself shrink watching the biggest loser in the Heather Glen Apartment Complex offer his friendship. Dios mío. This is what I've become, really more like unbecome. And yet. Pablito was the only loser who did not approach me with a Jesús brochure or a blessing or a *Got Jesús?* tank top suggesting I lose my Ramones shirt for some festive Caribbean colors. *You're colombiana, mami, where's your sabor.* Still. Homeboy gave me the creeps and I didn't dare to be seen with him in public (mind you, I didn't know anyone. Pero it was a matter of principle!).

Now, mi reina, do you understand why I locked myself back in my room (*No Pablo, hoy no*), blasting The Cure, staring at the MSN icon on the computer, waiting for someone, any of my friends back home, to say something? The first few weeks our conversations had lasted hours. They detailed all the gossip back in our school in Bogotá: who banged the panadero, who ended up drunk in the hospital, who was caught smoking, etc. I spent as much time as Mami and her devotion allowed me glued to that computer screen. But after the first two months the messages began to fade. New people were added to the groups. Who's that? Oh, you don't know him, he's María's brother que es un churro divino. Relationships changed. Carolina? No girl, she got kicked out of school for kissing Ana. Ana said she forced her. The nuns went insane. Who is Ana? Bogotá changing without me. Leaving me behind. New buildings, new bars. My own language kicking me aside. I remember noticing them using new words, *guapa* instead of *hembra*. *Darse besos* instead of *rumbearse*. I tried joining in, sprinkling those new words here and there, but they all sounded butchered, foreign, and I couldn't keep up.

Now the conversations lasted only minutes before hitting a dead end. The chat windows empty. Ceiling fan pressing down.

CHAPTER SEIS

The next Sunday at Iglesia Cristiana Jesucristo Redentor, a crowded group of women circled and touched a young woman's face. Homegirl couldn't have been more than twenty-five years old. She'd just gotten laser on her face. She'd had really bushy sideburns, *like a man!* and now, *miracle!* she'd returned hair-free, fully woman, and ready to testify about it. Apparently sideburns on girls are a no-no for God, especially if you want to marry the lead singer dude by the stupid name of Art, which she did, or if you want to join the inner church circle, which she did. The Pastores paid for the laser with church money and made a point of telling the entire congregation how they supported this dream. *Art now loves her! Look at their pure love!* Of course this was an obvious church expense since the girl now would be climbing the ranks with that smooth face. The men stood on the other side of the room while the collective female crowd worked as one big microscope on her face. We all wanted a piece of her transformation into a higher, more perfected female version. It was obvious that all of these women used to directly or indirectly make fun of her. It was obvious all the praising carried with it an underlying feeling of jealousy, of anger. Now we all touched our own sideburns, not as bushy as hers, but tiny hairs nonetheless—a reminder that we were still not as pure and definitely not as chosen. Nobody was paying for us to become more womanly and therefore more desired by the higher ranks of the church. And thus began the jealousy roller-coaster ride. All of us with hungry tentacles stretching out onto her body. Everyone took turns running their fingers along her silky cheek, commenting on her newly acquired beauty. She seemed thrilled with all the attention, nodding and repeating, I've wanted this all my life, I've wanted this all my life. Art is so excited for me. We're finally getting the church's blessing. Envious smiles all around. When my turn came to touch her, I declined.

It's okay, she pressed. Touch it, it's so smooth.

I didn't want to touch someone else's skin. She was already sweating from all the attention, and it felt disgusting to run my fingers on both sweat and skin. All eyes suddenly landed on me. Tata would later update me on the gossip of the girl's church history. She was a nobody and people spoke of her hairy face as if she was an abomination brought by Satan. Only in whispers. Only in passing. She was evidence of biology gone wrong, and all the women felt a sense of superiority when staring at her hairy body. Now she had outdone every single bitch and clawed her way to the hairless top. In Colombian Girl World this is called *arribista*. In Colombian Church World it's just called *a miracle from the benevolence of Papi Dios who refuses to let His daughters suffer*. Amén.

Of that day I remember running two fingers down her cheek, the girl's proud smile. I remember the feeling of being invited into the circle, of joining the women in this ritual. As gross as touching her felt, it was also an invitation. I too went ahead and ran two fingers over her skin. Something about it felt wrong. And yet. I was inside a circle, welcomed in. The Pastor called us from the podium, ¡Las mujeres! Please do us a favor and stop the gossip and go sit. Hairless Girl then hugged me. She said, Christ believed in me. I carried her face inside me that day, a weird feeling of closeness.

That morning I refused to join the Jóvenes en Cristo after the one-hour alabanza. It was salsa day, which meant one hour of nonstop holy salsa beats culminating in slow generic Christian music. Everyone's arms up high swaying slowly, in unison, almost choreographed, almost shadows of each other; the little, the big, the brown, the white, the arms with clinging bracelets; hairy arms, clasped hands, hands that had seen rough times. The scarred, the veiny, the wedding rings shining with light—all pointing to the baby-blue ceiling where Diosito metaphorically lived. This was the second most embarrassing moment during the service. The first one, of course, being the newly arrived sheep of Jesús walking up to the podium to share their Life Changing Testimonies in tears and recurrent fainting. It was the custom: every new devoto, every new Jesús heart, was encouraged to spill the beans of a past sinful life to the améns and tears of the congregation.

Mami, Tata, and Milagros had done so repeatedly. Dios mío. The embarrassment I felt, sinking in the chair as Mami told the entire congregation my father cheated on her. As she confessed how lost, how deviant from the True Christian Path she'd been in the past, dancing vallenato, praising the Virgen.

I could not look at her that day. People came up to me after her testimony in tears, pity spilling from their eyes and kisses. I too felt incredibly exposed by Mami's confession. As if the life she had led back in Bogotá belonged to all of us. I wanted to keep those memories untouched by this new wave of truths; I wanted them intact so that eventually we could go back to them and resume where we had left off.

When the alabanza finally ended, I remained seated next to Mami, who obediently bowed her head when the Pastor demanded, who obediently flipped through the Bible when the Pastora commanded, while I silently gazed at her, sometimes angry, most of the time in shock at her newly acquired unstoppable devotion.

When I refused to stand up, Mami gave me The Eye then whispered prayers to herself. Of course Lucía ran excited to the Jóvenes en Cristo room, hugging her Biblia. And of course Tata sat at the other end with the church gossip crew whispering about the putas doing it before marriage. She continued to call putas *putas* even though no one was supposed to curse inside church, but they let Tata curse because I could tell they pitied her. People knew. They must have. That La Tata practically ran Cartagena in her time, that she was known as La Muñeca, a voluptous hija of a renowned notary in the city and the most codiciada costeña in the late fifties. Now Alba Leonor de Jesús Juan was an overweight devota de Dios missing most of her teeth. Let the woman curse! A large alcoholic who had birthed so many children the skin around her hips drooped as if it didn't belong to her, as if it was dead and tired from all its use. For years, Mami ignored the tiny bottles of rum on Tata's nightstand, wrapping them in aluminum foil or, instead, pouring them into Sprite cans.

Oh she's just drinking her medicina, Mami'd say. Quickly. Then move to a different topic. And so we all forgot, until one day—many months from now—La Tata will step out into the streets en cuera, como Diosito la trajo al mundo. Until one day Tata will transform into a lost bird flapping bright yellowing skin, naked, talking to the sun, calling to her dead husband: Fabito, mijo, la comida está ready.

Ready, mis hermanos, the Pastor whispered into the microphone. All of you ready for some blessings, come on up.

Mami joined the crowd gathered up in front around the Pastor, who placed hands on heads and prayed over the kneeling sheep. I stared down at my hands, cold, dry from the AC. A half-moon mole on my right index finger (the only resemblance to my father), nails bitten to the core. Small, ugly hands that didn't say much. I turned them over and imagined someone tracing their lines. I day-dreamed of a huge mansion with an immense library, a lover waking up next to me, tracing the lines of my hand. I was sad, I was horny. I wanted a real party and a real dick inside me. There was nothing happening in my life. For hours I sat listening to prayers, listening to people want things from God. What did *I* want. Where was *my* miracle. There was no one staring at my hands. I was the only one witnessing this shitshow. I had dreams of pretty boys with long hair taking me away; dreams where someone showed up in a Jeep and drove me out of Miami to a quiet place where silence didn't hurt as much as it did here.

Carmen snuck up behind me, asked me to join the Jóvenes in the back room. Que no quiero, I said. But her arms were strong, clasped my veiny hands. She smelled of accumulated sweat and Vicks VapoRub under the veil, both soothing and disgusting. Face all drenched, satisfied, kinda ugly in that shekina outfit. Just as she was dragging me out of the main room, Paula, Carmen's minion and number-one holy criolla groupie, stomped down to the middle of the room tugging at Carmen, whispering loud enough for me to hear that she shouldn't be spending her time with me, shouldn't be wasting her energy on a useless soul like mine, clearly I was unsavable.

A ver, she mumbled staring at me, can we all just take a moment to look at this sad case? She wears black every single day. I mean, esa niña no se puede salvar, Carmen.

Paula wanted Carmen for herself and couldn't stand me because Carmen wanted to share herself the evangelical way with other people. Save people. People in need. Like me.

You don't have to save me, Carmen, I interjected.

But Jesús loves all His children, pela'a.

She really meant it, I could see that. It was painful for her to see I was not saved. It hurt her. It was part of her mission: to evangelize, convert, save souls for Papi Dios. I saw the pain in the low way she said *pela'a*, "girl," spoken by a true costeña but not as joyous as they usually speak, *¡Ajá pedazo 'e pela'a!* but sad and empty. I was an empty girl with no Jesús in me, and then she said she cared.

Of that Sunday I remember giving in to Carmen's insistence. I remember watching the Hairless Girl in the corner while her boyfriend, Art, showed the other boys her smooth skin. She let them touch her face and smiled at me when I walked past her with Carmen and Paula. Then I saw Mami fall to the floor for the first time. The power of Jesús in her, apparently. The Pastor pushed her slightly, and a bald ujier standing behind her caught Mami in his arms like a dead bird. For a second I panicked. Carmen noticed and whispered, She's okay, much better now. I saw Carmen calling Wilson with her eyes and saw Wilson appear by my side faster than you could say *la cosa está heavy-duty*, reassuring me that my mother was okay and I'd be too if I joined them. I didn't understand anything. Why did she have to fall and was it real? I didn't know Mami could faint on command, but maybe her faith was that powerful. I doubted the whole thing. Mi mami on that nasty carpet with a halo of brown hair.

Ven ven, Carmen and Wilson tugged at me. And why fight it? Clearly Mami was enjoying herself.

Y tú te preguntas, mi reina, did I go into the next room? Pero claro. Did I hold sweaty hands in prayer? Sí sí, cómo no. I prayed, and yes, when we left the Hyatt that day La Tata exclaimed in laughter that Carmen is a little recogida, adoptada with no class, and we both laughed uncontrollably, and yes, cómo no, I felt a slight satisfaction, and no, Mami didn't explain much else. She didn't care that I thought it shameful that a woman like her— hecha y derecha—fell on that nasty floor into the arms of some bald chirri from Valledupar. She didn't care. I sat in the van staring at Subway, Walgreens, Burger King,

McDonald's, feeling Mami moving away from me. Feeling she was past the point where I could reach out, grab her, shake her into remembering Sundays at Catholic mass followed by obleas and oncecitas at Tata's. I didn't know how to reach that part of Mami, how to get past the faith wall. A piece of me snapped. Like we'd been pulling a piece of gum and she'd run away without even trying to win me over.

Outside a man was sweating holding a *DEPRESSED? TRY OUR NEW OREO SUNDAE!* sign. It all felt like a joke. From behind, Mami still looked the same: wavy dark hair, quick shaky movements, freckled arms. Mami could come back to me if she wanted to.

Let me ask you something, Mami said at the stoplight. ¿Por qué la insistencia on going against everything I say, ah? When am I gonna see the day that you're going to stop being un dolor de culo and actually join the family, ah?

She searched for me in the rearview mirror. I stared at the man with the sign.

Before I could mutter an answer, she had her palm raised, stopping me short.

No, she continued. Don't answer right now, Francisca. Think about it.

~

Sometimes when we came home from church, Roberto, our neighbor, was waiting outside our house with a bag of tamarindos for La Tata. Red watery eyes from so much beer. Lucía ran to greet him and ask him for the millionth time to receive Jesús in his heart. He let her give him the Jesús Saves speech, always listening intently but eventually letting her know that he and the One Above had been through rough times. We don't speak much now, he'd say, it's better like this. He patted Lucía's head and mumbled something about Catholicism and corrupt priests.

I'd never seen Lucía so happy. It was probably one of the happiest moments of her life. Girlfriend found her clique, her life calling, and she couldn't care less that her juventud was wasting away, that she wouldn't discover masturbation until she reached twenty-two, that she would wake up one day many years from now crying and abandoned by Dios. Pero, for now, la rumba with Jesucristo continued.

Pablito and his parents were outside too. Pablito waved when he saw us step out of the car.

Francisca, allá está tu amigo.

Que he's *not* my friend.

His parents looked decrepit, goth, as if they'd literally walked from Argentina to Miami and now smoked cigarettes to pass the time. From the day we arrived finding cigarettes became an epic adventure, my day-to-day goal rarely accomplished because Mami always found the butts I picked up from the street and hid in my nightstand. Nasty, I know. Like, disgusting, girl—I *know*. I tried reclining against a wall outside of Publix Sabor near our house with a short skirt, showing all that body Diosito did not give me because I was plana like a tabla but still tried. I'd lean against shopping carts, waiting for the boys at customer service to take their breaks, flirting and pretending I'd lost my ID. They knew I was underage, but a grab of the boob three out of five times produced a pack of

Marlboro Lights. Until acne-scarred Jared dragged me to the bathroom and showed me his pipí, and there and then I knew Francisca needed new smoking avenues.

Maybe Pablito would come in handy after all.

I waved back shyly. Disturbed by Mami's "join the family" comment because what exactly did I have to think about? Against my own will she dragged me to that circus every Sunday precisely because I was Myriam's hija mayor and Mami needed to show her new sociedad that she was a dama, a good woman of Dios, and that her daughters were also devoted pious colombianitas, that we blindly followed her like all the women in our family had done with their mothers, that we—etc.

But what's an angry mamá when the prospect of cigarettes glimmers like the ocean we cannot see from our townhouse?

I joyously skipped over to and kissed both of Pablito's parents, who didn't even seem to notice my presence until I grabbed some groceries and helped carry them into the apartment. Pero 'tate quieta, you think Mami is dumb? Try again. Mami knew I was after the cigarettes and said loudly, Francisca, nena, if I see you smoking te las vas a ver conmigo, ¿okey? Francisca does not smoke. A grin to the goth Argentinians and a disgusted frown to La Tata for allowing Roberto to even hold her hand, plus a ¡Ya cállate! to Lucía, who did not for one minute shut up ranting about Eclesiastés.

Pablito's parents were two hippies, and he hated them for that. You could tell he despised their messy hair, Belén's hairy armpits, and the ghostly way they just drifted about barely touching the ground, ensimismados, perdidos, always in search of something invisible. He would later blame his parents for his failed social life, his addiction to porn, and even his foot fetish. Both Belén y Octaviano were part of the desaparecidos in the late seventies during the military dictatorship after organizing a sit-in against political censorship, and it seemed neither of them really got over it. It seemed both of them were still stuck in purgatory and were dragging Pablito along for the ride.

When I asked Pablito for cigarettes he mumbled that he did not want to be used. Is that why you came? he asked expectantly.

I felt bad and frustrated. I was here hanging with him, wasn't that enough?

I'm not using you, we're using your parents.

But I do not smoke, Francisca.

Basically, el perdedor felt guilty stealing cigarettes (brought by his tía from Buenos Aires porque here they were too expensive) and refused to disclose their location to me.

¿Por qué serás tan marica, Pablo?

As I have said before, he repeated, I am not a homosexual and I can prove it.

So what do you propose we do?

His room was scented with jasmine incense and papered with posters of dragons and comic pages ripped from magazines. The cleanest space in the apartment. With a whole cabinet full of cleaning supplies that I later found out he'd bought on his own. Figurines neatly arranged in war scenes stood along the bookshelves. An Argentinian flag hanging from the back of his door. I sat on his bed staring out the window at the orange rays dancing over dark cumulus clouds that contoured Pablito's belly as he scratched and asked me if I wanted to watch him slay dragons on his computer.

Ah Pablo, ¿en serio? Can't we just steal cigarettes and smoke?

Ya te dije que no fumo.

What if I teach you?

Pablito rolled up his Star Trek shirt, exposing cigarette burns all over his back. And I mean tons and tons of red circles splattered across his yellowy skin like a polka-dot sofa. He'd been burned by the venecos last week because he didn't want to suck someone's dick. I didn't want to look at him.

Ay, Pablo, why are you showing me that huevón? Cover yourself.

Porque no soy ningún maricón. I don't care about maricones but I'm not one, he continued. He clumsily rubbed some of the scars as if trying to wipe them out. He said he was now officially starting an anti-smoking campaign to eradicate cigarettes from the Heather Glen Apartment Complex.

Good luck, homie.

They're just fucking with you, I said. Smoking has nothing to do with it.

The venecos fucked with everyone in the neighborhood, the pool and Jacuzzi was their turf. I got away with walking in there sometimes because I was a nonthreatening girl with no ties to anyone, and usually all they managed to say was, *Mírala tan goth. Tan rico que lo debe mamar.*

But this fake campaign gave Pablito purpose, a way of

healing that was accessible to him. He couldn't just walk up to them and beat the shit out of their stinky asses, no ma'am. He grinned, hopeful, waiting for my response.

Maybe we can both beat them up, I said. Slay them like you slay those dragons. Inside I was all giggles imagining Pablito the Loser and Francisca the Goth raining hell on the cool kids by the pool. Lightning swords and all. Riding our centaurs into the pool, maniacally laughing while yelling, *¡Se me van de acá gonorreas!* Slay. Slay. Kick them out.

Nah, he said. They're so big. But you can help me with the flyers.

Out of his desk he retrieved flyers where dragons sat around in circles tearing apart packs of Marlboros.

I'd rather beat them up, I said.

CHAPTER SIETE

It was also around this time that Mami's Círculo de Biblia began assembling in our living room. I remember because the evenings felt endless. Alone in my room, I lay staring at the ceiling fan, sometimes reading, while three women plus La Tata and Mami and sometimes Lucía (when they let her) congregated with pen and pencil in hand filling out their *Jehová Vive* workbook. Each week they discussed one chapter of their workbook over some tinto and galleticas, filling out crossword puzzles, Jesús Saves the Unsaved (fill in the blanks), y El Quiz del Espíritu Santo. At the end of the eight weeks each one would graduate with a small ceremony at Iglesia Cristiana Jesucristo Redentor and a special diploma, which they all would hang proudly in our living room. And so every Tuesday I avoided our house for three hours, walking in circles, drenched in sweat the moment I stepped outside, peeking at the pool, sometimes longing to be in that Jacuzzi watching girls' breasts bounce up and down in excitement, fondled by boys who barely had facial hair.

There was also the lake. Man-made, green, impossibly dirty with cans, dead fish, and the fucking ducks squawking as if the world was about to end. And there was Roberto throwing moldy bread, petting ducks while grabbing the girls stepping in and out of cars, their round culos, the flashy one-pieces disappearing along with the reggaetón and the boys wearing dark sunglasses at night. I'd pick up the flicked butts landing close to me, smoking whatever was left, popping some gum and spreading pumpkin lotion all over my face and neck so Mami wouldn't notice I'd been smoking. But she did. Always. There was no way around her. The moment I'd come back to the townhouse she'd yell at me still looking down at her workbook, Te huelo, Francisca, ven acá, and right in her Círculo de Biblia she'd eye me over her rectangular glasses. Estabas fumando, ¿no? And in that nervousness I'd smile. The shame. Of course not, Mami.

Now, I know what you're thinking, mi reina, I do. Why wouldn't you just stand up to that madre of yours? What could she possibly do or say to you for having a benign cigarrito? Pero ay, that's because you clearly are not Colombian, you clearly didn't grow up with The Fearful Power of The Eye crushing your insides. The Eye that homegirl carried hidden in those lids—a genetic inheritance that only real Colombian matrons develop.

A ver, Francisca. Come here.

Pero Mami, I'm here, stop being paranoid. You guys aren't even done with your chapter tonight.

She wasn't having it. I said ven acá, Francisca, and the ladies can wait.

La Tata would look at me and bite her tongue as a way of saying, *Don't respond to your mother, mimi, do as she says. Muérdete la lengua*. Which always got me confused because she fought Mami about everything.

I stepped back, but Mami stood up from the chair, asked me to give her a hug. Only one of the women gazed at us, the other three busied themselves with pena ajena, stirring their tintos as if nothing at all was happening. One of them, I noticed, mumbled in prayer.

You know, cachaco, back in Bogotá I smoked my Kool Lights in the peace and comfort of my room, opening a window, blowing out the smoke that reached high enough to cover the tip of the mountains for a second. Mami only asked that the room be aired out and that I not buy loose cigarettes on the streets because, as she graciously explained to me, they could contain marijuana—which is totally untrue. Now she was determined to eradicate cigarettes from our lives almost as much as she was to militantly push Jesucristo into our hearts. So, here, give your Mami a hug.

Yours Truly spent the next week grounded, which didn't change anything because where else could I have gone? It wasn't as if Miami awaited my skinny, hairy body with exciting trips to the beach and tons of X. No way. I was helping Mami pass out flyers and wrap a Colombian newspaper that we then distributed first thing in the morning at four a.m. And, okay, I have to admit the sunrise in Miami pierces your brain like a headache you get from eating something so damn good. Its majestic yellows and oranges, its dampness, the shooting rays like darts penetrating the sky, a naked sun eating away at the receding night, and its beauty untouched by mountains. A rising hungry beast beating on the window where Mami outlined her lips, ready to begin the day. It was the most beautiful moment of the day and the most frightening. The sun was proof that this really was happening. This move that seemed like a mirage, a dream, an acid trip we'd unconsciously slipped into that eventually would fade. Before this week something in me still knew we would go back because Miami was evidently a failure, a wrong turn en el camino de la vida, and because we'd bought round-trip tickets para despistar a customs. That week our Avianca plane left for Bogotá with three empty seats.

We didn't talk much during our newspaper distribution and Tía Milagros always tagged along. Sometimes when reaching for another bag of newspapers, Mami placed her hand on my knee, showcasing her rings (the only remaining treasure she'd not pawned), and just left it there for a second. Then she asked for more periódicos and that was it. Milagros, on the other hand, did not shut up for one second.

Mira, sobrina, I've seen you hanging out with that argentinito. What's the deal? Don't tell me you're into gordos with no money.

Mami stared out the window. Two women fought in a front yard pointing fingers at each other, children around them played soccer.

Pablo? No, Tía, he's just a friend.

A friend, a friend. You know Wilson, Camilo, and Arturo from church are all single y dos de ellos work en Bank of America, she said, searching for my eyes in the rearview mirror and almost crashing into a Walmart truck.

I didn't have to see Mami's face to know exactly how it looked right then. How she pursed her lips, her hands accommodating the rings over and over, then retrieving hand sanitizer while she crossed the right leg over the left one, not daring to look at Milagros, who at every stop eyed me. Finally, at the light, Milagros turned all the way around saying Diosito would help me find a good Christian boy and that she understood why I didn't like Wilson, Camilo, or Arturo—You're waiting for a nice gringo. Good, good, at least someone is thinking of bettering our family.

Milagros, por favor, Mami's disapproving voice. She could be saying Merry Christmas, but the tone dragged the words, threw tomatoes at them.

Francisca needs to first open her heart to Jesús nuestro Salvador.

Claro, claro que sí. But she is opening her heart, right, nena? She's just not telling us. You don't want to end up como una cualquiera single y con malas mañas. Does she know—do *you* know, nena, that at any time and place you can recite the following prayer and Jesús will enter your heart and begin His saving?

Oh how Milagros enjoyed reciting The Prayer That Will Save You. How she then synced the radio to the Spanish Christian station and how she waved her hands to the beat, finishing each verse with an *Ajá Chuchito* and a *Ya tú sabe*. Milagros wore a pearl necklace bought at Sawgrass the week before because real pearls, mi reina, were a pawned thing of the past, a past with two maids dusting the ample living room and a job where people called her Doctora Milagros. And it seemed Milagros was dedicated to bringing back to life that high-class ejecutiva via secondhand, via outlet sales, via flashing them credit cards like tarot cards that'd determine her future, and via dressing—just wait till you hear—with pantyhose and paño. In Miami. With the remaining vestidos sewn in Bogotá by so-and-so designer that were, of course, way too hot for swamp weather but, nonetheless, cashmere turtlenecks (and leather botines) were worn that day to distribute Colombian newspapers that I was sure nobody read.

Mami mumbled the words of the song until she was also swept up by the now soft-rock beats, then joined Milagros in full singing. Her voice fueled by a certain conviction, channeling some deep inner hope—something she did quite often—her sweaty forehead wrinkled by the weight of her faith, pronouncing each word as if she was teaching it to children, vocalizing, leaving no *¡Ay!* or *¡Sí Jesús!* out of the chorus, her voice a pulley lifting Mami's troubles from her belly to the tip of her tongue and out to the air-conditioned oxygen we breathed inside that white van at eight a.m. watching the bumper-to-bumper traffic going south on I-95.

I knew something about Milagros's question troubled Mami. She only sang tightening her eyes with such fervor when something real was happening around her. She was in-your-face about everything except her feelings. Those were channeled via grand gestures and sad singing in the car. I tapped on the window and rolled my eyes until they hurt because Mami was so predictable. Pleaaaase, give me something to work with. Always—that invisible volcano of annoyance hidden under layers of makeup, a poker face that could cut your tumbao in two. Or three. Even before we jumped the Caribbean charco, girlfriend didn't have to mutter a word because her eyes, nose, forehead glared with neon subtitles: *I do not approve of that shirt, I abhor that friend of yours with the black shirt,* and *What do you think you're doing coming home at this hour, and showing off those legs?* But this tightening of the eyes, this hand-waving pointed to something else being concocted inside her: a gray mass of disapproval waiting to be dumped on my head.

CHAPTER OCHO

When we arrived home that afternoon, Mami let slip that as part of my punishment Carmen would be picking me up in two hours to join the Jóvenes en Cristo in their flyer distribution at Sedano's.

No way, Mamá, I said slamming the van door. Ni por el putas.

Cuidado, Francisca. Words have power, culicagada, and in this house we don't curse, agreed?

Agreed mi culo. I smelled foundation powder on her face more now with the heat and watched the wrinkles around her eyes accentuate when she squinted at La Tata, who carelessly chatted it up with Roberto, window open and all. Like Julieta. Cual muchachita de fifteen años. La Tata noticed Mami but barely smiled, paid no attention, and continued talking down, exchanging nods and smiles, so that you could only see a moon of white hair with streaks of blond (she'd unsuccessfully tried highlighting her hair) hanging like a carpet put out to dry over the windowsill. Don Francisco's voice yelling from beyond. Below, the townhouses packed together, pale-green sardines. A few of our neighbors decorated their entrance stairs with fake potted plants and their windows with Venezuelan, Dominican, Colombian, Argentinian, Cuban flags in an effort to express their deep patriotism for a country they'd left because they were all pussies who didn't want to stick around when shit went down—at least that's what Roberto said.

I thought Mami would stomp right on their faces, confront them about this make-believe romance, or, at the very least, yell at La Tata for her indecency porque qué dirán los vecinos. Porque una mujer que se respete. Porque this, porque that. But what did Mami do? She walked—not even—she *strolled* one foot in front of the other with such glamour, such elegance, con una clase que, Dios mío, you'd think she was still entering her office in Seguros Bolívar, waving at the doorman opening the door for her, greeting her, *Doctora Myriam, ¿cómo está?* Ay cachaco, even the weight she'd lost the past months was working for her, lifting her thick varicose legs from the cement parking lot.

Mami was on the runway of her life, crushing that thick hot air in jerky steps, now long strolls, now clattering murmur of the neighbors, now wavy black hair blocking Mami's view so that for a second it seemed as if she was stopping this race, pero, no señor, Myriam del Socorro Juan flitted across the parking lot hushing Helena who mindlessly sang boleros next to the dumpster, now with determination, now Mami a circle of prayer around Roberto, arms extended and yelling for the entire Heather Glen Apartment Complex to hear that *he!* es un sinvergüenza, that *he!* doesn't understand what he's doing because, por el alma de Jesucristo, this hombre is a sinner, unsaved, who, amid the skirts of widowed viejas, searches for lost life taken from him by the evils of la borrachera, las mujeres, because there is no doubt, oíganme bien, no doubt that *he!* es un pobre mujeriego who knows nothing about respect, who was probably kicked out of Cuba because he was an embarrassment to his family. You got no family, she said now pointing at his face, so you come trashing mine. ¡A ver! she continued for the handful of spectators, Mírenlo, por favor. Please God—now eyes shut to heaven—take pity on this sad soul, let him find you.

Uy Mami, no seas cruel. No es para tanto.

What Mami really meant to say was she was tired of seeing La Tata hanging out with a bueno para nada borracho near the house. If they could just not be visible. If they both could get drunk hidden from view. Because we'd come so far (so far!) for La Tata to ruin this Migration Project by lowering herself con un pobre cubano, not only black, but in a wheelchair. Por Dios.

La Tata closed the window furious before Mami finished her speech. Poor Roberto was left babbling, head down, hunched over, picking the dirt from his calloused hands. You could tell homeboy felt shamed or defeated or both. You could also tell some of what Mami said was true. He didn't fight her. Even his eyes showed a different type of watering. Different from the drunk pool that made his eyes yellow, sometimes red. This time the water was clear and the babbling stopped.

My punishment did not last one day. It lasted three, four, five days that turned into weeks in which Carmen picked me up in her white van decorated with so many golden Christian fish it looked like we were a tourist excursion on vacation to the beach and not Jesús advocates on earth. She arrived right at noon. Puntual esa niña, como si no tuviera más que hacer. She arrived right when the heat lost its gaseous elements and the air transformed into a solid cotton ball of warmth pushing at bleeding nostrils, successfully inhibiting normal breathing so that just stepping outside felt like drowning in hot caldo.

Hola, Carmen. *¡Pela'a!* She arrived right when the gray asphalt of the Heather Glen Apartment Complex was a hot plate seen through a veil of gas. All a mirage. Carmen at noon when Miami was a closed kitchen with a terrible gas-leak problem.

The car door slammed. Then her eager knocking on the door. Francisca! She didn't ring the bell, didn't wait patiently for me to open the door. Carmen's confidence stood firm in her black leggings and white flip-flops.

Francisca!

By the fourth day Mami knew it was Carmen, and by the fifth day Mami complained about Carmen's manners. ¡Esa niña! Can you tell her to ring the freaking bell?

I dreaded this moment almost as much as it excited me to leave the house. Because what waited for me inside the townhouse? Aló, cachaco. Nada. But, also, what waited for me inside that white van with the energetic youth leader? Three cold empanadas, boxes of *Jesucristo Vendrá, Are You Ready?* flyers, and Carmen's fruity cold-medicine smell. I went along with it. I took Plath's *Ariel* poetry collection with me for comfort because Sylvia was always there for me, always made me feel like this suffocating sadness went really well with black eyeliner and one hundred degree heat. With her emo ways Sylvia Plath was teaching me inglés, cachaco, teaching me that you can be brilliant and terribly alone.

Day after day dreading Carmen's smell but anxiously waiting for it.

My daily choices fluctuated between licking white envelopes with Mami, watching Pablito slay dragons, forever couch surfing with La Tata, or driving off to Sedano's with Carmen. This is what summer looked like. Veraneando con Jesucristo. In Bogotá we didn't have summer, time wasn't divided between seasons. We didn't even have seasons. We had rain and then we had aguaceros where the sky opened up to an ocean.

Leaving is always the best option.

At least you're moving, pretending you're off somewhere else. At least the dread of the house doesn't hook onto you like a screaming child wrapped around your leg that you have to drag. In a useless effort to conceal my identity, I wore a black hoodie thinking the cool kids by the pool wouldn't notice it was loser me, loner me, still-no-friends me seated shotgun with this excited blessed costeñita. I wanted to scream out the window, *I'm not even Christian please believe me!* I wanted to unzip my yellowing skin, leave it behind. But we didn't roll down the windows here. AC was our oxygen because real oxygen was unbearable.

On the first day she picked me up, I made the terrible mistake of asking for music. A stack of CDs with titles such as *La Luz del Señor and Other Hits, 30 Ways to Love Jesucristo, I've Been Rescued: 10 Hit Songs by Former Prostitutes* were our options. I fed *La Luz del Señor and Other Hits* into the radio. As soft beats bounced from the back speakers to my ears, and as Carmen hummed the lyrics of the song (which she did not have memorized entirely), I watched the few people outside. A homeless man held an *I FOUGHT FOR YOUR FREEDOM* sign with a tiny US flag perched on his web of hair; a dark woman sold red roses. People in and out of cars. Blond babies in the backs of SUVs. Both the translucent white people and the black people here had shocked the entire familia. Bogotá's diversity only went so far (meaning most people's skin color fell somewhere between yellowish olive and dark brown. Meaning not too pale, not too dark). The black people in our city were poor, very poor, displaced by the violence in rural areas and begging for money at stoplights. Here black families bought eggs next to Mami at Walmart and albino children sold cookies outside of supermarkets. I had very little contact with the gringo population those first few months, those first few years, really. In Miami, you don't have to. Gringos were somewhere out there beyond the tiny Latin American flags, beyond the church. It was all so different and yet so similar and yet so boring. I noticed these slight differences with zero excitement. They passed right through me. Like riding a tour bus with a jaded guide who nonchalantly points at the city's attractions: to your right, here, another Pollo Tropical.

The Christian music was annoying and heartfelt. The guy sang so passionately it was impossible not to feel some of that passion too. At some moment in the chorus I felt a tug at my stomach, a mix of eye roll and boredom. Carmen wore some ridiculous reflective sunglasses that I'd only seen on men riding motorcycles and a fish symbol on a gold necklace over another gold necklace reading *CAR-MEN*. God. I was constantly feeling shame for her.

So this is the deal, pela'a, she said. Pay attention, ¿okey? Why are you all distracted? We haven't even reached the pretty part of the road yet.

Francisca, she said tugging at my hoodie, por Dios, niña, it's a million degrees outside. Why you wearing a black hoodie?

Carmen, like Mami, was full of questions for me: Why don't you join the familia? Why don't you receive Jesús in your heart? Why are you wearing a black hoodie? ¿Por qué, Francisca, por qué?

Because, I said, I need to balance out those colorful flyers.

We were now way past the homeless guy, already on I-95 North.

You want some empanadas? she said, pointing with her mouth to the square Styrofoam next to my feet. I would eat cold empanadas every day for the next few weeks even though La Tata cooked the best arroz con coco with chicken sudao in all South Florida. But this was a little white spaceship taking flight. A small gateway outside the house. I pretended Carmen and I were running away:

Hello, this is radiocriolla reportando from our runaway car. Over here Jesús, over there some dirty tampons.

One is espinaca, she said, and one is carne.

Catholic school in Bogotá sold fat empanaditas with yellow rice and meat. Every day my friends and I waited in line for Glady's empanadas then broke into the chapel to play Ouija. On my last day at school we slid a pocket knife across the tips of our index fingers and promised the four of us would be mejores amigas forever and ever while mixing the drops of red blood. The rice on my empanada turned pink, then red, but I ate it anyway. I didn't cry. Not then and not at the airport when I ate my last empanada because whatevs, there's no way Bogotá would leave me. There was no way I was really leaving Bogotá.

Y aquí de nuevo, damas y caballeros. Radiocriolla reportando: This is us leaving the Heather Glen Apartment Complex. This is the white van and the kids by the pool squinting and pointing at the Christian fish, y el más musculoso winking at Carmen, winking at me while cracking open another beer. This is us leaving. Flying high. This is us slamming the van doors while the venecos move their heads in disapproval then tongue-kiss their jevas, then gently slap their butts. Their brown necks glowing in the sun.

On the fourth ride, after munching on the empanadas, I noticed two wobbly heads on the dashboard holding hands and blurted, Do you have a boyfriend?

It came out of nowhere. And once I heard the words leave my mouth I wanted to swing my hand in front of Carmen, pluck each word before it reached her. I pointed to the wobbly heads.

Carmen bit into the empanada, chewed for a good ten seconds before responding.

Pela'a, I was about to tell you our distribution plan, you ready?

I wasn't ready.

I continued, ¿Y es que no te dejan o qué? Is the Pastores' daughter not allowed to have boyfriends? Is that why?

I don't know why I felt this sudden spurt of intimacy with her. That I could cross that invisible line. Maybe it was the empanadas. Maybe it was the fact that we'd been spending so much time locked inside the van (the drive to outreach was longer than the outreach itself).

She turned to me quizzically, trying to decipher my intentions, so I said, Tranquila, mi reina, I'm not here to judge you.

All of a sudden my spark coming back. Like I could tease her.

She chuckled. Of course you're not judging me! Duh.

What does that mean? I said slightly offended because deep down I *was* judging her.

We'd arrived. She turned off the car, turned to me. Her right palm landed on my left knee. Cold from the AC. Freezing, actually. But also small with dirty nails painted a horrible off-yellow.

She left it there with no explanation. I waited for her to respond that, of course, I could not judge her but, of course, she judged me because Jesucristo was not yet in my heart, etc.

Pero reinita, nada de nada.

The weight of that hand warmed my leg. Dark fingers, cuticles eating away at the nail. On her wrist a small band with the Colombian flag and a brown one with yet another Christian fish.

The hand remained there until she said: You are very important to Jesús and He is waiting for you.

It was all about smiling. All about *Dios te bendiga, hermano*. All about patting them on the back after handing them a flyer. That's it. Our three-step program for Jesús flyer distribution and outreach efforts. Some forced a smile, others yelled thinking we were gonna jump them. One guy pulled me aside whispering that he didn't want a flyer but wouldn't the two gorgeous chicas join him for fried chicken and a good time? He lifted the bag, showing me the fried chicken, then pointed at Carmen who joyously (and without a bra) smiled in excitement every time she approached somebody.

I laughed at the fried chicken lover. Iluso, huevón. He called me una calentahuevas and limped toward Carmen.

Of course girlfriend didn't notice the skinny stick of white hair approaching her. She didn't notice when his eyes traversed her legs, landing on the *Jesús Lives* spread across her shirt, or when his reading glasses finally found her neck, studying both gold necklaces.

Two things occurred to me. First: it would do her good if this psychopath attacked her so she stopped trusting every motherfucker with such joy and began to distrust everyone like a true Colombian. My mind went there. It went to this fried chicken lover reaching for Carmen's waist, forcing a kiss on her neck, people around us busying themselves with their kids, everyone (including me) looking the other way, at their groceries, at the inflatable dinosaur selling Excedrin, at the sun. But the fried chicken lover just stared over his sunglasses, squinting at her necklace. He wanted her, that was clear. What if he *did* touch her? The probability of drama, of Carmen yelling and blessing, opened up right as the fried chicken lover slowly and clumsily gestured in front of Carmen, pointed at me, receipts falling out of his caqui Bermuda shorts like feathers.

Second: I'm not getting involved in this. Carmen is a big girl, big enough to handle an old man and his fried chicken. Let Jesús handle this. Let Diosito step in. Isn't He omnipresent? He must know one of His sheep is about to get slammed. Or kissed. Plus, I don't even know her. Let me just turn around and face the storefront. Let me just move away from them and hand this señora a flyer, a blessing, pat her kid on the back, tell her that *no, mi señora, we're not Catholic*, pretend I didn't see her shaking that rosary, sprinkling agua bendita, demanding we return to the real Iglesia católica and not this embarrassing circus you call una congregación, carajo. We agree on that, mi señora. If the fried chicken lover touched Carmen, the police would come and in broken English I'd say, *Mai neim is Francisca an ai guas bord*. And if the policeman was Cuban I'd say, *Mira, mi hermano, yo no vi nada, yo no sé nada, a mí ni me preguntes*. I'd let them know I just met Carmen, you see? I'm not even supposed to be here, I'm grounded and this is how Mami punishes her kids. And when Mami showed up at the police station dignified, completely disappointed but not letting anyone see it until we're inside the car and it's just Mami and me, she'd say, *Of course you wouldn't do anything to help Carmencita but just stand there. Por supuesto, qué vergüenza*. And I'd nod at my own predictability. I'd never been the courageous one and I was not about to start my superheroína career in the Sedano's parking lot.

And yet. Sometimes I imagined myself courageous, my skinny legs sprinting, my veiny fingers choking the motherfucker who dared touch that girl to the clapping and cheers of the growing audience. Francisca! Francisca! Francisca! The girl in my arms.

But mostly I stand motionless and look away. At times screaming for someone to do something. Like that one time back in Bogotá when, right before my very eyes, Ulises, my hamster, choked to death. The furry old ball thought his tiny mouth remained elastic but then it didn't, his eyes lost, his miniature body on loop. Garoso el nene, he choked on too many almonds and it was only after Ulises plopped on his side that I screamed and screamed and screamed and mindlessly ran holding him in my palm to the kitchen where María was washing the dishes and singing vallenato. Immediately María rinsed her hands, dried them on her apron, and proceeded to execute what she called dándole-vida-a-la-rata-esa. Chubby fingers all up in his small mouth. I remember knowing that, in some way, I killed him.

Now back to fried chicken lover.

I wish I could say all my third-worldness won, that I remembered I came from the land of the panela and the yucca-that-never-dies. That I channeled some of that fierceness that fueled my criollo ancestors when defeating the Spanish (but, also, fierceness that made them hate each other and never agree on one single thing). I wish I could say I remembered La Tata's wise words about womanhood and strength (people always seem to remember having remembered a third-world granny saying shit that saved them) but, really, La Tata believed a trimmed pussy and one hundred dollars would get you anywhere. I wish my legs hadn't been so limp and stupid, I wish they could've taken a freaking stance in life and walked me over to that security guard checking people's receipts. I wish I had yelled, *Carmen, there's a viejo verde next to you!*

Fried chicken lover gazed back, winked at me, kissed two of his fingers then placed the two kissed fingers in a metaphorical kiss on Carmen's shoulder. As she turned to greet him thinking homeboy was looking for some Jesús loving, fried chicken lover grabbed her face with both hands, leaned in, and whispered something.

Another señora argued Catholic things at me. We weren't the only Jesús-loving group at Sedano's that day, the Jehovah's Witness ladies in pantyhose y zapaticos negros had set up a cardboard bookshelf that advertised similar apocalyptic booklets. I watched them watching me watch Carmen and a pang of shame ran through me. Dios mío, the señoras *knew*. But Carmen gently pushed the fried chicken lover and continued distributing flyers to a family of six, and when the fried chicken lover gave her the finger, she smiled thinly and annoyed, then shouted some blessing at him. I stood with my shame holding the Jesucristo Vendrá flyers in one hand while Carmen triumphantly nodded at me.

You're a terrible outreach partner, pela'a, she said after the first week. You complain about the heat all day, you don't smile, and what's this? She snatched Plath's book from my backpack. ¿Qué es esto, Francisca? The car pulled to the curb, stopped. She eyed me. This depressing, manic poetry is only distancing you from Jesucristo, ¿qué vamo hace contigo?

I was both shocked and excited. Nobody in this shithole read anything beyond the church's canon.

You've read Plath? I said unable to hide my surprise.

She grew a little desperate. That's not the point!

But that *was* the point. This Jesús-praising jevita, this adopted child of God, this greasy-haired costeña and her perfected aleluya tumbao knew who Sylvia Plath was. Carmen totally regretted this intervention.

Está bien, I said trying to calm her down. We don't have to talk about it.

But there's nothing to talk about!

I winked teasing her. Something broke loose between us, our tightly pulled-back hair buns freed Pantene-commercial style. An easiness that made me feel we'd been friends for a long time and that I could do this, I could tease her. And there, right in front of I-95 South, my own plain mouth contorted, pushing itself to the sides in what can only be described as a plain ole smile, a small wakening monster.

~

Of course you could argue this was coming. Que si es culebra te muerde, mi reina, but I guess my vision blurred. I guess the days piled one on top of the other like balls of dough kneaded in a pile on the kitchen counter, next to the fake fruit and the porcelain angelito. It was the end of August, which meant Mami got into a fight with Milagros because Milagros mentioned my father. I inadvertently became Carmen's outreach mano derecha, and the palm trees swayed in the same direction as they did in June, as they did in July, as they probably do now.

If Mami avoided talking about anything, it was, uno,

dos, tres: Colombia. She did not touch The Subject, did not compare places; she cut Colombia off like a nurse cuts an umbilical cord with silver scissors. Chin-chin. It was gone. There were, of course, more specific Untouchable Colombian Subjects including my father, the previous shine of Mami's hair, and Mami's former job as a gerente general of a multinational insurance company. Subjects she'd dismiss with lies such as *You know they murdered a cuchillo limpio three muchachos from good families in Bogotá last week? A ver, can you bring me that notepad?* Nodding, pointing to the notepad with her lips, then resuming inserting flyers for Facial Surgery Discount! and licking the envelope twice. Mami dreaded licking those envelopes and eventually used a brush dipped in water; mindlessly, repetitively, she'd dip and brush and dip and brush until a white stack grew cave-like around her.

Mi papá no es un misterio. If my father has yet to make an appearance it's because Mami overreacted to his stupidity. My eyes rolled all the way back in my head every time she said, *Tu papá ruined my life.* He was not a secret DAS agent or a senator snorting paramilitary money or a good machito grinding corn for arepas on Sundays for his family. Homeboy was there and then he wasn't. Nevertheless, Myriam del Socorro Juan, a.k.a La Mami Mayor, took it to heart to tattoo the pain all over her face as a reminder that my dad was an asshole. It was like a glow-in-the-dark tattoo, only visible when the lights were off.

Milagros dropped some comment about my father being one of the best things that ever happened to Mami.

The real tale goes something like this: ¡Y dice! Mami was *this* close to joining a convent, a real convent with full habits and no sex. She was *this* close when she met my dad, then boom boom I want you in my room, Lucía and I plus a dead baby all breaking in from the cosmos. Mami said Milagros knew how much he ruined her life (that's all she says. Do not ask for specifics. Mami's reply is always: This is not the moment, pass me the glue), but Milagros is also jealous that the Pastora chose Mami as the lead ujier and knowing Milagritos, well, ya tú sabe. Mami says—and La Tata is not taking sides on this—that Milagros's face almost exploded with anger when at the Mujeres Valientes meeting (not to be confused with the Círculo de Biblia at my house) La Pastora announced that Mami showed leadership and a devoted commitment to Jesús. And she did. I can attest to that. Myriam del Socorro arrived that night with a dignified look, a look that reminded me of the times I visited her office in Bogotá. A look that said, *I manage people, I make shit happen, do not mess with my tumbao.* Mesmerized by her own energy, Mami sat munching arroz con coco with a terrifying look of satisfaction.

Was Mami back?

Ay Dios mío, reinita, do not get ahead of the story.

Obviously during the next few Sundays Milagros did not sit with the familia in our reserved spot on the right side next to the diezmo box. Milagritos walked around us, kissed everyone except Mami, and continued kissing people like it was a cocktail party and not a holy service. Y para colmo Mami in turn searched for La Pastora, laughing and gesturing with her as loud and obnoxious as she could while wearing her favorite red pantsuit that returned that boss glow to Mami but also made her sweat profusely.

I arrived early with Mami to help Carmen set up the Jóvenes en Cristo space. Wilson was already there to help us. We arranged purple pillows, stacked Bibles, bullet-pointed the material Carmen would cover on the whiteboard, and placed a small stack of flyers in front of each pillow that the Jóvenes en Cristo distributed sagradamente to their peers each week. Paula (Carmen's number-one minion now suddenly relegated to number two because *this* pechito was going places) and the other shekinas were there arriving earlier and earlier each Sunday, gifting Carmen cookies in the shape of crosses and even an iPod Mini with a Christian fish on the back. I'd later listen to some of those Christian songs. You could tell Paula was perdida. If la nena hated me before, now she just could not stand me. She kept bumping into me, policing my every move, pointing to my clothes, my hair, digging about my "dark past" as she called it via Lucía, quizzing me on the New Testament every time Carmen was there.

Francisca, she said to me, if you now have Jesús in your heart, you have to stop wearing all negro. It's like kind of an insult to El Señor. Wouldn't you agree, Carmen?

The bathroom mirror reflected our three heads. Mine was the smallest. Carmen in the middle pinning up her hair, readying her shekina outfit.

I don't have Jesús in my heart, I said while Carmen obviously tried to ignore the question by pushing bobby pins into her tangled hair.

You don't? Then to Carmen, She doesn't?!

Carmen's response was a simple: The Lord loves all His children, Paula. Now pásame that brush.

This wasn't enough for Paula; she clearly worked hard to climb the blessed ladder at this church, clearly wanted to go to high holy places, and where was she now? Where was Carmen leaving Paula by choosing me? And why, really, was Carmen choosing me?

Furious, Paula entered a stall and peed. I thought of leaving them alone—girlfriend was trouble and Carmen needed to set shit straight with her—but the thrill no me dejaba vivir. *This bitch wants to make trouble with me. She's jealous. I'm making a name for myself in this shithole church.* During one of our days at Sedano's, Carmen mentioned that Paula had some unresolved issues with the One Upstairs, that she was too competitive, always kissing the floor Carmen walked on. And you don't like that? I said envying her power. And with a genuine face she replied, Does it look like I like it?

I thought of walking out of the bathroom and bumming a cigarette from the kids at the 7-Eleven across the street. Maybe I needed to leave this Jesús Diva Tournament before it all got too messy. Pero cachaco, who am I kidding. Let it get messy. Homegirl wanted blood? I'd give her something to complain about. Carmen didn't say a word. Bobby pins fell like hail around her. Dry hair a tangled mess. She caught herself before saying *fuck*.

I eyed her frustrated face and she giggled. Carajo, she whispered, you see how dry this hair is? Carmen's attention was the only spark in my life right then. I was so distracted I didn't realize I was slowly becoming Carmen's mano derecha. That the other Jóvenes came to me for advice. And who did Paula think she was anyway? Let's be honest, mi reina, I spent all those hours with Carmen distributing flyers in the sun, aguantándome el dele que dele de las señoras católicas, eating stale empanadas. I clearly deserved to be the Pastora's daughter's number one, y Paulita se lo podía meter.

Even if I didn't have Jesús in my heart, so what?

I took Carmen's hair in my hands, so dry it could snap any second. Do something, Francisca, por fa! I took the comb out of her hands. For once, carajo, for once I was spending my days doing something other than writing Don Francisco letters or waiting for the dial-up internet to connect or watching Pablito slay dragons or staring at the fucking ceiling fan. Time, although still circular, wasn't piling up on itself.

This isn't gonna work, I said. Let me braid it.

Carmen handed me a gold hair tie. In Catholic school we weren't allowed to wear our hair down so Mami taught me in front of the hallway mirror how to braid my curls in different styles. I was a braiding pro and Carmen's dry hair was perfect. And, yes, I felt some malice trickling all around my flat chest as I saw myself climbing life's ladder and staring down to find Paula begging for un poquito. Uy tutuy. I had something people wanted.

I braided Carmen's hair like I owned it. Every string of hair I combed through my fingers twice. When Paula walked out of the stall, I was all over that head, hair spraying the shit out of it then sprinkling it with gold glitter (Carmen was the Holy Spirit that day), not even caring (but knowing) that Paula was washing her hands totally heartbroken, holding back tears, searching for Carmen's eyes in the mirror, and when they met, Paula blurted, I picked up the new *Got Jesús?* shirts this morning. They're on the counter at the entrance next to the fake bowl of grapes.

You gotta give it to her: She tried. Over and over.

Carmen thanked her. Then Paula asked if there was anything that needed to be done before she got all done up in her shekina dress. There wasn't anything. Wilson and Francisca already finished the setup, Carmen added. I kept my gaze to the dry hair, untangling here and there, feeling Carmen's dandruff, amazed at my newly acquired girl power.

~

I made the terrible mistake of telling Pablito about my rise at the church, about Carmen and the way Paula literally opened doors (more like closets where we kept the pillows) for us. In his room we were watching yet another rerun of Star Trek. Excited I yapped about doing Carmen's hair, having VIP access backstage where only the important people at Iglesia Cristiana Jesucristo Redentor were allowed, where the Pastores kept all the church merchandise and money.

Pablo, es que you don't understand, las chiquiticas, las shekinas lined up for me to do their hair.

I went on and on about brainstorming with Carmen for our weekly Jóvenes en Cristo youth-group meetings, how after Paula left almost crying that day in the bathroom, Carmen and I bought a friendship necklace at Walgreens, you know, the ones where each person keeps part of the moon on a necklace. I was on a roll. Didn't realize I had launched into a monologue when Pablito interrupted me.

I thought you hated that place, he said scratching a scab on his arm.

¡Yo sé! I *do* and that's so not the point.

Well, entonces? Excuse me, Francisca, but if you abhor that institution, as you claim you do, then it seems contradictory that you care about this Carmen girl?

He always talked to me like we were high-class Spaniards who, instead of embarking on a low-class trip to the New World, had stayed in the Motherland, grateful for the purge of bums. Only we had no money, no crown, no motherland.

When he looked up at me, I realized he never shaved his upper lip and thin black hairs shadowed in an awkward, uneven semicircle around his mouth. I had something similar going on and I felt a weird sense of closeness to Pablito. The hairs were mostly dry except for the tips of some, wet from his constant licking.

You're sooo missing the point, huevón. That's what I get for trying to tell you anything important.

He chuckled. So esa iglesia is important now? God, Francisca, are you Christian for reals?

Shut up! I'm not! It's not important. Get me a cigarette please? I said frustrated, picking up *Ficciones* by Borges from his nightstand, trying to change the subject. He tried to resist but eventually caved and brought back a pack. Keep them, he said. Now would the señorita care to watch me slay zombies?

We slayed zombies for hours that day. Pablito let me smoke in his room with the windows open while he crushed my zombie soul because his parents also smoked inside the house so it always stank of cigarettes and anyway they wouldn't be able to tell. I secretly wished I had parents like those for at least a month. Can you imagine what I could have done with all that freedom? I couldn't imagine all that freedom. Mami would find me. I just pictured myself chain-smoking in a room plastered with Joy Division and Kurt Cobain, eating home-cooked meals where nobody used mustard or fried plantains and nobody watched Don Francisco and you couldn't find one Bible. Pablito kicked my ass and killed all my zombie tribe. You suck at this game!

I sat on his *Dragon Ball Z* bedspread smoking, a faint smile on my face. Out the window it poured like it only knows how to in the Caribbean, soaking even beneath the skin. The rain did not come in drops, was not subtle or comforting, but like someone gashed the ballooning gray sky with a giant knife and every drop of ocean rushed out. It's like the sky has a fever, Pablito said, and it's sweating all over us. Whenever it rained in Bogotá (which, reina linda, every day), Mami said it was God crying, and my father replied, No no, Myriam, it's Dios pissing on us. It's His revenge.

Tropical fever. Tropical revenge.

Maybe God cries, sweats, and pees at the same time. If I was the Creator of this world I'd be sobbing and peeing too, all the time—I also would have done things a bit differently. On the other hand, I never would have applied for that job.

I never understood Pablito's obsession with video games but I didn't care. I enjoyed being numb in the head, focusing on ripping off people's heads and killing everyone to feed my zombie tribe.

¡Muere, pendejo!

From time to time Pablito's mom yelled from the balcony, still in her pj's, smoking, reading, asking him to check on the gnocchi. This house, so chaotic and godless. Pablito told me he sometimes heard his parents having sex and he knew where they kept all the condoms and none of it bothered him. That's disgusting! You pervert. How can it not bother you? I couldn't believe his parents had sex—they could barely fucking walk.

That day while peeing in their bathroom, I found a box of colorful condoms and took a few. In my room that night I ripped open the extra-large cherry-flavored pink condom and blew it up into an imaginary penis. So slippery and gross. I couldn't believe Pablito's skinny gray father wore a cherry-flavored pink condom. Pablito was such a pervert. I caressed the gooey surface, massaging the tiny bumps with my index finger, pretending at first this was a scientific pursuit and I was just doing empirical research on the matter of weird neighbors who fuck. But then I moved into the bathroom and forgot about Pablito's parents.

In the bathroom mirror I am a long yellowish stick. Sad small tits and a jet-black bush that I refuse to trim (for what?) plus this new cherry-flavored pink cock. I picture what it must feel like to carry such a thing between your legs. I turn sideways, I twirl. I give myself a shameful fake hand job pretending Carmen opens the bathroom door and sits on my lap and I braid her hair while she whispers my pink cock is the most beautiful dick she's seen. I hold the pink dick on my pelvis looking more like a tragic bal-loon animal than a sex toy for Carmen. I'm horny and scared. I try thinking about boys sitting on my lap instead of Carmen. Wilson, Pablito (I went there), my cousins, Camilo, Arturo, every boy at church, every boy hanging by the pool, every boy I know. I'm stroking buzzed heads, flat chests, penetrating them. Five minutes pass before one of the boys grows long dry hair, greasy skin, thick legs. Five minutes and their dicks disappear and I'm braiding Car-men's hair again, hair spraying it, gold necklaces between her breasts, her deep voice praying over me, and before I know it I'm praying too, before I know it I'm thanking Jesús, then regretting everything and asking for forgive-ness over and over until the condom deflates from all the touching and Lucía knocks on the bathroom door.

CHAPTER NUEVE

When Mami talked about El Apocalipsis, it always ended badly. She slowly removed her glasses, flipped her hair, eyes closed, index finger and thumb pinched between eyebrows so we knew we had to pay attention. There is a sort of magnetism in Mami's gestures. A hypnotic force that pulls every bone, freezes all muscles with a nod or a touch or, in the Apocalipsis case, an eyes-closed, grabbing-bridge-of-nose combo that indicated something troubling Mami was about to be released as a "piece of life advice" or a passive-aggressive story.

It started with a loud silence.

Then she'd sigh (eyes still closed). Again. And again and again, until after five minutes one of us asked, Mami, ¿qué pasó? And she'd say, ¿*Qué* pasó? Que ¿*qué* pasó? Leéme esto. And one of us would read: *Porque El Señor Himself con voz de mando, con voz de arcángel and with the sound of the trumpet of God will descend from heaven And the dead en Cristo will rise primero.*

She was obsessed with the coming of Christ. More than anything in the Bible it was when the heavens parted and she'd fly into Papi Dios's arms that had Mami mojando canoa about being Christian. It was also because of this obsession that she couldn't stand my apathy toward the Apocalipsis. Because what happens with those unsaved souls, mi reina? They burn and burn and Satan inscribes *666* on their butts like cows while having a big orgy.

I told Mami I didn't care and asked for money. *You don't care? How can you not care about this?!*

I knew money was so tight, I knew we barely paid rent, I knew every time we talked about budgeting homegirl landed on the Apocalipsis just in time to avoid explaining why the Pastores had bought our groceries that week.

Mamá, just tell me we don't have money, I whispered angry. And that, mi reina, is how the Apocalipsis talk ended. Door slammed. Mami prayed at me, La Tata drank, Lucía wrote Christian songs.

But Mami wasn't the only one worried about Satanás burning numbers on my ass. The Pastora had already pulled me aside many times for "una charladita" on matters concerning my soul burning after the Rapture and yada yada yada Cristo was still waiting for me and yada yada yada wouldn't it be nice to join my family eternally? I wondered what exactly Mami had revealed about our house to the Pastora that made her think we all wanted to spend our afterlives together. I also couldn't imagine Jesús and Dios like kids in a dentist's waiting room checking in with the receptionist every so often, *Did Francisca receive my son in her heart yet?* (said no god *ever*), then He sat again and consoled Jesús, who couldn't stop sobbing because the answer was: *No*. I evaded those questions with nods and grunts and emergency bathroom breaks.

And yet. Reina mía, reina mía, guess who else loved

the Rapture? It was so hard to dodge Carmen's insistence. Mami and La Pastora I could handle, Lucía and La Tata were a piece of cake, but Carmen? Damn. I was with her when she chased a woman from Sedano's into Walmart and out again because the señora said, *Okay, I'll think about it.* You couldn't tell Carmen you'd *think about it* because that meant giving her hope about one less person burning in hell, which was something that greatly troubled her. Plus, Carmen and I had become inseparable. It felt like at any moment I could close my eyes and tell you exactly how many pimples she'd had on her forehead that day. Like I could mimic her jumpy giggles and if given enough time count the freckles on her brown skin from memory. After Sedano's we hung out at her house even though the Pastora still wasn't 100 percent on board with her primogénita kicking it so much with an unsaved soul. Nonetheless, this unblessed cuerpito criollo sat on their couch every day before and after outreach and every Sunday after church, Wilson sometimes joining us, but mostly just la jefa Carmen y this persona debriefing and planning our next Jóvenes en Cristo outreach, the next Jóvenes meeting, while Carmen's bare feet lay on my legs as she complained about Paula insisting on sleeping over at her house.

Estoy mamada, ¿sabes? Technically I can't say that, but I'm so over her, pela'a.

Every time she talked shit about Paula, a piece of my skin danced in enjoyment. It was rare that we got to talk shit, but after a few weeks Carmen started letting her guard down and I did everything to encourage her.

Yo sé, why doesn't she look for another church?

Primero, why don't you let Jesús save you y ya? Salimos de esa. She sat up, her head falling on my shoulder like she was almost begging me to be saved.

Pela'a, you smell like shit!

We'd been passing out flyers all morning, then lifting boxes with new youth merchandise in and out of the church. Of course I smelled like shit, although I didn't notice.

Francisca, she laughed, let me lend you some deodorant.

Don't bring me anything! It's fucking hot outside, Carmen. Además why are you smelling my armpit, you weirdo.

She sniffed under my arm again and laughed. Nena, she said, Francisca, hueles terrible cojone.

I refused her medicated Dove deodorant with its miniscule hairs. The mere idea of having pieces of her in my pores gave me an excruciating thrill that I just couldn't stand.

Okey pues, I can lend you a shirt. Take that nasty thing off.

It was pouring outside. The rain banged against the windows, the wind whispered through the tiny cracks. Sometimes I still closed my eyes and pretended I was back home in my room and the rain was cold, misty, full of darkness and danger, that if I stepped outside a bunch of señoritas in miniskirts would rush past me with plastic bags on their heads. The AC always killed the daydream. This time it was the AC plus Carmen holding a pollito-yellow shirt from her own Catholic school back in Barranquilla.

A ver, she pulled up my arms, let me help you.

I could've done this on my own, Carmen knew I could

do it on my own, but she held my waist tight. Her arms around me like a soft straitjacket, like they could have stayed there forever and eventually blended with my Ramones shirt. Carmen was in charge and I let her. She breathed close, mumbling one thing or another about using the right deodorant and about my tiny arms, which she thought were cute. How can arms be cute? How could she think my hairy stick arms, now up in the air waiting for her to pull up my shirt, were cute? Her hands were cold. They were on my skin and then they weren't. As she pulled up my Ramones shirt, my earring got stuck. I yelled but she kept yanking at it, trying to break it loose but making it all worse, sending a ripping pain from my left ear to my left toe. I heard the earring hit the floor but the shirt wouldn't come off. Great. And now half of me was exposed and I couldn't see anything and the shame of her staring at my belly, my gray bra, at the mole with the hair I forgot to pluck because *I did not know* someone was about to see me half-naked and the boiling heat of shame slapping my face and fuck La Tata for suggesting those earrings made me look so churra, so guapa, so señorita, when I never, ever wore stupid pearl earrings and now I only looked like a maldito joke with no tits y Carmen que nada se lo toma en serio y Carmen giggling—Mierda, pela'a, your ear is bleeding—and her cold hand on my waist again not comforting but supporting herself because homegirl could not stop laughing.

¿Cuál es el chiste, Carmen? ¿Cuál es el chiste?

It's no joke, she said cagadita de la risa. Sit on the couch más bien.

She pushed me onto the couch then landed next to me.

She smelled my armpits again and I couldn't do shit about it. Then her fingers gently slid underneath the shirt collar, brushing my neck, almost poking my ear but finally the shirt was off. I wanted to pretend it wasn't over. My ear was still bleeding. I pretended I was angry at her, touching my ear like it was hurting so much, searching for the missing earring on all fours.

She rested on the couch looking for the first time like a cool dorky girl who just happened to be wearing a shirt with a bleeding crown bisected by a blue dove. That morning when she picked me up, the venecos had yelled at her to please come bless their dicks with her dove, but don't bring your friend! Blue dove shirt kicking the Ramones' ass. I didn't say anything but felt so glad I was with her.

I have a secret remedy for your ear, you wanna know what it is?

Pff sí, claro. Like I'm gonna let you anywhere near my face right now.

She waited for me.

Leather couch on white tiles, faded bra on yellowing skin, and my belly still exposed, still too real right now and allofasudden Carmen's hands, also too real, on either side of my head pressing on my neck, my toes contracting in fear. I may have closed my eyes? Or grabbed her leg? I may be making shit up but I know at some point I grabbed the couch as if we were flying off and her breath stank of Cheetos. Stay still, Francisca, she whispered. The thrill of her warmth approaching y yo frozen on the spot until I felt her tongue, like a mollusk entertaining its prey with its tentacles, licking and sucking on my earlobe.

She did not kiss me, mi reina. Well, kinda. Not really.

She put my entire right lobe in her mouth like those hamsters the shekinas bring to church sometimes suck on tubes of water. Eyes closed or open or staring at pictures of the Pastora because I didn't want Carmen to stop but also I had no idea exactly how my earlobe tasted or if I'd washed my earlobe that morning or if Carmen would turn around disgusted. Her teeth barely touched my skin and I couldn't make out the form of her tongue, just its waves of water.

Not sure how long this lasted. Maybe real-life thirty seconds, maybe a minute, but it was eternal. We were there sixty years until her tongue grew wrinkly and we passed out from old people's disease. We died side by side while she still sucked on my lobe, my faded bra holding my sagging breasts, her shirt threadbare. The warmth of her saliva on my ear was abruptly followed by the cold wind of the AC right above us. I dared not look at her. The thought of a disappointed face—I didn't want her taking back all the seconds of saliva spent on my ear, I wanted her to be proud of licking a part of my body. The fear of Carmen suddenly snapping out of it.

CHAPTER DIEZ
Bogotá, 1970s
Myriam's Presidenta Dreams

But let's go back to Mami—to Coffee Land, to the *bum bum bum* of the seventies, the Sagrado Corazón and the Virgen María supervising the early days of perico that brought us ay Jesucristo here comes Don Pablito Escobar and there's nothing you can do about it. In those days Mami lived in Bogotá. Seventeen-year-old Myriam sang Ana y Jaime in a blue checkered school uniform that hung below the knee, daydreaming of Cartagena and Mansur, her ex-novio—that dreamy machuque with the papi tumbao and the perfect mustache—and a desk with a plaque: *Myriam del Socorro, presidenta.* La Tata yelled at her to help with the sewing, the baking, amazed at Myriam's ability to lose herself todita in a sueño. Sometimes La Tata found Mami en el patio, book in hand, eyes closed, daydreaming of the machuque opening doors for her larger-than-life oficina, shiny imported wooden floors below her feet, gardenias framing the floor-to-ceiling windows with a view of the expanding Andes, and at the center, Bogotá: small, infinite, dirty, and all of it at the tips of Myriam's fingers typing behind an imported German typewriter, but never *ever* helping La Tata sell another candy or bake another cake for rich people (toca aclarar, her *own* people). She would be Señora Myriam estrato seven, mi reina, and her office with a view, plus the machuque with his caterpillar eyebrows, would be proof of this.

¡Myriam! ¿Qué carajo are you doing?

The sueño's bubble was tough to burst, La Tata knew this. No passive-aggressive banging of pots and pans on the door would bring Myriam back from the leather office chair, the secretaria providing a run-through of her daily schedule, lukewarm tinticos, a perfectly arranged set of blue pens across the mahogany desk and Mansur by the window, full of testosterone and love for her. In her notebook she detailed exactly how the plants should be arranged, how many sets of blue pens and blue binders should fill the shelves, and even the room temperature, cachaco. Girlfriend had it down to a T. That office had always been inside her, bien despierta, poking at Myriam before she could say *billullo*—even before her father, Don Fabito, fucked the family's estrato there was baby girl Myriam, calculator in hand, charging three pesos to anyone entering their house, making them sign her *Jean Book* notebook with a clear explanation of their visit. Back then homegirl had just turned seven and she had La Tata calling her Doctora Myriam.

Once La Tata burst the sueño's bubble it was the small house with its rusty wooden fence and old buckets of paint that welcomed Myriam. Hola hola, buenos días, princesa. Over here half-dead roses crumbling by the entrance, over there browning leaves against thick gray clouds. Against a drop of light blue, the same blue. Same cielo. Every. Day.

¡Ay Mamá! I'm coming.

Nothing ever changes in this city. She looked up and as she cursed the damn clouds, a pajarito shat on her shoulder. That's good luck, mimi, La Tata would say. Bogotá's mornings of sun and a sky so blue you thought it was our mar, another of Diosito's third-world jokes because the sea did come from the cerros, from el sur, thick dark cumulus clouds circling la city, so that by four in the afternoon the sky ripped open in a fierce aguacero that transformed Bogotá into a blur of water. Myriam enjoyed the rain. The one thing about Bogotá she didn't hate was the weather, cool and crisp, rainy, blow-dried hair lasting an entire week without puffing into an uncontrollable frizz as it did in Cartagena (and she always carried a plastic bag for her hair). La Tata complained the hijuemadre aguacero created puddles, drowned the roses, and made her run around the house with buckets catching every leak from every crack in the ceiling. The labyrinth of buckets depressed Myriam, angered her, reminded our girl of their previous casona in Cartagena not leaking or cracking, mornings where pajaritos sang instead of shitting and Armenia heated quibbes, chocolatico caliente, calling Myriam *señorita*. A good maid. And the spiral stairs? The smell of cleanliness, Chanel perfume, imported vanilla candles.

The thought of her childhood was dreadful. Days in Cartagena before el idiota of a father fucked—lo que se dice *fucked*—them over investing money in land all over a country that was quickly overtaken by this mafia and that sicario and no use paying vacunas to this narco or that guerrilla; in the end they didn't know which poor-turned-evil-rich motherfucker stole the fincas. Lost in the swaying bureaucracy of the seventies when her father reached out to his rich buddies at Banco Popular, all them criollos gave Don Fabito the finger, and before you could say *se armó el coge coge* Don Fabito was fired. And so, unable to pay the private club membership, private school, private this and that in Cartagena, and Cartagena's tight social circle whispering of their loss, the family could not take the embarrassment and moved to Bogotá like nobodies, mi Dios! Like Milagros and Myriam never took tennis lessons, nesting en una casita in a so-so neighborhood surrounded by *those kinds of people*. Gentuza, pura gentuza rara en ese barrio.

Myriam detested the thought of her wasted childhood but never lost faith. La niña kept drawing her office as a purification ritual, coloring important parts: the view, her perfect hair, Mansur in aviator sunglasses. La Tata poked her and Myriam responded she was working on her homework, Mamá.

But you're asleep! Drawing mamarrachos.

Mamá, it's called *thinking*.

As she said this Myriam stepped back, waiting for La Tata's manotazo to her face.

Respondiéndole a tu madre, muy bien. Come here right now, I need you to finish the icing on this cake for Martica.

From time to time La Tata slapped the girls to keep the motherhood mojo going. Not this time. She was in a good mood: her cakes were booming in the barrio and everyone craved a piece of Alba's sugar. A line of pompous hats appeared outside their door every Sunday after church, women tasting (and loving) her new bizcochos, ordering three, four for their grandchildren's birthdays. Y allá deep inside the house where nobody saw him was Don Fabito, the only man of the house, a ball of aguardiente murmuring to himself, glued to the radio. Against all odds La Tata's income fed the house. And because La Tata wore the pantalones, earned the monies, instead of nuptial bliss the main bedroom became her workplace, and in the tiny room adjacent to the kitchen, a room for the maid they couldn't afford (at the moment), sat a double bed for La Tata and Don Fabito where no magic happened. La Tata called him Señor Martínez: *¿El Señor Martínez ya almorzó?*

The sight of Don Fabito angered Myriam now. Radio on all day, old newspapers scattered around the floor and draped like blankets over the couch next to the invincible media de Néctar. Myriam rarely invited her friends from Catholic private school—sobra decir paid for by her mother's sisters who of course couldn't sit and watch the downfall of the girls into district schooling—she couldn't stand the embarrassment of the harapiento daddy mumbling curses at the radio, fighting with his own shadow, broken TV antenna and bags, plastic bags, clothes, porcelain angels scattered around the house, and the house itself small and screaming a bare estrato three. From Mercedes to buseta. Na-ah, mamita. At school she performed the high-class elegance memorized so well from the early days cn la costa, her sister Milagros playing along but barely caring, sometimes forgetting their father *was* on a trip to Italy, remember? Myriam didn't let La Tata set foot on the perfectly trimmed lawn of the Santa María school unless La Tata's outfit had been scrutinized, scanned for any possible poor choices. And La Tata was no dumb bitch. Her heart knew. She told the girls to be thankful, at least they had food on their plates, a roof over their heads, at least they weren't begging on the streets. Look at those poor children with snot and ripped clothes. ¡Dele gracias a Dios, no joda!

But Mami couldn't thank God. And yet. Although angry at El Señor for letting their lelo father ruin their lives, she still prayed during school mass, after communion, and at night in front of the Virgen, asking the blood-teared Madonna to please let her rise above this nightmare, let her be the businesswoman she was meant to be, let Mansur find her again, etc.

~

A block from the house there was a small mercadito de las pulgas where mujeres campesinas sold handmade clothes, jewelry, and those ugly chivas tourists get when traveling to Colombia. Those sold cheap. The jewelry even cheaper because nobody in that neighborhood could pay more and of course the campesinas got what they could, having been uprooted from their land by the same poor-turned-evil-rich motherfuckers plus the military. They were the new poor class of La City arriving en pleno Bogotá, sometimes barefoot, always lost, always pushed to the margins, up the mountains, beginning what would be known as *invasiones*: a clog in the arteries of Bogotá. Assemblages of shacks coating the mountains with their sadness, their lack of electricity, their mud and rats. Mi reina, the campesinas had it so bad even the poor people en La City were like, *I ain't sharing my barrio with* those *people*.

Myriam walked past the mercadito every day on her way to and from school. Today she stopped, caught by the truly intricate and beautiful jewelry: tagua necklaces, wooden bracelets engraved with precolonial designs, silver earrings. She picked up a tagua necklace and held it to her chest, checking herself in the long, blurry mirror. The campesina said she looked good. *Sí claro, and what do they know about looking good.* The next day she stopped again. This time she tried on the silver earrings that accentuated her cheekbones, transforming the carajita into a high-class businesswoman with a checkbook and a chauffeur waiting outside the school. And this time when the campesina reiterated how good Myriam's face looked, so exótica, like from the movies sumercé, she handed her a few bills and said, Por favor be serious, hiding the internal goose bumps behind a bitch face. The expensive-beauty pride. The bling-bling film gently smoothed over her body, clinging to her ears. At the Santa María school all the niñas de papi drooled over the delicate stones hanging from Myriam's ears: *Que oh my God where did you get those, que oh my God if I give you money can you please buy me some in red.* Even Leonor, the coolest chick at school who never ever gave Myriam the time of day, *even* Leonor stopped Myriam during recess because she had not seen those earrings in that color—Are those *French?* You'd think Myriam would just feel superior, welcomed, a new sense of belonging for finally cracking the friendship code. Pero, cachaco, that's not our girl. Our girl smelled the dough, the business opportunity, a miracle, an ajá momento sensacional.

And so began a new entrepreneurial phase for our girl. The next day Myriam went back to the mercadito and with half of her savings bought every set of earrings, negotiating for them at half the original price. The next day, hair up in a beautiful bun, braided, sprayed, and a notepad with Sad Sam on the cover where she kept a detailed inventory. Homegirl hung around the school bathroom where all illegal transactions took place—think cigarettes, black eyeliner, and partially nude mags—offering earrings from French designers François Blah Blah and Pierre Blah Blah at six times the price she'd paid the campesinas. Mole penciled above her lips. She transformed herself during recess from Catholic schoolgirl to Catholic businesswoman, and motherfucker did it *work*. She stole one of La Tata's last glamorous possessions—a leather Chanel pouch—and arranged the earrings.

A small semicircle around Myriam. Girls on their toes pushing each other—the glimmer of the stones outdoing the stench of shit, period blood, outdoing the goody students who couldn't care less about French-designed jewels, who seriously believed relinquishing all feminine vanity was a woman's number-one priority in moving closer to God, and so, smart and avispada as she was, Myriam set up her own puestico inside the biggest stall at the end of the restroom, lit two vanilla candles the next day, harmonized her space with a small handwritten sign: *Joyas Francesas*. Next thing you know the culicagada is investing all her savings, plus some of La Tata's, in the campesina's jewelry.

She was rolling deep in it, cachaco, te digo.

And La Tata ni bruta que fuera of course freaking out.

Are you stealing money from your own mother? Myriam denying it all then counting and entering the money in her Sad Sam database. And where does the señorita think she's going with a box full of earrings? Are you stealing? Mira, Myriam, we may not be rich pero Dios es mi testigo that if I find you stealing! But La Tata quickly forgot her rage.

Myriam dared not reveal her secret business to anyone, anyone but Milagros who was sometimes distracted— sources say Milagros fell head over heels enamorá with el moreno Alexander working the corner store and just imagine what *that* did to La Tata and the tías en Cartagena. Milagritos was aloof but still noticed the new circle of preppy girls around Myriam. Her hermana rapidly acquiring superstar status.

Quickly, and purposefully, drifting up the popularity ladder, now spending weekends in Fulanita's penthouse in Santa Marta or Sutanita's country house in El Peñón, all paid for by the new BFF's disposable income. Buying her way back into each estrato. Powerful feelings of control energizing her heart, Myriam saw a future now and it had a panoramic view of Bogotá plus three secretaries. I've been told she looked stunning and scary, stone-faced but glamorous, running about the house hiding things, using too much hair spray. And I imagine her after school, unbraiding her hair in the bathroom, peeing, what did she think about when she saw her face? She could be beautiful, but you had to stare at her face for a while, wait for her dark eyes to settle, for the corners of her thick mouth to stop twitching until suddenly a face would appear, voilà.

Still, she couldn't afford designer clothes, but with the

pesos gained from the jewelry, she purchased the campesinas' clothes, worked on them for days on La Tata's sewing machine, adding gold lace here, silver buttons there—copying every outfit Rocío Dúrcal wore in the fotonovelas she read religiously.

Sobra decir: if the nuns caught Myriam selling she'd be kicked out of the school, and if the girls found out she sold cheap jewelry she'd be kicked out of the sociedad.

And did Myriam get caught?

She did and then she didn't. Already a queen at school, already La Tata dropping her killer eye on her, already buying white Reeboks and perming that hair, already those chubby fingers working that calculator in gold rings. Myriam spending so much money like it was nobody's business, shortening the school uniform—already colonizing the patio with jewelry boxes, hunched over balancing the books! The books! Was this surreal or what, cachaco? Seventeen and in one hand as many bills as any niña de papi. The Dream!

Milagros approached her one day midrecess.

¿En qué carajo'e lío andas metida tú, Myriam?

To Myriam, Milagros was just a jealous pendejita with no drive. She thought her sister had some brains, but she missed the volador por el culo and had no discipline.

Ay ya Milagros, you're making a spectacle.

Spectacle? Spectacle is what Tata is gonna give you. She knows what you're doing and she doesn't like it one bit.

That night when she got home, La Tata was waiting for her, belt in hand. She'd found the Sad Sam notebook while searching for some extra flour in the boxes stacked along the patio. La Tata's eyes conjuring a memorized motherly anger, the same anger brought on her by her sick mother, by the vecinas, by her patronizing sisters, an anger spilling out of every single mother, a rehearsed womanly conviction, a learned frown, hands arched on hips, pursed lips, eyes vaguely shut vibrating to the rhythm of the vocal cords—the posture of every Colombian mother, a hologram passed on through generations to land on the next girl's body in a Now you are gonna tell me ahora mismito where carajos are you getting all that money y ay Myriam del Socorro Juan that you lie to me.

Y agárrate muela picá que lo que viene es candela.

Myriam didn't say a word.

She felt betrayed by the failure of her own system. By her negligence. Why did she hide the notebook in the patio? Por bruta. La Tata wouldn't understand.

Is *this* how I raised you? No me respondas. That's what I get for letting your tías enroll you in that school . . . in and out of this house like it's a hotel, and those friends!

¡Mamá!

Mamá nada, Myriam. Mamá, nada. Those friends that I don't even know who they are . . . Why don't they come to the house? Why haven't I met them? You can always bring your friends here.

Myriam's face sent a *you-know-I-can't-bring-them*-here. La Tata froze, stunned that her daughter saw her in such a pobrecita way. She knew what Myriam meant, the shame, the fear, the rupture—something broke inside La Tata that day. She would later tell me it was her fault, she raised Milagros and Mami like that—*But el descaro de tu madre,*

Tata shut her eyes as she continued her story, *the shame in Myriam's eyes nearly killed me*. La Tata worked hard, and *the three of them were a pain in my ass complaining all berraco day, Fabio silently drinking himself to death, useless in a corner listening to every damn fútbol match and news program—and here comes this culicagada staring at me with* shame.

Like I also didn't once wear so much hijuemadre gold, like I wasn't La Muñeca with three maids just to cook for me, did I tell you I once had a suitor who shipped a German horse all the way to Cartagena for me? ME. La Muñeca of Cartagena, and Myriam's shame shocked me. What had I become?

Years later in Miami, La Tata would fight Mami over the verifiability of this story. Because as La Tata tells it: *I told your mother she was not going to jeopardize her education—and lying about jewelry? Where did she learn those mañas? And I may just be a vieja but didn't I have dreams too?*

Myriam didn't want to come clean because she knew La Tata would throw a fit for "exploiting" the campesinas, lying to the girls at school, and jeopardizing the expensive education paid for by her sisters—and who was going to tell the tías? Plus, why was she not helping with the bills?

Because, ¿aló? An apartment en la 94 was not paid for with smiles, and the carajita knew this. La niña was a soñadora but she wasn't dumb. Además, every day coming home to her mother's exhausted eyes drained her, watching La Tata's hands peel and darken, eating fucking arroz con huevo and plátanos every Sunday. She needed to be vindicated, ¡no joda! Myriam knew there was a way out of that routine, out of that sadness that bit her in the ass daily, that if she hit that sadness in the face enough maybe the house would shatter. She didn't want La Tata to disappear; she just wanted her mother to stop the same poor gesturing and please massage some cream into those hands.

The house did not shatter, so Myriam left. She packed all the jewelry, her school uniform, two pairs of bell-bottoms, Reeboks, and left a very dramatic note on La Tata's worktable: *Please do not come looking for me, Mamá.*

~

Myriam moved in with Leonor, her rich friend whose father traveled all the time, their place so big Myriam was barely noticeable. Leonor de las Mercedes Santos was the daughter of a widowed senator that we'll call Pepito Santos. If you've been paying attention to this story you now know that, yes, corazoncito mío, Pepito was one of those rich hijueputicas money laundering for our dearest Michelsen, shaking hands with the cartel's top gangsters in exchange for silence, billullo, and tons of uncut perico. And what. Do. You. Know. Leonorcita, being a spoiled only-child brat herself, managed her own perico habit on the side, a hobby really, a relief from her shopping trips to Miami and tanning trips to her papi's apartment in Cartagena. When Myriam entered the equation Leonor was in the midst of her own small coca business, obviously just a way of entertaining herself because, hello, what senator's daughter in the late seventies needed money? Days spent in Leonor's guest room where things shone and they had different towels for the hands, face, and body.

She took trips back to her neighborhood en el sur only

to buy jewelry from the campesinas but detoured into her street, watching her small house from afar, sometimes longing for La Tata's bizcochos, but usually angry at the disheveled entrance with its graffiti and dying trees.

Once she caught sight of La Tata's hands, white from the flour, trimming the roses. Still—just as her stomach quivered in a yearning knot, the image of Leonor's doorman, silky perfect hair, and equestrian boots shattered the spell.

From the moment Myriam stepped outside the household La Tata did nothing but pray to Dios y la Virgen del Carmen. As La Tata explained it: *Every day this devota de Dios lit candles, prayed three rosaries, and donated money to the neighborhood chapel.* When I asked Tata why she didn't just stop by the Santa María school, she said that with el dolor de su alma Mami needed to learn a lesson. *Myriam wanted an easy life? Then in no way was I gonna stop her from hitting her dumb head against the world. Life is hard. I had cakes to bake, dresses to sew. Life didn't just stop because your madre wanted to play superestrella.*

Ay Dios mío were these two stubborn.

In the midst of the fake-jewelry blowout, climbing the pompous estrato ladder with Leonor, returning to the exhilarating comfortable feeling of superiority so prominent and deeply rooted in the clase alta of our patria: doormen opening doors, maids making beds, cheeses aged for years traveling the Atlántico to land on her plate, hair blow-dried twice a week, Marc Jacobs purse, drifting quick and far—hooked to Leonor during every party because of course Myriam couldn't say no to all the parties, cocteles, dinners at Leonor's house. Parties with a live orchestra, live magician, every culicagado under twenty-five whose daddy had a foot in el Senado (let's admit it, there were no women), jarras upon jarras of aguardiente, salsa, and— you guessed it—perico until five, six, seven in the morning y a seguirla. There they were: Leonor and Myriam passed out drunk on champagne. Leonor and Myriam in Santa Marta in mini-bikinis. Leonor and Myriam driven in a Mercedes arriving at the Santa María school with sunglasses and poker faces. Leonor and Myriam getting their mani-pedis. Leonor and Myriam binge drinking whiskey with the number-one niño rico Nicolás Betancourt and his friends. Leonor and Myriam speeding down the Circunvalar. Now out of her house Mami fell head over heels deep into the luxury and wealth of Bogotá's Elite. I am afraid to say—despite her denial—that Myriam became the Life of the Party, demanding more aguardiente after everyone lay passed out on the floor, stealing little bags of coke from Leonor's drawer to stay awake and fully watch the sunrise. Cachaco, the late seventies! Colombia was just getting started in the perico business. That shit was so sticky and good your face felt numb for hours.

When Milagros tells the story there's a lot of frowning and sighing and *imagínate*, and when La Tata tells it there's blaming, prayer, and some light cursing. When I imagine Mami's life during that time, I see her searching for glimpses of herself. I see Myriam sniffing the last drops of the Ariel detergent that La Tata used on her uniform, I see a thinning arm opening heavy doors to rooms packed with silence. I see Myriam at night unable to sleep, the thought of Leonor figuring out her jewelry scam, the dreadful longing for the warm smell of her house—every feeling pushing upward like a colony of hungry ants in her stomach. She looks at herself in the long bathroom mirror and laughs. She eats strawberry popsicles and ruins the only dress La Tata sewed her. She wakes up on the floor more often than on a bed but laughs it off with Leonor, laughs it off with herself, doesn't even braid her hair anymore because someone will eventually take care of it, the hairdresser, the maid, or Leonor herself will pull Myriam by the hair, sit her down, and brush it gently, like a dog. I see bits of skin falling off her chest, her arms, chunks of hair next to dirty underwear; she gathers the pieces, stores them in a drawer.

Pero mi reina, there's no processing. No time for Myriam to stop and smell the skin falling off her. There's only a sense of teenage dignity and pride powering through her bones.

And there she is: foulmouthed, dropping hijueputas here, malparidos there, showing up coked out of her mind to chemistry class, kicked out of Spanish for chewing gum. I mean, what did she care? Leonor was now her sister from a rich mister. She was living The Life. But it didn't stop there. Mami swears my father took her virginity, swears on the Bible, in front of the Pastores, her Círculo de Biblia— but the reality is a bunch of carajitos hijos de papi were cruising those bell-bottoms. Nicolás Betancourt especially charming her with his light brown curls, green eyes, and endless source of dough.

Sometimes while Nicolás anxiously grabbed her breasts, she thought of Mansur. Warm Mansur, caterpillar-browed Mansur, olive-skinned rich Mansur with that

Lebanese accent mixed into his Spanish. *How's the seño-rita doing today?* The politeness of his ways: the opening of doors, the pulling out of chairs, the perfect dabbing of mouth with cloth napkins. His big hairy hands. The way they grabbed her waist, hard, pulling her close so that everyone knew that hembrita was his. Mansur who read Shakespeare, recited poetry, and serenaded Myriam outside her house in Cartagena with roses. You, queridísimo lector, may be bored out of your mind with the sight of this Romeo, but try saying that when an hombre with so much tumbao knocks on your door with freaking mariachis and a love poem. And homeboy *respected* her. In the seventies. In Cartagena. You're gonna fly high, my pajarito, he'd say whenever Myriam rambled about the big office. You, mi princesa, will run this town and possibly this godforsaken country of miserables. They walked around the Ciudad Vieja, hand on waist, the breeze of the night finally cooling the infernal heat of the day. The sea dark, infinite, monstrous, sprinkled with couples here and there, naked teenagers swimming and giggling. Whenever they spent the day at the beach, Mansur's skin quickly turned dark and when she'd turn to play with the curls on his chest Myriam would whisper: Mi negro bello.

Mami was fifteen, new to the love business. Blindly following her negro bello into this motel, that restaurant, that other playa, ignoring the days when he did not call, the nights he hurried home, the weeks of silence, and before you could say *Se armó la gorda*, Mansur's wife knocked on the Juans' door.

Now below Nicolás's hairless body, Myriam did not know La Tata apologized to the woman, visited Mansur's office, demanded el hijuemadre restore her daughter's reputation by disproving his wife, by disappearing from the girl's life. We are to assume the negro bello loved Mami, but guess what? Myriam also avoids reminiscing about the Lebanese papi. Apparently Mansur saw her one last time before the family moved to Bogotá, but if Myriam still waited for him, still longed for his eyebrows while Nicolás thrusted, then the papi probably didn't keep La Tata's promise. And so Myriam imagined his big hands opening her thighs until Nicolás's heavy breathing, smelling of strong cologne and cigarettes, slapped her back to Leonor's house, to the six months of hellish wealth.

Six months that felt like a lifetime.

And it surely was a lifetime, for when Milagros finally caved in and approached her during recess, Myriam's once Coca-Cola cuerpazo had now transformed into a sad skeletal dry carcass with protruding teeth. Girlfriend was all teeth! *I cannot emphasize how flaca your madre was*, Milagros would say. Eyes popping, more bones than cuero. Ay mi niña but those emerald stones and new haircut y Nicolás's chauffeur picking her up in a Mercedes after school. I mean, who needs body fat when there's a rich muchachón willing to fuck your brains out in his penthouse? And we'll get to the brains-out part of that fucking. But first, Milagros approaching Myriam:

¿A qué tú juegas? Milagros handed her an empanada. You need to eat.

Myriam chuckled. You don't think I have enough food?

What Myriam really wanted was Milagros begging her to come back. She couldn't admit this high-life plan had gone cuckoo off the rails, and now homegirl was losing her freaking mind, half of her hair, the booty that took her places—losing her soul with no idea how to get it back. Secretly for the last two months Myriam had yearned for this moment. Secretly a yawning loneliness clogged her heart. She stared numbly at the ceiling at night after el niño Betancourt finished his humping business and came all over her. But she needed Milagros to plead, implore on her knees, supplicate in a poem, something that would soothe the shame. The pride of this culicagada! Myriam needed Milagros to drag her to La Tata, where she could curl into a ball while La Tata rocked that wounded body, and a punta de aguapanela con queso and vickvaporú she'd heal Myriam's soul.

¡Pero ese orgullo!

And, sadly, this is not a children's book, mi reina.

Milagros tried stroking Myriam's cheeks, but she recoiled and left her sister standing in the middle of the parking lot while she hurried into the Mercedes where a stack of wrapped gifts waited for her. It was August. It drizzled. The school a haze of impressionistic grays and greens, blue dots in skirts covering their heads, white smoke speeding out of mouths like they were all dragons. Myriam rolled down the window, letting in the thin water blades like little silver bullets obliterating her face. Her entire face damp. Her heart knowing exactly what she wanted: the touch and care of her madre. But she couldn't just show up at the house, she couldn't just admit she needed La Tata, she couldn't throw away everything she'd gained. And that teenage pride coupled with the still-delicious numbing feeling of the perico plus those gifts on her lap tightening Nicolás's grip on our girl.

A week before her eighteenth birthday, on one of those rainy mornings Bogotá does so well, Leonor banged on Myriam's room and when Myriam opened the door, sleepy, dazed, confused, Leonor dragged her by the hair, wrestled Myriam's bones to the ground, angry, yelling— surely rolling on whatever was left from the night before.

¡Te me vas ya! Leave my house ahora mismo. Perra de mierda, ladrona, hija de puta levantada. Here I am opening the doors of my home to you? And what do you do? Ah? What do you do? Responde. Ahora no, now you don't want to say anything. You're stealing my jewels and my drugs? You low-class bitch. *Out.*

La Tata would always fall silent at this point in the story, but I managed to gather a confession from Milagros. No, she did not sell any drugs. Por Dios, tampoco. Yes, Myriam *did* steal Leonor's jewels, sold them *right at the school*. La idiota. Right underneath the niña rica's nose. Sold even to Leonor's friends. What was she thinking? How desperate had she become? Nobody in the family wanted to dive deep into her desperation. No one wanted to remember. But if you watched Myriam close for years, you could almost peel the amnesia off her skin, like an onion, layer by layer, until you reached a yellowing coat wrapping her body like a mummy, and *here's* where she had stored her gray bitten-down nails, *here's* where she stored bruised knees, numb heart, deadly popsicles. She must have been frenetic, manic, sleepless. So hopeless, almost no light shone inside her.

Por supuesto once and for all Myriam should have walked her ass home with the cola entre las patas and begged for forgiveness. Pero niña, if that country of reinas had a contest for Miss Stubborn, Myriam wouldn't even have to enter the competition to win.

There was always Nicolás: the drunk messiah. Ay el niño rico always willing to save her, the Mercedes always stacked with wrapped gifts. Always willing to drive that skeletal body to his penthouse, fuck the bag of bones, maybe slap her around a bit when she refused his dick. A whole week she spent there.

This junkie motherfucker would eventually go to rehab in Miami then move back to Bogotá to run for a senate seat—and win!

~

Milagros picked up Myriam in a taxi. When they arrived La Tata had transformed the living room into a healing cocoon: carefully laid-out pillows, ruanas, and blankets, warm water, aguapanela for an entire batallón, chicken caldo, beef caldo, vegetable caldo. Vickvaporú for days. Isodine, Dolorán, gauze, a rocking chair. Curtains parted, the midafternoon sun warming Myriam's frail body. When I asked La Tata how she knew her daughter was beat, La Tata responded she *felt the pálpitos, mija. A mother knows, a mother knows. And I knew,* she continued, *that Myriam's pain ran deep, and I was right. Her soul came back broken.*

They didn't speak. Mami's silencing shame didn't allow for any small talk but also she *still* could not just outright ask for forgiveness. Cachaco, you do not know stubborn. And more than orgullo, it was the saddening gaze, chills running down her spine every time Nicolás's memory imposed itself on her like a bucket of ice slowly released on her back. Myriam was más allá que acá. And the sueño! The riches! Not only broken but pulverized. Mansur at times a beautiful mirage warming her toes, her neck, the tip of her earlobe—then quickly swallowed by the darkness rippling inside. Heart clouded by an uncomfortable heaviness but Myriam dared not cry. She would never admit it (even to herself) but girlfriend hit her first rock bottom (congratulations!) and La Tata right there, wrapping her in a motherly blanket of tenderness and Merthiolate. La hija pródiga returning home. At night Myriam would wake up panting, sweating, like Bogotá didn't rest 2,600 meters closer to the stars, running a 104 fever only lowered with sliced lemons in her socks and leche magnesia. In Milagros's words: *Francisca, tu mamá was nothing but a threadbare trapo.*

Dios mío.

And it was during those sleepless nights, between nightmare fevers and mumbles, that Myriam started speaking to Dios.

Just outside the bedroom La Tata left the radio on for most of the day, humming boleros, listening to the few old radionovelas that still aired, but mostly it was *El Minuto de Dios* tuned in day and night. The unofficial official white noise of the house was Padre Ignacio's fervor in the name of the Father and the Son and the Espíritu Santo. Padre Ignacio's muffled voice, like someone speaking into a plastic cup, directing todos los oyentes to leave their worries at the door and give themselves to the One Above. Like most souls in our berraco country, la cartagenera was a cultural Catholic attending mass on Sundays, crossing herself when in front of a church, sometimes lighting the Virgen a candle but never taking The Power of El Señor too seriously. The fever changed that. Rock bottom changed that. The murky forest of gloom swaying inside her called for release, and girlfriend understood she needed help from someone bigger than herself, perhaps that mister from above? A foam of clouds began appearing during her dreams. A gold radio right in the middle of the gray cotton clouds and Myriam sitting on those clouds stroking the radio, repeating the songs and prayers.

For years she'd watched how La Tata's devotion built the tesón and motherfucking backbone that had her mamá feeding the entire family. La Tata's obsession with the radio always a mystery to Myriam. Now la niña felt the power of la radio, the way her heart opened up every time Padre Ignacio prayed for the sick, prayed for your confessions, for you, sinner. Something happened that stirred her insides, and before you knew it the girl was kneeling next to the window, rosary in hand. Our girl crossed herself, recited the Jesucristo prayers memorized during childhood, at times chuckling at the embarrassing sight of her frail body in the middle of a room speaking to no one, but this too faded, and as the nights progressed, Myriam demanded (you think she'd ask?) forgiveness, healing, Diosito she'd been bad but did she deserve all the shaking and headaches and insomnia? She prayed and prayed and sometimes she didn't even know what she was praying for. But now she had something to do, something to expect out of every day. The *Minuto de Dios*, the prayers. Kisses were sent to Jesús's knuckles crucified on the wall. Kisses and finally tears.

Every day La Tata changed the bandages on her arms, rubbed vickvaporú on her chest, sat silently listening to a radionovela while Myriam sipped on caldo. Humming a bolero, La Tata combed and braided Myriam's hair every night so it could recuperate its original voluptuous mane proportions and strength, then the praying of Ave Marías, Padres Nuestros over Myriam's sleepy body, Myriam suddenly—to La Tata's surprise—joining in prayer, conjuring every santo, and even inviting Padre Pablo, the family's priest, to bless the girl.

Milagros excused her sister to the nuns at school. Telling them Myriam had caught a terrible flu. Yes, the one that's going around. Horrible. Leonor and her amigotas whispering levantada, mal nacida, ladrona, but Milagros was not Myriam and she passed it off with a smile.

If you ask La Tata, she'd say Myriam broke the silence after five consecutive days of prayer when her cheeks blushed with some color, some cuerito shaped around those bones, and she was strong enough to hold La Tata's hand and say I'm sorry. But of course we are to doubt La Tata. Myriam lay praying in secret asking stupid questions to God, *Why am I here? Why is my skin so yellow? How can I be like Rocío Dúrcal but own an office?* She was head deep in la-la land. La Tata grew desperate and finally said to Mami, Bueno, Myriam, ¡ya!

Myriam's fingers played with the ruana until she blurted a It's not going to happen again.

Of course it's not going to happen again! La Tata replied amused. You are a desvergonzada, Myriam, is what you are.

Okay, I'm a desvergonzada. But I'm paying for it, no?

Paying is what you are gonna do when you knock on San Pedro's door and he slams it in your face.

Of course, mi reina, if you were to ask me I'd say it was the caldo, the Merthiolate, the Dolorán, the rubbing and caring of motherly love, Bogotá's warmth radiating on her body. But knowing Myriam's obsessive personality, once Diosito entered her head it was *He* who guided her. She craved some spiritual relief, I get that. The numbness of her drifting body needed to be anchored, grounded in some straightforward way, directed, instructed to pray three Ave Marías plus two Padres Nuestros for lying, plus an extra rosary for stealing. It was a system. Myriam loved systems. Plus, praying calmed her. It relieved her from the responsibility of dealing directly with the ball of solid pain roller-coastering in her belly. Praying hid the memories of Leonor and Nicolás behind a black curtain, to be dealt with later (or, as is the case, never). If you guessed this was Myriam's first heart-opening to Dios, then you guessed right, cachaco. A moment she would remember twenty-something years later inside a room at the Hyatt Hotel as La Pastora shook hands over her body and, overwhelmed by Jesús's presence in her heart, Myriam fell into the arms of the lead ujier while I watched in silence.

We know Diosito's mystical power can only take one so far. It definitely took Mami to faraway places (and still does). Pero everything that rises must fall, reinita, and the holy highness eventually faded, the haze of the Espíritu Santo evaporated, letting the broken pieces surface from the underground of her heart.

But first, let's enjoy that moment of glory for a second. Let's savor the gloria gloria aleluya and the sudden lucidity waking up Myriam with a renewed sober determination that said, *Today is the day*. Today I'll make lists of this and that and check them off whenever they get done. Today I will wear that uniform and walk through the school with dignity. A sense of control, of change.

In front of the bathroom mirror she'd rehearsed saying, My mother sews dresses and bakes ponqués y bizcochos. I live en Suba. Milagros is prettier than me, I wish I had her hair, *¿y qué?* ¿Y qué? Girlfriend rolled in her own twelve-step program of holy rejuvenation and acceptance. A walking self-help bible even before there were self-help bibles. In Dios she could have everything: the office, Mansur, and a spiritual transaction with the One Above. She didn't have to give up her dreams, right, Diosito? But then again, that longing had carved a hole in her soul. She had stabbed herself in the back—pero pa'trás ni pa' coger impulso. A prayer to Diosito came to the rescue. A wooden rosary now hanging around her neck (*Tacky*, she first thought, *but necessary*), the weight of the cross calmed her, the beads tickling her chest a reminder of the cambio: a new mujer, a mujer that carried a rosary and God.

~

It was September and that meant rain. A cántaros. It meant the opening of underground rivers overflowing the streets to sea proportions. A Colombian Poseidon backstabbing La City. Gray sky and gray roads melting into a blur of impressionistic umbrellas, tall buildings, red brick, red brick, red brick. Hazy mini-faldas clutching purses tighter than life. Tighter than the masses of bogotanos herded into this buseta and that taxi, now the street kids poking purses, horns screeching like it was the end of the world and they were all late for it. The stench of wet soil, of gasoline, of loss. The cerros fogged and infinite. Rain meant endless plastic bags covering blow-dried hair. It meant jumping puddles, dodging splashes from motorcycles, and cars sharp-turning whenever they saw a girl in uniform. ¡Estos hijueputas! But now she held a rosary and didn't say anything. Didn't give the finger. Myriam hid behind a floripondio tree when a car drove too close to the sidewalk, praying, trying to keep that feeling afloat, attempting to let Diosito know she needed Him. Needed peace, calm, was scared shitless of the rotting forest now faded to the back of her mind. It was all a theater show of the body. A ballet. This shift from rotting forest to a Clorox-smelling peace—brought to you by Ave Marías— it was a car driven by a drunk driver that at any minute could crash against a tree and *boom*. A tiptoeing of emotions. But she tried, cachaco. She prayed. Counted the Ave Marías with her fingers while searching for Leonor who evaded her a toda costa.

While Myriam was bedridden, Leonor called the house countless times demanding the return of her jewels, drugs, emphasizing que she nunca, oígame bien, *never* wanted to see Myriam again. La Tata answered with a *Señorita you got the wrong number* but after a few days of nonstop ringing she disconnected the phone.

Nobody wanted anything to do with her at school. Just like holding hands with the niña de papi catapulted any hembrita into superstar status, fucking it up with Leonor sent you below the social grave with the worms.

Plus Myriam returned with a different air that screamed *nerdy nerd please bully me* all over that recuperating cuerpazo (a cuerpazo building slowly but surely), with the uniform now past the knee, almost touching the pavement, a tight bun and only two fake pearls adorning her face. Even the translucent girl from Popayán with colorful braces, thick motherly glasses, and a limp wanted nothing to do with her. Even the girl from Popayán threw shade. The unspoken vow of respected hierarchies, so alive and well in our patria. Myriam transformed into a loner loser but also the consentida of the monjas, even telling Sor Patricia she was considering joining a convent. A convent! Because if Myriam was enrolling in this God-believing business then she wanted to do it all the way. When Milagros told La Tata about the rumors, she sat Myriam on the rocking chair exasperated.

Why can't you keep it together, mimi? Now you want to be a monja? A monja? Por Dios, Myriam del Socorro. Why can't you walk through life like a normal person. Look at Milagros, she's doing it. A monja and give me no grandchildren.

Myriam didn't care. She fell hard with God, with His discipline, she wanted to marry Him so that feeling would keep her warm forever. The nuns at school had it good. They enjoyed a comfortable life, no? They were teachers. They lived together in a comfortable old Spanish house next to the school. They occupied gorgeous offices with a view of the cerros. The Madre Superiora managed the entire school plus the monjas plus her room all mahogany with paintings dating to the virreinato—or so we were told. Myriam even daydreamed about being named the first woman pope. That gold Christian Dior cassock, waving at a crowd.

Photographs of that time show Myriam smiling thinly, impeccably dressed in the blue checkered uniform, long wavy brown hair parted right in the middle, locked behind her ears. And if the background were not the flowery couch and the disarray of La Tata's sewing supplies, Myriam could pass perfectly for an apparition of the Virgen.

Ay Myriam, you tried keeping your chin up, tried rejoicing in that blessed tumbao even when at school they filled your bag with worms, stole the tightly wrapped sánduche La Tata packed every morning for you, cornered you in the bathroom to slide ice cubes down your blouse. Some nuns disciplined a few of these girls but none could do shit about Leonor, her daddy the number-one donor at school, sending blank checks every time daddy's girl was in trouble. Even La Tata met with the Madre Superiora after finding Mami's notebooks dripping with worm goo, the nun's response a mere *We're doing everything we can, señora. But, you know, girls tease each other.*

Indignant, La Tata knew this had everything to do with the monies. Everything to do with becoming a *no one* in a city built for *someones*. The frustration overwhelming, and before she could stop herself, a *Váyase a comer mierda monja hijueputa* sped out of her mouth.

CHAPTER ONCE

Carmen did not freak out.

That really did work, I said breaking the silence. Longing for my earlobe to stay inside her mouth a little longer.

Although her cool dorky look was replaced with a greasy church-girl side-eye when I finally turned to her, the holy costeña wore that signature smile on her face. A smile that meant something—something I didn't know.

A sudden electricity in my head and my crotch pulsing with excitement. A dog waiting on a bone. I could still feel the imprint of her mouth on my ear. I didn't know ears were so sensitive. I didn't know they were connected to your backbone, your inner thighs, sweaty palms. I didn't know her sucking on my ear could make me fear sitting so close to her. What. Is. Going. On.

Please say you want me, Carmen—please.

And what did I say, pela'a? Carmen continued now, gesturing with her hands so close to my face I could smell their sweat. But you think I'm puro embuste, puro mequetrefe lying to you, no? Of course it works. Just like Jesús also works. I give you the truth plain and simple the way Jesús has been giving you His truth for months now.

She inched closer inspecting my ear but didn't touch it.

Carmen's excitement, what did it mean? There was barely any excitement back in Catholic school—it was all about stealing cigarettes and wearing the shortest skirt possible without the nuns calling you out. There was always Jesús. But different. The nuns' excitement about Jesús was soft, silent, and a little indifferent. You knew they were excited because they reminded you every day: *We're excited about Jesús,* they'd say. And you believed them. But Carmen's holy energy called for something else, something beyond the nailed cross, higher and warmer than her tongue on my ear, and for the first time I really prayed to Jesús to reveal it to me, for the first time I felt something real catch in my throat, some wind that needed my care, my attention. I wanted to be close to her, to feel that ball of excitement. I wanted her in my ear again. Licking and touching. I searched for what was missing. Clearly something was hidden in the way Carmen's tiny teeth popped behind that smile. Come on, Jesús.

And so I give in. I don't want to. But, maybe, I do. I do.

I brace myself for the worst, fearing the goodness that may come of this. I anticipate the change. The way my skin will suddenly glow bright instead of yellow, the way I will hold Carmen's hands and actually give two shits about prayer. The way Mami's face will soften. El Sagrado Corazón de Jesús dropping from the heavens open-armed, sharing some of that halo with me. The way Carmen will now keep licking my ear because there will be no reason to stop. I knew Jesús was waiting for me to hop on the holy train. I could feel it. For the first time since the morena from Barranquilla and I met, I stared at her fiercely and said, Carmen, I want to receive Jesús in my heart.

The biggest smile on her face.

And so, queridísimo reader, with eyes shut and holding Carmen's left hand while her right hand landed on my forehead, we both said in unison the prayer repeated over and over for the past six months:

Jesús te abro las puertas de mi corazón y te recibo como mi Señor y Salvador. Gracias por perdonar mis pecados. Toma el control del trono de mi vida. Hazme la clase de persona que quieres que sea.

We remained silent for a few seconds.

Francisca, picture Jesús entering your heart. He's knocking on the door of your soul, bringing you peace, bringing you love, bringing you truth. Pura verdá, pela'a, pura verdá. Saving you. ¿Lo ves? Do you see Him, Francisca? Do you see Him descend on you and cover you with His holy blanket? He's releasing you of pain, of worry, of evil. Do you see Him? Are you letting Him inside? Don't be scared, pela'a. I'm here with you.

All I could picture was her mouth on my ear. All I saw was Carmen distributing flyers next to me, chewing on an empanada with her mouth open. I tried harder. I reached for any image of Jesús I had in me and sighed deeply so she knew He was really entering me. I said *Amén* over and over. I breathed deeply and shut my eyes and pictured a bearded Jesús de Nazareth in muddy sandals dropping from the heavens à la Mary Poppins. I said *Señor* over and over. Then her hands pressed over my heart in circles.

What are you doing? I interrupted.

What does it look like I'm doing? I'm helping ease your heart from the light-rip, she explained.

I see, I said. I thought it was metaphorical? But okay, I get it.

Carmen clearly distraught at my reaction. Upset because I didn't understand the steps it took for Jesús to enter a sinner's heart, but also because her leadership skills were failing her terribly at this moment. I chuckled and she frowned.

You're not taking this seriously, she said letting both of her arms fall to the side.

But I was. I grabbed her right arm, clumsily placing her hand on my heart: Okay, please heal my heart from the ripping.

I shut my eyes longing for the ripping to happen. Her hand moving again in circles over my heart, the left side of my body warming, Jesús entering, ripping my heart. Blood vessels spurting blood all over Jesucristo, who slides down the aorta and into my beating cave. I said to myself, *Take this seriously pendeja por favor. Everything else has failed. You're doing it. Here is Jesús settling inside your heart. He's bringing peace, he's bringing truth, he's bringing love. This is your only chance.* And just like that, that sudden wind caught in my throat rolled up to my head not before shaking my eyes then vibrating on my toes, my knees. Carmen's blessed radar must have activated because she hugged me, gently we lay on the couch, Carmen now reclining, now whispering prayers in my ear, now holding my hand and praying, now holding my hand, holding my hand.

Está bien, she said. It's okay. Let yourself go. He's with you now, pela'a.

~

I didn't want to tell Mami about it. How do you go about revealing such things to people? I wanted everyone and no one to know about my new devotion to Papi Dios. Also, I didn't want Mami thinking she had anything to do with it (although in a way she did) because she'd get all proud and start lecturing me about how a mama knows best. But of course she started noticing some differences. After that afternoon with Carmen a weight lifted off my shoulders. The black curtain between her and me, between Mami and me, lifted. We were acting in the same play of life. We now shared a ground fertile with prayer, inner peace, and sacred devotion.

Look at me, mi reina, I am part of something.

I am there passing out flyers in Sedano's; I'm packing lunch with Carmen for the youth group, my hands swaying for the One Above; I am up there at the podium reciting my Life Changing Testimony; I am there and Carmen is with me, next to me, always holding my hand, always inviting me over for dinner, for a movie, for a sleepover where we pray in total darkness. Jesús had settled somewhere underneath my aorta and I was now saved. If the Rapture surprised us tomorrow, my soul would fly far beyond the murky Miami sky to the heavens next to Papi Dios, where I would watch everyone who stayed behind burn in apocalyptic fire. I know it's hard to believe, but I was into it. I was into talking about Satanás like homeboy was in every corner, imagining being pardoned from flames and instead resting in comfy clouds with a flat-screen TV and a myriad of books. Eventually I even wore a *Got Jesús?* T-shirt and stared in disgust at people who picked Spider-Man, Batman, or SpongeBob toys (satanic toys!) for their kids at Walmart. Once I handed a woman a *How These "Toys" Are Opening Doors for Satan in Your Home* flyer and she stared at me in disbelief. But there was always Carmen's light up ahead letting me know *this* was right. This feeling of closeness. With her, with Jesús.

But even before the shirts and the evangelizing in Walmart, in service after service my hands slowly sprung up like shy worms squirming to the surface until they swayed in unison with the rest of the congregation, women of course noticing, of course winking at me, and at the end of the service congratulating you, nena, on your fervor! Then congratulating Mami for performing an excellent motherly role. Your niña has found the truth! Gloria a Dios.

At first, it was embarrassing.

The godless girl inside yelled *Plath, eyeliner*. Yelled *social suicide*. Sometimes in an effort to cling to pieces of this girl, I'd step outside the service, light a cigarette, recite Plath's "Lady Lazarus" from memory. Then the magic faded. Who was I kidding with this shit? I remembered Carmen's prayer the night before during our sleepover—*Satanás is a liar, he wants to block my blessing and he will not succeed*—and I asked Jesús to forgive me, to take me back. Put out the cigarette and join the alabanza inside. Worried someone would see me, someone who would tell Carmen or La Pastora and I'd be removed from my church duties and be back at square one, where I'd started many months ago. I didn't want that. What with all that energy metastasizing inside me every time Carmen danced and clapped next to me, every time I braided her hair before service, every time the Pastora seemed to be pointing at me when in the midst of a sermon she said, *You've been lifted from the depths of hell, hermana! Now give El Señor your life, soak in our Savior's blessing!* All this new attention and the youth group looking up to me and Carmen calling me late at night to go over the outreach plan for the week and people *needing* me; and dinners at the Pastores' house where I sometimes slept over watching Carmen babbling prayers in her sleep.

During sleepovers we lay on her bed in complete darkness. Instead of glow-in-the-dark stars, Carmen's room glowed with tiny green crosses and clouds like a cosmic cemetery engulfing us with its mystery and silence. Just the two of us plus the glimmering green heavens, and I wanted nothing but to stretch out that cosmic cemetery forever, make it last until the end of time, be buried in that bed, next to her. I felt like the moment we turned off the light we'd suddenly plunge into a dark abyss where only her breath was audible. Her breath and then the AC muffled by the music coming from the living room. The Pastores left "Nadie como tú, Señor" playing the entire night so the Christian voices would cleanse the house of any evil spirits that may have entered during the day.

Carmen hummed the songs.

I could feel the waves of sound leaving her mouth, dissipating in the air then landing on my face where I tried catching them. I didn't want to miss a thing of her. My body was as alert as it had ever been, and every one of her movements—when she tied back her hair, when she sneezed, when she scratched her arm and brushed past mine—sent an excruciating thrill to the back of my neck, down my butt. We prayed together. She grabbed my hand tight, real serious, interlacing our fingers slowly, and we prayed that way. We prayed and she massaged my fingers with hers, and by the third week she was joking with Jesús and we were fighting with our big toes: Oh Señor, we thank you for today's blessing, Padre nuestro, we thank you for Francisca's soul, oh Lord, por tu misericordia. Please let Francisca know the sun is free and she can use it anytime by just stepping outside. She'd say this all serious but pushing her big toe against mine, running it on my hairy leg—You're a pale animalito, she'd say.

After a few sleepovers I also started joking with God: Diosito, thank you for today's blessing, Padre, thank you for letting Paula trip in the bathroom (Carmen giggled). Gracias, mi Rey, for keeping Wilson from staring all day at Carmen, homegirl needs a break (another giggle). Gracias, mi Dios, for Carmen, who now can almost say an entire sentence without eating the end of every word, who can now speak real Spanish. I've taught her well, amén.

And so we developed this ritual. Every single time I slept over, we watched the ceiling in total darkness, then prayed and always joked, trying to outdo each other— talking so much mierda, cachaco, sometimes about people we didn't like from church (Paula always making an appearance), sometimes asking Dios for random shit like thicker eyelashes and softer cushions on the church's chairs. With every prayer we built a world for ourselves. I built a world with her. Please Diosito, can Xiomara wear less perfume? Can Wilson stop bringing out the pillows before we get there? Can Octavio not snore during the alabanza? Can he please not kiss us goodbye ever again and leave traces of snot on our cheeks? Can Paula stop buying Christian books for Carmen that she's never going to read? At some point our prayers got real deep, real intimate, and we went from joking about someone's nasty-ass Dollar Tree makeup to praying about our moms, our lives, our fears. This is how I found out that La Pastora slapped Carmen's hands for not eating correctly, that the Pastor slept on a blow-up mattress by himself, that Carmen never wanted to find her biological mamá but whenever she went back to Barranquilla she looked for people that resembled her—this is how I found out that her hair was naturally greasy, that she had a mole on her back which she totally detested, that she'd had sex with some boy— Way back, pela'a, way back. I couldn't help but detest that boy. I built this anger every time she mentioned him all dismissive like it was nothing: Bluyineamos a little, just over the clothes, pela'a, y después tan-tan, we did it. I now think that Carmen probably lied to me, that she enjoyed how jealous I got, all tense, letting go of her hand. ¿Qué pasó? ¿Qué pasó? she'd say all giggly. What was she really thinking?

Once I asked her if she wanted to be a Pastora.

Sí, she said.

Like with your own church? Here in Miami?

Carmen wanted to lead a church but wasn't sure if she could live in Miami for the rest of her life. This is still gringolandia, she said. Y los gringos son muy aburridos. What about you?

I never thought about my career path as a Christian woman, didn't know I had to. I had no idea how faith worked, I didn't know you could go places with it. I also couldn't imagine myself older than I was; I couldn't see myself in five or ten years and I didn't want to. But when she asked me, I imagined opening my own church in Hialeah (because it's cheap), writing sermons in my little office in the back, delivering my outstanding speech, and bringing the congregation to tears. People would know me because I could change their lives with my words. They'd come from all over South Florida with anchetas and gifts of all kinds so I could pray over them. I'd get myself a little Jesús fangirl group.

After the congregation sobbed from such intense prayer to Dios, after everyone left, Carmen would be waiting for me in the first row. For some reason wearing a hat and some blue heels she'd never really wear, but there she was: gorgeous in that greasy-hair church-woman way, pointing at my Bible. Carmen as my Pastor. Carmen as my husband. Carmen collecting the diezmos, inviting people to the Círculo de Biblia at our house. Carmen and I evangelizing together, batiendo palma, Pastor and Pastora praying over their herd of sheep.

I told Carmen I didn't know what I wanted. I'll probably just go to your iglesia a joderte la vida, I said.

~

At home, life became more peaceful. Except for La Tata's silent drinking and the secret meetings with Roberto that I still arranged because it seemed the old Cuban drunk brought her a glimpse of felicidad, a moment out of her museum of sadness. Except for La Tata's glassy eyes, now gloomy and glued 100 percent to the TV watching every single telenovela on Telemundo, there was some harmony now between Mami y yo, yo y Lucía. The three of us like the Holy Trinity. Lucía even lending me her favorite book, *A Young Woman after God's Own Heart*, where I learned about devotion, sin, and daily prayer. I never read the book but I liked sitting next to Lucía. I liked watching the ceiling fan together. Junticas we fed the nasty ducks outside stale bread and screamed disgusted when they shat on our doorstep. Ew! ¡Qué asco! Her blessed wall of protection crumbled some, not completely, but we now had some moments in front of the TV where I rested my head on her shoulder.

We all took turns filling La Tata's Sprite can with more water than rum, but it was pretty much left to me to help fasten her bra every morning, rub her swollen feet at night, give her ibuprofen before she went to sleep so she wouldn't wake up with a hangover. For some reason everyone forgot about La Tata. She hung around the house like a dusty ornament, quietly hoarding photographs cut from magazines that she taped around her room, paying Roberto for tiny bottles of cheap rum—a darker spot growing on the sofa where she sat religiously to eat and drink until it was time to help her stumble to the bedroom.

Mami's motto with most undesirable events was (and continues to be): If you ignore it long enough, it will go away. What she ignored: Bogotá and her windowed office, my father, the new greasiness of her hair, a thick web of that hair asphyxiating combs around the house. She shut out anyone who dared mention María, our maid, or Alex, her hairdresser, or our handyman, doorman, etc. At the top of the amnesiac list was, of course, La Tata's drinking. And I was not about to disturb the slight chance at peace and winning in life that the church provided, so I too pretended La Tata *indeed* drank a ton of soda. I silently cared for her so Mami's Migration Project could continue. Admittedly from time to time I stole a few bills from La Tata's hidden envelopes, sometimes also from Mami's purse, and did nothing with the money. Just felt it. The comfort of those bills wrapped in a small bag inside my Plath book. I didn't ask Jesús to forgive me since that would have meant admitting I was doing something wrong. I wasn't. I felt justified since La Tata's meager income was spent on rum. Justified because that black plastic bag was the family's savings account. Duh. Just in case something went wrong, I had a cushion stashed in the middle of "Lady Lazarus."

Every week Mami entered the church proud next to me in my pastel-colored shirts, next to Lucía, La Tata dragging herself with little steps helped by a cheap cane. She sat in a special chair where everyone at some point during the service would stop by and kiss her cheek, ask for a prayer, share some juicy gossip. Never failing to show her devotion, La Tata shared her Life Changing Testimony more than three times and, helped by her morning rum, sang so loud during the alabanza I had to tug at her dress to shush her. The tension between Mami and La Tata was real. Mami glared at La Tata, and La Tata eyed her back and shut her eyes with such force and fiercely shook her hips to the salsa beats and tightly hugged La Pastora asking for prayer over her legs. The thin veil separating La Tata's drunkenness from our perfect church bodies always in danger of ripping.

El Señor doesn't like grays, the Pastora reminded us.

Either you devote yourself entirely and follow His word or you don't. Nobody is coming here a calentar silla!

We were finally all together in Christ as a familia, como debe ser, and Mami kept inventing new illnesses when people asked why La Tata fell asleep during el sermón, why she chuckled so loudly. I ignored Mami's complaints and poured La Tata water, helped her to the bathroom, told everyone she had a tough night sleeping with that arthritis. I did not want to focus on my abuela, thankyouverymuch. Why were we focusing on La Tata when I had Jesús in my heart? When the shekinas ran to me and demanded advice on their boyfriends? When Carmen and I spent entire weekends together planning the youth group on her bed? When Carmen and I prayed together? When she lent me her pj's?

But it was La Tata who, after church one Sunday, told me she knew what was happening with Carmen.

¿De qué hablas, Tata?

Eyes shut the way she closed them whenever she was angry or frustrated, as if she needed the darkness to concentrate, as if the weight of what she was about to say lay heavily on her eyelids.

Ay, Francisca mami. You know that's gonna kill your mother. Who cares if you kill me? Pero tu mamá, Francisca, she may be a pain en el culo but . . .

I didn't say anything. The accusatory tone was new and it was lumped with some gossip thrill and a hint of acceptance.

Yo sé lo que está pasando contigo y esa muchacha, Francisca. Ay mi Dios libre a tu madre de un ataque.

I hugged her. She didn't return the gesture. Her eyes still closed.

Tata, I'm Carmen's right hand! I'm helping with the youth group! What you need is a refill!

Turned on the TV. Poured Tata her refill, shouted out the window searching for Roberto. Mami out with Milagros and Lucía, so I heated up some Hot Pockets for La Tata and her secret boyfriend, served them rum cocktails (a bunch of rum and a slice of lemon), and placed both lovebirds in front of the television. Told them they had thirty minutes before Mami got back. La Tata closed her eyes at me again, but then Roberto's hand landed beneath her summer dress and I disappeared.

For the next few days I avoided her. I had no idea what she meant by "killing Mami" and I didn't want to know. Or I did know, but I *still* didn't want to know. I applied Mami's Forget About It wisdom and moved on with my life. Wait, scratch that. I didn't "move on" because that was the entire problem with Miami: there was nowhere to "move" to. I was forever stuck in the Heather Glen Apartment Complex, the man-made lake now cooler, less infernal with fewer mosquitoes buzzing around. November in the blink of an eye, mi reina. November when I'd sworn I couldn't last more than a few weeks here and now look at me: wearing shorts (still no flip-flops because I respect myself) and sometimes when speaking to people in broken English I'd say, *That's exciting* and *Oh my God*. Cachaco, so alien! But still my tongue delighted in trying out new moves. November and the trees and flowers remained the same, just like Bogotá. I used to cherish my city's stagnation, how August and January could only differ in rain and the weather was never severe, never snow then flowers then heat then fallen leaves. The same. And now here there was no change either, and sometimes that sameness came with waves of recognition. I understood tropical weather. But November was different. I could move myself to Carmen's house whenever I pleased and I could move my body next to hers and watch her drool in her sleep. It was November and the weather seemed Andean. Still no mountains or redbrick buildings but a softer air, one that didn't get stuck in your nostrils. No thick Jell-O passing for oxygen. A thinner, cooler breeze that killed some of the ducks unable to fly outside of the pool.

We continued our days of devotion and prayer. We continued heating up Pop-Tarts for dinner and fried plantains with rice for lunch. I ate Hot Pocket after Hot Pocket until I couldn't poop for three days. Continued my sleepovers at the Pastores' house, Mami enthralled by my relationship with Carmen, nodding every time I walked out of the house with my Jesús T-shirt on, sighing in relief when I joined prayer during dinner, even leaving a Christian CD wrapped in gold paper on my bed as a gift. I lay in bed every night trying hard not to touch myself, repeating *Jesús is with me* over and over in an effort to contain my hands— but who am I kidding. *El que peca y reza empata*, I also told myself. *Jesús, I'm so sorry. Please know you're still welcome inside me, don't leave.*

Then the hardest part: don't think about Carmen. Pero cachaco, inevitable. By now I had my own routine, the same pink-dick bathroom fantasy alive in my fingers without thinking. My hand knowing exactly what to do, when to stop. The moment I left my room to get water La Tata called me.

Francisca.

¿Qué?

Mi niña, por favor.

¡¿Qué?!

We both knew. I felt she could read it on me so I avoided staring into her eyes. The TV showed a blond woman thrusting her hips, stretching her legs, with a Spanish voice-over selling a $19.99 aerobics video. La Tata clasped my hand tight. Bring me more Sprite. We sat side by side watching reruns of *Caso cerrado*, La Tata's hand patting mine from time to time letting me know, Dios loves all His children but He still demands those children align with the Evangelio. I know that. Okey, she said. But then she'd repeat it all over again. I combed her dry white hair with my fingers. Curly white. She let it grow into a tiny afro that she called the Crown of Old Age even when Mami suggested she dye it blond like most old women at church—or at least a light brown. La Tata refused saying she'd fought plenty for her white hair. Las canas son la corona de la vejez.

Mija.

¿Qué pasó, Tata?

Ay mija.

But, again, nada. Just patted my hand over and over, rocking herself back and forth back and forth guarding my palm in hers like a treasure. As if she could control my destiny by keeping my hand close to her.

~

The next week the Pastora facilitated the Jóvenes en Cristo workshop around the "urge to touch yourself and let boys touch you." Carmen helped, handing out worksheets where a blue-eyed blond smiled, the caption underneath reading, *Jesús helped me wait for the right man. In Jesús I leave all my carnal longing.*

This is a period of transformación, cimentación, formación of values for all of you. You think Jesús was not a teenager like you? You think He wasn't offered the temporary pleasures of drugs and sex? But all these roads will eventually lead to unhappiness. The only eternal road is the one going to heaven!

Paula's enthusiasm catapulted her to the make-believe stage, where she shared her testimony in tears after the Pastora encouraged us to share our terrible youth experiences. Paula told us a boring story about some boy back in Bogotá fingering her underneath a desk during math class, sobbing because she still could not believe Jesús was not in her heart at that moment.

The Pastora hugged her. Had she repented?

Then came the endless repertoire of regrets from every single girl. Marijuana. Perico. ¿Basuco? Yes. Fingers here. Penis there. Money. Money. Tongues. Condoms. No condoms. A surprise abortion. Más perico. Etc. In the back I sat restless. Like hell I was going to share my intimate one-on-one with everyone. Yes, I was down with Jesús. Yes, Jesucristo (and, let's be honest already, Carmen) unknotted something around my belly every time I sang during church. But this? We all knew there would be judging. If La Pastora felt the sexual encounter being revealed truly crossed the holy line, then out that secret went to those parents' ears and no, mi amor, Mami did not need to hear what she spent so much time avoiding. Plus, it had been a good month since Mami's last lecture and ¡Jesucristo! did it feel *good*. Besides, what would I share? Lining up in Catholic school outside the bakery to tongue-kiss the baker? Cruising up and down the fenced lot of the school, skirts all the way up, demanding some sexual attention from the boys from the school next door? Or share the saddest hymen-breaking story that was losing my virginity to my neighbor who just humped like a rabbit inside me? I chuckled at the thought of him. So tiny and desperate. Then I remembered Jesús and a terrible shame overcame me. *I'm sorry, Señor, but there's nothing I can do about the past.* With my eyes I told Carmen I wasn't going up, and with her eyes she called me outside.

La Pastora stopped us midway.

Is there anything you want to share, Francisca?

Not really.

She stared at Carmen, eyes demanding she get a testimony out of me. *She's your friend, carajo! Get her to confess.*

There's nothing to fear, Francisca, Carmen said.

But of course there was. Confession *was* fear.

Confess. Tell Jesús y de paso every repressed soul in there that I want to wrap my arms around Carmen and live with her for the next fifty years. Go ahead. See how that settles in this group, mamita, a ver berraca, where are those cojones that carried you in Bogotá? You think you're punk now, bitch? Go ahead—tell all these harmless hijosdeputa what you *really* want to do with the Pastora's daughter. Tell Jesús you love Him but that for some fucking reason you love Carmen's greasy smell more. A ver.

I know, I said. But I don't have anything to say.

I was left on my feet alone, everyone judging me for not confessing because of course we've all done some shit and all of them knew I was reluctant to join the church in the first place and that Ramones shirt screamed heroína, sexo, STDs, or at least perico.

What did I do? The only thing I knew how to do now: pray. When that didn't work and everyone grew quieter, I made up some terrible youth story.

I let a boy touch my tits once and I'm sorry, Jesús. I know now to wait for my husband.

Unconvinced smiles all around. Amén. God forgives you, hermana. Etc. Carmen nodded but we both knew I'd held back. When the workshop ended she drove me home wanting to know what went wrong.

Nada. I just don't like sharing my stuff, you know?

One hand on the peeling steering wheel, one hand resting on the window. Out of that shekina dress her legs dark and thick with tiny black hairs and those chapped lips that she continued to bite and peel. Carmen glowed when she worried about me. I played with the Christian fish hanging from the rearview mirror.

I've never told you this before, pela'a, but I wasn't 100 percent on board with my mom and dad when they became pastors.

She searched for a reaction and I nodded.

I was in a very complicated relationship with an ex boyfriend. And let's just say I'm glad I'm not the guaricha of a low-class sicario en Barranquilla.

Sí, claro. You're the closest to a Christian Virgen María in Miami.

Embuuuuuste. Is *that* what you think?

She stopped the car and stared at me for a long time.

If only. Right then. I would move close to her, would hold her face and kiss her. She might panic for a second but then say, *Ay pela'a you are so slow, what took you so long,* and demand we leave this shithole together. I'd grab her thighs and tits and awkwardly admire them. She'd do the same. We wouldn't know how to properly fuck inside her car but it wouldn't matter because it'd be warm and we'd be naked drawing stick figures of ourselves on the misty windows.

Jesuuuuuuucristo.

Dame paciencia. Mi queridísimo reader, you think you're frustrated with this? Enough is enough, you say. Stop the pendejada and own your shit, Francisca. Francisca, carajo. Yes, reinita, but you're not the motherfucking criolla scared shitless of losing the one relationship that at fifteen brings you enough joy to ignore the hell outside.

I told her I didn't really know what to think. I thought that's what Christians wanted to be, that's what we aspire to in life. To be pure and righteous and right all the time so God would not kick us out of His eternal mansion when we died.

Tú sabe most people at church—including myself—have gone through some real stuff. She continued, Vainas berracas, no te crea. I know it's been hard for you but come on, Francisca, it's time to get over it. Over it, muje. You're doing so well.

I am.

Look how far you've come.

I have.

She keeps driving.

From that quivering place behind my knees I gather the cojones. I put my left hand on her thigh. Warm. She tenses but doesn't say anything. I give in to the quivering. I open up to that place deep inside me calling for her warmth. I wait for her to relax and then I slowly caress her thigh. We both keep our eyes on the dark road, from time to time a few lights like shredded silver light up her eyes. I feel myself disappear into my knees, my fingertips. Pulsating like a dying animal. No one can see us. I wait for a slap, a push; I wait to be kicked out on the curb, I wait for an explanation. Eyes deep into the darkening road, I know somewhere inside this car there's hope for us. There's some humming on the radio and she turns up the volume. The radio spits soft Christian rock: *And to whom has the arm of the Lord been revealed? We are growing seeds. Calm your desires. Calm your desires. We are growing seeds.*

When she drops me off I don't get a kiss but a low Dios te bendiga, pela'a.

CHAPTER DOCE

We're up in the mountains but we don't remember how we got there. It's an unusually sunny day, the skyline of Bogotá perfectly traced against the deep blue of the Sabana. Not one cloud. Behind us a rose garden covering every wall of Monserrate, behind us a seño selling mazorca, chunchullo, churros. Carmen wears those unflattering motorcycle shades, hands on the railing, pointing to this bird and that airplane and over there where you can get the best arepas de queso in the entire city. I stand behind following her fingers. We buy mazorcas and eat them. The grease from our lips collides in a clumsy kiss and I want to stay in that moment, perfect and suspended. Knowing I've never been happier. When she turns to pay the seño, the coiled rose stems rip from the walls, they rip break tear, the rose stems surround her, thorns aimed at me. Paralyzed in fear I watch as the pink serpentine dances in circles with Carmen inside. Then I move closer. I approach the maze defiant, my hands fists of fear until thorns knife my left cheek, until the pink roses swallow Carmen.

I woke up panting, nauseous, touching my cheek over and over, traces of the dream following me while I peed, brushed my teeth, sipped coffee, watched Telemundo next to La Tata.

~

I tried calling her twice.

By the fifth day I had no nails left, my fingers all craters pooling with blood. I found out three days later on a Tuesday, and a sudden grief, a momentary sense of complete loss, launched inside me.

Mad, I thought, or cutting me from her life completely, or telling the Pastores y de paso Mami, all of them coming for me, their tears and rage, Carmen's disappointment— or was it shame?—barring her from my life.

Carmen left without saying adiós. Mami walked into my room ten days later with printed photos of Carmen and the Pastora dancing in some church in Bogotá, eyes sizing up my reaction. I muffled my surprise in a toothy grin.

Of course I knew she flew to Colombia! A ver, duh. We're super close friends, we tell each other everything.

Mami looked me over, suspicious at my excitement.

Nena, you didn't know she left? Mami fanned herself with the photos. I thought you two were like *this*. She twisted her fingers in a super close way.

Obvio sí, we are. She probably just forgot, Ma, ¿sabes? With all the work at church and running the youth group.

She didn't forget. I knew that. My heart knew that. I couldn't believe she was gone. Why. How. After she drove me home, we didn't speak for an entire week, and when she didn't show up at church I thought, *Okay, she's sick.*

Okay, girlfriend's got the fever or maybe she can't face me. And who should I ask about her? Who should I tell that I never felt closer to anyone, that I know she felt it too. Right? She did? Were we both in the same car? Was she there when her heart beat on my palm against her thigh, calientica. Was she feeling that. Of course it had to be about us. *Us.* Ay por Dios, Francisca. *Us.* The sinful weight of those letters.

Mami kept her eyes on the photograph. Hands no longer so soft, smooth, but cracked with deep thin lines criss-crossing them. She was standing directly underneath the AC, hair softly blown in a frizzy halo.

La Pastora said she's acting all rara since you last shared testimonios, Mami continued with a look that said, *There's some shit here and you better drop it now.* In her email she said it was the first time Carmen refused to lead the Jóvenes that week. Imagínate tú. La hija de La Pastora. Any ideas?

I couldn't tell if she blamed me or if that was a genuine question. Mami had developed this devoted face in the past few months that said, *I'm better than you,* and also, *I fear for your soul,* and sometimes even, *What are you doing away from Jesús?* The judging, the condescension all there wrapped in a thin-smile bow.

Que no sé, I raised my voice. Annoyed. How am I supposed to know what she's feeling?

She drove you home that day, Francisca. Yo no soy estúpida.

Mami: Jesús's bitch and now Jesús's detective. That couldn't be it, the car? She would have said something: *Francisca, stop. Pela'a, what in Jesús's name are you doing. Is this a game. Francisca, Jesús is very disappointed.* Girlfriend is the hands-on, aggressive, overtly direct niña de Dios. Why hadn't she said anything? And what could she have possibly told the Pastora? If the Pastora knew I approached her daughter in a minimally sexual way, before you could say *Ay Chuchito* our entire family would be banned from Iglesia Cristiana Jesucristo Redentor and Mami would be sobbing, digging for a belt. Everything that we built here, gone. Domingos de church, Círculos de Biblia, dinners at the Pastores', monthly food giveaways, Lucía's endless phone conversations, the Jóvenes, the phone ringing nonstop for Mami. Carmen. Monday Tuesday Wednesday Thursday Friday Saturday Sunday: all gone. *Jesús, sálvame de esta. Chuchito hazme el milagrito.* I prayed for Carmen's silence. I was so confused. *Jesús, what should I do?* What could I do? I couldn't imagine a different self that did not desire the costeña. Couldn't see a way out of wanting her. And I knew she did too. She had to. I did not exist without that longing, the ball of feeling around my shoulders, the hunger to touch her, to fuck her. To wrap myself around her and sniff that greasy hair.

Ma, you know Carmen is weird. Why don't I help you with the Christmas celebration for church?

You want to? Ay, nena. I have so much work to do. There's the children's danza, the Holy Ghost cupcakes, the tree to buy at Walmart. ¿Vamos a Walmart?

Right now?

Mami eyed her watch, she still had the photos.

Primero, let's finish this conversation. What about Carmen, nena? You two didn't fight?

And fearing for my life I said, *What* exactly did the Pastora tell you?

That Carmencita did not come out of her room the next day. Or the next day. Didn't feel like leading the Jóvenes. Spent all her time inside her room doing nada, and you know how that niña is loud! Between us, nena, you know Carmen talks talks talks, habla como lora. No se calla. So the Pastores took her with them to Colombia on that evangelizing trip, remember? I think they're in Medellín right now but the Pastora is worried. Young people don't understand sometimes how important it is to follow the Lord's word, ¿me entiendes? Gracias a Jesús, you've changed. Me tenías los pelos de punta. But see the good Jesús has done in your heart? And it's hard when you're young, I know. But like the Pastora says, it is the most important moment to create the base for later. Jesús was tempted too! I was tempted too! Obvio que sí. But He teaches us to call on Him during those temptations. And, quién sabe, maybe Carmencita is falling onto a bad path? I don't know.

The yellow light filtering through the window made Mami's features stark and manly. Shadows breaking her face into puzzle pieces, tiny golden boxes, black liminal space. I wasn't sure how much she believed. How much she questioned, how much she knew but dared not ask, preferring to pretend like niña is all good, is all fine, is all dandy-pandy, pass me the glue. How much was the "Pretend Mami" she performed so well, had refined in the last months so that the real Myriam lay mummy-buried somewhere in that body. Because let's be clear: Mami was not dumb. Jamás. Mami *knew* her shit.

Ma, it's nothing. La Pastora is probably exaggerating.

Okay. But just in case, I'm gonna ask you one last

time, listo? Did anything happen with Carmen when she dropped you off?

~

I tried not to cry and succeeded. Tapaditos los feelings, bien tight. I begged my eyes to keep their water from flowing. But I could feel the pressure, behind my lids, inside my ears, all the way to my chest. Rushing in. Trying to find a way out. Una cascada a punto de reventar. The water was coming, reinita, the water was coming.

For the next two days I walked aimlessly around the townhouse.

Nobody knocked on the door yelling my name, eating all the vowels. Nobody complained about my bitch face. Nobody held my arm in the dark. Nobody sucked on my earlobe. I could barely eat. Tenía un remolino en el estómago que no me dejaba vivir. My body boycotting itself. I went back to wearing all black. Back to staring at the ceiling fan contemplating the blades, but now praying to Jesucristo to helicopter me away to Colombia, to that church where Carmen was surely dancing, surely thinking of me.

One afternoon of fierce rain I sat with Tata watching Telemundo. A rerun of *Marimar*. Both Tata and I loved Thalía so much we kept having loud conversations with the TV. We sang the opening song together and I twirled dramatically for Tata's amusement at the end. Mami and Lucía were out. The rain outside swinging its force against our window, buckets of water, one after the other. It seemed like the rain dripped not only from the sky but was lifted from somewhere below, somewhere unknown, deep inside the swampy soil. The rain its own musiquita, its own traca-traca, its own fever.

When Tata asked for a refill, I served myself a shot of rum. When homegirl asked for another refill during commercials, I took another one. And another one. My conversations with the TV turned into fights, turned into cursing, turned into ¡Hijueputa! Do not hurt Marimar, hijueputa! Tata patting my leg, Ya ya, mimi, it's just a novela. Tata's glossy eyes dared not look at mine. But my insides were running. My bones alive. I kept yelling at the TV, gesturing with my hands, holding my head—the impossible rain knocking como loca on the window—until Tata grabbed my hand, kissed it, and said, Mimi, déjaselo a Dios. Leave it to God.

On Friday I lay in bed skimming my Jóvenes en Cristo book, waiting to go to dreaded Walmart with Mami. Pablito called a few times but I didn't want to see him. I couldn't get the roses swallowing Carmen out of my head, my hand unconsciously checking my cheek for any knifings. I couldn't properly look at Tata. I checked inside the Plath book for the money I'd stolen and saved. The $347 that got my blood running every time, knowing there was a possibility of escape, a one-way ticket. Where? No bus went to Bogotá. New York then. I'd seen *Sex and the City* when La Tata gave the TV a break. Just in case Jesús backstabbed me, gave me the middle finger and bye-bye.

During the last Jóvenes en Cristo meeting the temptation discussion led to a sex discussion which led to this tiny puertorriqueño showing everyone a newspaper clipping of a man in an orange jumpsuit being interviewed about proudly killing men in South Beach.

These are men having intercourse with each other, the tiny boricua continued. How should we feel about this? What is El Señor telling us to do?

Everyone had a sad opinion: Convert them. Lock them up. Make them fuck prostitutes. Evil souls. Dead spirits. Soldiers of Satanás. I had no opinion but I had money. Just in case. In case Mami, sobbing, belt in hand, disowned me, left me to the ducks. And what about Tata? I didn't dare think of Tata. Think of what she knew. I had crisp green bills. Bills that I ironed when the house was empty, mumbling prayers to El Señor, *Please, mi Dios, make me like a boy, any boy, make me think of a boy*. The vapor from the iron rose, the bills stacked flat.

We stopped by Xiomara's house first. Two enormous palm trees enclosed the entrance where Wilson in shorts trimmed the bushes waving at us as we parked. Pink, gray, and so big you could fit five townhouses in there. Hurricane season was officially over and the sky shone an electrifying blue as if it were lit from inside.

All the women at Iglesia Cristiana Jesucristo Redentor envied Xiomara. Praising her jewels, her designer purses, the handmade leather case etched with a gold cross covering her precious Biblia. I mean, Xiomara was the first one to own a BlackBerry and a hands-free Bluetooth even before the Pastor allowed them as nonsatanic devices. But. While that gringo second husband was an engineer, we all knew girlfriend grew up in rusty Pablo Sexto and those thick gelled curls, those accentuated *eses*, were proof of her low estrato. You cannot fool the trained Colombian eye, mi reina. So there you have it. Señoras de bien of Bogotá, cachaco, the wives of that bank president, that part owner of Pan Pa' Ya! that never before had to be in such close proximity to la chusma, el pueblerío, now swallowed the stone of pride and let Xiomara sit wherever she wanted. ¡Jesucristo! If this was not the Apocalipsis, Jesús definitely had a dark sense of humor.

Her son, a.k.a. Wilson Jesús, led us into the house. Inside, Xiomara perched on a red velvet chair as another church woman hunched over coating her toenails. The television blasting Joel Osteen in a football field packed with people in white T-shirts painfully shutting their eyes and smiling at the same time.

¡Pero entren! Sin pena. Francisquita mi niña y tú Myriamcita. You want some tintico? Some tea? Papito, bring Doña Myriam some of that French tea in the yellow jar. I'm telling you, Myriamcita, Frank brought it from his last trip to París and it made me lose fifteen pounds like *this*! She snapped her fingers in a Z like El Zorro and pushed in the sides of her waist showing us the imagined cuerpazo.

Ay pero no se ponga en esas, Xiomara. We only came to pick up the tree decorations you are donating to the church?

Mami was better than anyone at hiding envy, and to be honest she sometimes enjoyed Xiomara's outlandishness. Both went way back. If you were to ask Mami she'd just say Xiomara worked briefly for her and that was it.

When, Mami?

You know, before.

If you asked Xiomara, which you didn't have to because "la guaricha" ran to the Life Changing Testimony spotlight every four weeks, you'd know she was once Mami's maid, or cleaning lady, or *special assistant* as she now wants to remember it, and is proud of the drastic turn in her life. Look where I am now. Look!

Wilson will get them for you, Myriamcita, but you are not leaving so quickly, no? Sit down. Yaira can do your nails too, right, Yairita? I'm paying.

No, no de verdad. We have to get going. Francisca, go help Wilson with the decorations.

Wilson returned with tea in a Miss Piggy mug and then awkwardly stood next to me. Xiomara didn't listen. She kept rambling on and on, talking to herself while picking up the pink cushions that supported her back and placing them in a semicircle on the other end of the sofa like a nest of Pepto-Bismol.

Right here! She patted the cushions. All that stress is gonna kill you, Myriamcita. Not to mention the wrinkles that you already have but that will get worse! ¡Relájese! Did you know stress is the number-one cause of wrinkles? I'll bring you some Cocaditas. You two go pack the Christmas balls or do something. Wilson needs to finish the flyer for the Jóvenes, why don't you help him, Francisquita? Or should I call you Panchita?

That's okay. Francisca is fine. I'll stay here.

Xiomara laughed and Wilson echoed her.

Yo no muerdo, he said. I don't bite.

The thickest curls crowned around his head dropping to his eyes, so that every few seconds he brushed them back but the black rings of hair cascaded down again. Objectively, I thought, Wilson could be a good-looking muchacho. If he didn't miss spots when he shaved, if he wasn't an awkward bag of bones. If those chicken legs were pumped up with some muscle. If he didn't walk diagonally as we entered another room, his one long fingernail pointing to the plaque next to the doorframe, *Xiomara's Biuti Studio*. I tried fixing it, he said, but she wouldn't let me. His faint mustache curving in a smile. The mustache not unlike Carmen's upper-lip shadow. Black hairs on brown skin. His was thicker, coarse. But the droplets of sweat reminded me of Carmen's. Her vulgar way of eating, which, according to Mami, meant the Pastora needed to teach esa niña how to chew with her mouth closed. She'd lick her fingers, one by one. Pollo Tropical was her favorite. After outreach at Sedano's we always stopped by Pollo Tropical for some pollito, plantains, fried yuca. The chicken overcooked but motherfucker did Carmen eat through it like it was her last meal while Yours Truly just chuckled, amused, as she devoured wing after wing like I'd only seen men do before. No shame. No apologies. Dainty manners thrown out the window. With a napkin Carmen wiped her mouth, missing spots on her upper lip that afterward shone in the sun like she'd hidden tiny precious stones under her skin.

Bueno pues, Wilson said, here are the Christmas balls. And those two other boxes under the purple shelves.

And a ver, where's the flyer, Wilson? I said.

I missed helping out with the youth meetings. You know, what I did before you-know-who left. But mostly I missed being useful to God, etc.

You really don't have to help me. I know my mom can be pushy sometimes.

I tried suppressing a laugh. What? *Sometimes?*

After it became known at Iglesia Cristiana Jesucristo Redentor that I had converted, Xiomara pulled me aside many times whispering she'd rather see her son with a niña from a good family than a morena with unknown roots. The Pastora can say misa! But I haven't worked this culo off for nada. And despite knowing Wilson chased after Carmen, phoned her, consecrated her the most beautiful shekina in the world, every time she had the opportunity Xiomara reminded me her son needed a novia. And how was I not pursuing her hijo? He clearly was un partidazo.

Oh por Dios, I know! She's *always* pushy, right? said the partidazo. I'm sorry.

It's not your fault.

His dark green eyes smiled at me. The thick gold curtains glowed in stark contrast behind him. Who has thick gold curtains in Miami? I'll tell you who: Xiomara. I didn't know how to smile with my eyes so I blinked. Blinked. Blinked until Wilson's brows furrowed.

Are you okay? he said.

Not only was I okay but I was so okay I stumbled on the rolls of fabric behind me and knocked down a picture of Xiomara.

¡Muchachos! Xiomara yelled from the living room. Don't destroy the house por favor!

I stood up like it was nothing but another part of my performance. ¡Tará! How do you like that, I said. Then I picked up the drawing of bulgy-eyed Jesús playing fútbol with a bunch of boys.

Is *this* the flyer?

Yes.

Is it a boys-only Christmas?

No.

¿Entonces, Wilson? ¿Dónde metiste a las niñas?

He said he didn't think it mattered that there were no girls. We're all hijos de Jesús but I can't paint *all* of humanity. Right?

Okay, I said. But if you want people like, say, *me*, who are already part of the church to come to this Navidad en Jesucristo, you need to try harder. Why would I want to go to a soccer match full of boys?

Why *wouldn't* you?

He winked. I couldn't tell if he was flirting.

Maybe at least draw some breasts and long hair on one of the boys?

We decided it was best if I drew the girls for the flyer. I sat at a red desk and waited for Wilson to bring the markers. Tiny porcelain dolls smelling daisies leaned on the edges. The room entirely decorated with dolls of all sizes. Some of which Xiomara had painted. Yes, homegirl was also a painter. Paintbrushes of all sizes perfectly arranged on a mounted shelf. Dolls crying blue tears, googly-eyed dolls, black dolls, doll-girls holding hands with doll-boys. At first I hadn't noticed the shelves behind me, next to the closets, lined with dolls clothed with actual textiles. But as the sun set, the sunlight glare from the window shone, deforming their faces. I wondered, on the scale of satanism, how satanic were these dolls?

We stayed inside that room for hours. I taught him how to draw hair and watched him take my hand discreetly. Like I wouldn't notice it was my hand inside his, now the fine tips of his nails, now sweat that I couldn't help thinking—forgive me, Lord—smelled like balls. At first I felt like a traitor. But I let him run his fingers over it. Why not. I let him clumsily intertwine his fingers with mine because I yearned to feel wanted by someone, because Carmen was far away and she didn't want it, she never did, because I wanted some of that joy of two hands together, the electricity. Then I noticed him staring at his boner, trying to hide it with a pillow.

CHAPTER TRECE

Cartagena de Indias, 1956
La Muñeca Brings All the Boys to the Bar

Before there was Miami cradling Mami's holy high addiction, before the Sabana Cundiboyacense swallowed everyone's pride with its mountains and the redbrick buildings killed Tata's husband, even before Yours Truly was a lost criolla spermatozoon, there was—*drumroll*—La Tata hiding in prayer underneath a bed in Cartagena. Every time the Dandy Lawyer, her fourth suitor that year, knocked on their door, she ran up the stairs holding her naguas and whispering to her sisters, That hombre *again*? Pero Dios mío. I'm not here, I'm not here, I'm not here. But under the wooden bed she was clutching her rosary. Annoyed, sweating bullets. Our Alba. Just fifteen but a total mujerón with hair so long Rapunzel cried envy tears, hips so smooth and thick Coca-Cola should have modeled their bottle after her. But silent and shy like a worm. Swimming deep into a cave, diving into the wood of darkness. Some earthworm, this niña. Like she'd inherited some bad blood and not the tra-la-la tongue del diablo of the cartageneras. *Pero what's going with this pela'a? Ajá is she slow muje?* seemed to be the song sung on repeat around her. The niña was cursed with shyness. Okay, that's not true. Let me rephrase that: a love for solitude misunderstood as shyness.

And there she lay: eight in the freaking morning and already inhaling all that dust under the bed, inching backward while her daddy whispered angrily that if she didn't come down a hacerle visita al Don he'd pull her out himself. How dare she. His screams annoyed her, but she'd devised a way of keeping them out by always carrying cotton balls in the pockets of her skirt, placing them in her ears and humming while he yelled. Did he think this jeva was some dumb bitch easily manipulated with bug-out eyes and belts? Of course he did. Pero mi reina, our girl was *re-source-ful*. You wanna yell, papi? Bring it on. I'll be waiting on the other side humming some Panchos and filing them nails.

The room smelled of burned candle. Next to the door the long mirror reflected the lit candles emitting a trail of smoke as if there were a thin thread tied to the planks of wood in the ceiling, as if the room were held together by a thin evaporating miracle. Next to the candles, estampas of El Sagrado Corazón de Jesús, La Virgen de la Candelaria, La Virgen de Chiquinquirá, La Virgen del Carmen, Santo Tomás. Unopened gifts with love scribbles stacked against the armoire like shiny green grenades. La persistencia de ese hombre. Is he ever gonna give up so I can listen to my radionovelas in peace? No joda. You'd think any jevita during the fifties would be jumping on one leg if a partidazo like the Dandy Lawyer approached their father with two bottles of whiskey per week, serenaded them with mariachis, and gifted them a freaking German horse with a red bow and luscious mane. Do you know, carajita, it took three months for that horse to travel across the Atlantic? Albita didn't know and didn't care. Por mí, that horse can die y yo no muevo un dedo. The horse stayed outside in the sizzling sun, shitting so much the Juans' house became known as La Cagada. *Oye, mi niña, tu casa es una cagada.* Papi couldn't take the sassy whispering of the vecinas and the condescending pats on the back from the hombres—hermano, por favor, one can only take so much shit in life—so instead of killing it, everyone in La Cagada just let the stunning four-legged beast die. Right outside their windows. Inside the patio. Drooling away any water left in him. And every day during breakfast Papi pointed to the patio announcing to the entire family: The groans? Alba's fault. The snorting? Alba's fault. Letting no one else feed the horse but reminding them every morning his oldest daughter cared for nothing, had no respect. No soul. Alba closed the curtains and placed cotton balls in her ears to avoid the painful moaning, but it was only when the radionovelas came on and homegirl turned them all the way up that she could refocus, that she could *live*.

Eventually, when hearing his gift drowned in mosquito shit, the Dandy Lawyer sent three of his machitos to deliver a letter to Alba with just one sentence: *¿Qué tú quiere, muje?*

Because nobody rejects a Veléz papá, not your mama, not your papi, not your fifteen-year-old radionovela-driven muñequita self. And who did Albita think she was, picking and choosing which macho forever humped her?

The cabrón's family owned the Ford dealership in Cartagena, carajo, knew the presidente by name. His family dealt emeralds from the moment the Spanish landed in the Nuevo Mundo and said, *¡Aquí me quedo, hijueputa!* The warm breeze of Cartagena plus its rhythmic military chants luring every motherfucker willing to make a buck in the ever-growing markets of the slave trade and shiny stones. Cha-ching. The Dandy Lawyer could trace his lineage all the way back to Arnoldo Veléz, a famous Spanish jeweler known for his cat fetish who, in 1786, jumped on the next boat out of Sevilla chasing El Dorado and found himself switching out his top hat for a guayabera. Papi Veléz fell head over heels hard for the smell of the ocean, the cats, the Sinú women who tended his house. Now that, mi reina, is a *real* baller. Two generations after Papi Veléz died asphyxiated from all that cat hair—homeboy brushed his fifteen cats three times a day, yes, I know this because there is a statue in La Ciudad Amurallada of the dude's stony face holding a kitty—the Velézes started losing money big-time. What with all-of-a-sudden having to pay their workers, all-of-a-sudden Las Leyes de Indias protecting people and shit. The Spanish crown couldn't make up its mind, cachaco! Are the Sinú people or are they not? Talk about wishy-washy. Por Dios, the familia had no patience for this. The Dandy Lawyer's grandfather sold the emerald company just when Mr. Yankee Ford was looking into expanding his wheels and, Madre Santísima, the dough was real. They were right at the port! When closing the deal the Dandy Lawyer's grandfather's famous words: *This is proof that Jesucristo is part colombiano.* Was it not? Everyone wanted a piece of that fancy Yankee cake on wheels. Shiny black machines roaring around Cartagena like futuristic monsters, naguas in and out of cars, hairy hands in and out of naguas. The Veléz empire, known for its harem of beautiful wives smoking outside on a terrace with sad looks, fake moles. The Dandy Lawyer needed to continue that tradition with an Albita in a pompous pink dress and French updo by his side. So he promised land, cars, any number of maids, entry to the country club, plus he wasn't even that perro. Only slept with a few guarichas. What else do you want, mujer?

But have you learned anything from this story yet? These women ain't gonna fall that easy. Cachaco, por favor. Cars nauseated her. She hated the country club. She hated hairy men in white suits. And, above all, she hated her father's smiling eyes, the cross ring on his pinky, serving whiskey and cracking jokes with the Dandy Lawyer while they waited for her downstairs.

¡Albita!

She sneezed. It was bug season. It was mosquito fever season. Outside: muddy streets staining long skirts. Outside: sheets of rain coating Cartagena. The colonial Caribbean beauty once the most important Spanish port through which slaves came in and only gold came out. A boiling pot of riches, Dios te salve Marías, and gunpowder.

Alba scratched the red mosquito bites on her legs, enjoying the pain, scratching harder each time, checking the bumps until a red head popped and bled. She'd been out in the garden with her radio until late last night even though her sick mama had begged her to come inside before Papi woke up, but no use in begging. Now her legs looked more like corn than skin.

It was only a matter of time before she had to walk down those stairs, our girl knew this. A matter of time before Papi yelled an ultimatum, before her mama's coughing fit, before Lurdes or one of her other sisters teased her, threatened to cut her hair, burn it, break the radio. *¿Qué tú hace all day with that Crown radio, niña?* They knew, cachaco, they just *knew* Albita and the shiny brown box had a tight connection all of them secretly wished for but could only dream of having. Our girl did not give the time of day to anyone in that house, anyone but *El derecho de nacer, Maruja La Sangrienta,* and, her complete favorite, *Lo que nunca muere*—That Which Never Dies. A murmur trail followed Alba wherever she went. Her very own son y ton, her personal soundtrack. Sometimes her mama found our girl sobbing while plucking chickens, and Albita would explain to her with a smile that when she tried to escape poor María did not make it to Madrid, they killed her, Mama. For wanting a better life, Mama, they killed her.

Ay mimi, you do know those stories are not true?

Who cares what's true. That's not important here. And what did her mama know about truth anyway? Would Truth wear a brunette wig in a bun? Or pencil in a mole above her lip? Or, better yet, soak in soap y Clorox a husband's kiss-stained work shirts pretending that rouge was some spicy ají? Would Truth visit a palanquera begging for some magical happiness potion that had Mama locked in the bathroom for hours on end?

Alba snaked out of the cave. She wanted to stretch that time like a piece of tutti-frutti gum. Wrap her body in that tutti-frutti gum hoping for an invisibility cloak or, if possible, knead it into a thick cocoon around her. A bubble-gum nest of infinite time. Pero, mi reina, tutti-frutti gum quickly hardens and before you could say *Se armó el bololó* she was sitting next to the Dandy Lawyer inhaling his cologne and sweat.

Could you please wear a different cologne next time? she said bothered.

Alba, carajo, how dare you? Papi whispered muy offended.

I can barely breathe next to him, Papi, and you want me to marry him?

Papi could have slapped that mouth shut, but gente de bien keep their dirty laundry in the family. So he just wiped the sweaty trail of anger around his forehead with a handkerchief, poured the Dandy Lawyer another one on the rocks, then yelled at Delsira that she could come play with her dolls now.

When Delsira dragged over her box of toys, Papi clapped and swallowed another shot, Alba grunted, and the Dandy Lawyer reached for her hand but not before Papi coughed as their fingers touched. Because women are like cars, the moment they step out of the car dealership with a macho inside they lose value by the second.

Come on, hermano. We're almost family now.

Close up the Dandy Lawyer lost fifteen points of swag. Alba held his dry hands, suppressing the giggles climbing up her throat when seeing the thick road of bumps and scars mapped on his face. Homeboy was all acne and acne was all makeup. Just for that she held his hand tighter because, whatever, underneath that yes-imported-from-Paris makeup lay the face of a boy beaten up in school for looking like a damn queer. Hidden platforms raised his shoes and by now Albita knew he wore shoulder pads underneath the guayaberas and was never seen shirtless.

He smoked cigars and had thick gold necklaces hanging over a carpet of curly hair to compensate. Papi's drunken eyes either knowingly missed or were selective and just saw what everyone five meters away from the man looked at: a testosterone-fueled toro, an irresistible Veléz, a loaded bank account, a motherfucker who could have your sister for breakfast, close a deal with some Yankee white dude for lunch, and down a few whisquisitos with Rojas Pinilla for dinner.

Alba was zero impressed by this. She cared zero for men like him. Actually, she cared zero for men in general and did not understand all the fuss about thick curly chest hair that, according to Marina, the flower lady outside the Santo Domingo church, drove the jevas *nuts*. For instance, Papi won the Man of the Barrio contest and was respected among the women in the family *because* he was a real pelo en pecho man with so much chest hair Mama sometimes trimmed it in the bathroom, a rain of thick brown hairs covering the white tiles. Women knocked on the Juans' door repeatedly demanding to see Papi, crying to Alba when she told them he wasn't there. He is not coming. He doesn't want to see you. Her mama served the women tinto, pastelitos, exchanged recipes, and discussed the new smell of the Santo Domingo candles, which crept into your clothes and stayed there for months, even after washing it with Jabón Rey. Some of them brought babies, and Mama sent Alba for the priest to baptize them and sometimes the priest would refuse to baptize the bastardos so Mama lied and said they were her own. Los pobres criaturos, it is not their fault.

What is it that you love so much about Papi? Ay niña,

have you *seen* that chest? Alba sometimes imagined gluing the fallen tufts of hair on her chest, walking out of the house into the streets where everybody, upon noticing the pillow of brown hair, would throw themselves on her like fangirls wanting to be cast as the new up-and-coming radionovela voice. *Maybe this way someone will take me seriously.*

The three of them watched Delsira playing on the floor, chewing on a rag doll.

In a perfect triangle: Papi, Alba, and El Dandy. The Holy Trinity in the pursuit of marriage, happiness, and hopefully a discount on a new car. Mama's coughs audible from the next room, that endless phlegm rhythm beating on the walls, reverberating in the flowery couch, the nailed Christ, the life-size statue of the Virgen, the Coca-Cola bottles, that ca-ca-ca of her throat infesting every moment of peace, interrupting Papi who just now was about to negotiate a 40 percent discount on a new auto. Pal diablo. Sister Yamira ran back and forth from the kitchen to the room with a pot of boiling water, eucalyptus, and what would become the most cherished miracle worker en Colombia: vickvaporú. The four sets of eyes watering from the intense eucalyptus-menthol smell, Papi murmured to the nun to shut the door, can't she see he's got important company? I'm doing what I can, she's very sick. Sister Yamira came three, sometimes four times a week with holy water, eucalyptus, and a ton of other magical shit to cure Mama's lungs. Pray for your mother, she said to Alba and her sisters.

Is she gonna die?

We're all going to die.

Well, duh. She could have figured that one out. Is Mama going to die soon is what Alba meant, should she be preparing to lay Mama inside a coffin, would the next mama role be assigned to Alba, who didn't want it, who prayed her mama be kept alive so she wouldn't have to serve pastelitos and tintos to Papi's novias, dress her sisters for church, sew stuffed animals with chicken feathers, draw a fake mole on her face. Sometimes her mama said she not only had to be strong, Alba, you gotta be the strongest one, mimi, porque cuando yo me vaya you'll be in charge of this house. ¿Me entiende? Mama, Alba said, deja de hablar pendeja'a, you still got plenty of time. Her mama sighed, plucked more chickens. Our girl did not want to be in charge of the house, but how to tell her mother that she had to stay alive so Alba could move to Bogotá to write and record the up-and-coming radionovela sensation. The sickness already a regular in the household, already normalized like the lizards, Papi's notary stamps, the girls' rag dolls, Sister Yamira's churchy smell, the dead chickens. The chicken feathers incubated inside everyone's lungs mixed in with eucalyptus, cigar oil, dust.

Sister Yamira couldn't find the bag of herbs she'd left in the kitchen. Alba drew her hand away from the Dandy's, excused herself, sidestepped Delsira's saliva-soaked doll, and handed Sister Yamira the remaining herbs. From the kitchen she saw Mama take a gulp of whiskey, cross herself. She'd permanently taped black cloth on the bedroom window so nobody from the outside could see her in that state. Yes, mi reina, taped windows in *that* heat. Forty degrees in the shade and a tiny white fan the only ventilation. Papi didn't sleep there because he always woke up sancochao, oliendo a tigrillo. But Mama's atrophied internal thermometer allowed her to resist the highest temperatures without a drop of sweat. Papi actually liked this about her. Nobody wants a sweaty female, por favor. The women of Cartagena (las mujeres de bien, that is) suffered terribly because of this because ain't nobody gonna look cute with four layers of pollerines on plus a dress in that infernal heat. And talk about smell. If there's anything memorable about the fifties in Cartagena, it's the tigrillo-dusty smell. Like stuffing one's head inside the bedroom of a teenage boy.

Alba crossed herself. Sister Yamira then drew out a rosary, held Alba's hands, and began praying a few Ave Marías and a Padre Nuestro que estás en el cielo, santificado sea tu nombre, etc. When she was done Sister Yamira told Albita to pray for her mother.

Is she gonna die?

We're all gonna die, Alba. Sister Yamira picked up her things and wiped the sweat from her neck with a kitchen towel, which Alba thought disgusting and inappropriate. She would have to wash that kitchen towel later, hang it outside to dry, say hi to the vecinas who always asked about the men coming in and out of the house and told her to send some of the machos their way. Suelta eso' hombre, jevita. The thought was dreadful. Y la berraca monja continued to wipe, pushing back her habit so that Alba could see her bare hairy arms, the drops, no, the *clots* of sweat transplanted to the kitchen towel. Who raised this woman? Alba knew Mama would slap her in no time if she saw her wiping her body with a freaking kitchen towel. She couldn't imagine Sister Yamira as a young woman. Alba imagined all nuns were born nuns: they had no childhood, no youth, they didn't come out of anyone's vagina, they were just *there* being nuns all the time. Sister Yamira sighed, wiped her forehead, *again*. There was no way she could stop this. Sister Yamira handed her the kitchen towel. Gracias, mi niña.

Is there anything else besides prayer that I can do, hermana? Alba tried hiding her disgust.

You can pick up more holy water from the capilla later on today, she definitely needs it.

How the holy water was going to keep Mama alive so she could be a radionovela star was a mystery to Alba, but she respected the church, respected Sister Yamira—despite the kitchen towel—and above all, this was the only hope she could cling to. This water.

~

Mi reina, but what you really need to know is this: They showed up without any prior warning and sometimes stayed for days. They came from Arjona, Barranquilla, Santa Marta, Corozal, from Mompox, Distracción, San Martín de Loba, Turbaco. Muchacho, espérate. They wore top hats, dark mustaches, a scar or two on their faces, sometimes a distracting limp, a man purse, a case of cigars, and if they were lucky a novia or two waiting for them in the back seat of the car, fanning themselves and stealing anything they could. There was Filoberto, the skinny shoemaker with an eye tic who salivated every time he talked about gluing shoes together, and Manuel

Jesús, more corpse than body, a rich terrateniente always interested in knowing if our girl Alba was any good at foot massages and shooting shotguns. She wasn't. Eliécer arrived with three hunting dogs, a pierna de pernil, and a note he secretly passed Alba: *I'm into you plus your chickens, together.* Dare I mention Miguel Ángel? The bald dude from Cali sobbing the entire time he was there, sweating profusely, refusing to leave the house until someone left with him. Álvaro, Jesús José, Mariano Alberto, Ulises, Carlos Pedro. They knew each other, hated each other, loved each other, shared the tight entrance space to the house while wasting no time and doing business transactions right there, three horses, five cases of whiskey, two new supermarkets, bum bum bum. Some of them knew each other from their wife-searching adventures and exchanged anecdotes about fathers willing to give away their daughters too soon or some who inquired way too much about their lives. Que dónde van a vivir, que how many times is she gonna visit, que do you have enough maids to care for her hair, her special feet, her special diet. Cachaco they wanted a wife, period.

Alba's mama barely able to keep up with all the coffee, palitos de queso, the line at the bathroom, the urine everywhere around the toilet, to the point that she demanded Papi hire someone to tend to all the men's needs. ¿Me viste cara de empleada o qué? Mama also wanted Alba to marry but found the spectacle outside their house deplorable. People were *saying things* during mass. At first Mama held her head high, orgullosa of course that her oldest daughter could cause such commotion, that men traveled for days to see her. Pero después it wasn't all that cute. They stank after a few days, drunk from all the whiskey and the sun, cursing at passersby, catcalling the vecinas and even Sister Yamira when she entered the Juans' house. *Monjita, pero qué linda está la monjita, carajo.* But that wasn't the end of it. The worst? People setting up puesticos, selling tamarindos, lemonade, fried fish, palenqueras handing out fruit salads for a few coins, street kids blasting music—all of it in front of *their* house. The city even sent a few volunteers to help with traffic.

Mama's cough worsened during those times. You're gonna kill me, Alba. None of them good enough for you? Jesucristo as my witness, niña, you are killing me. Get me some vickvaporú. Alba didn't bring her the vickvaporú. She let her cough and cough, closed her door, turned the radio all the way up, and when María La Divina started imploring for her life, Alba recited from memory the lines before María La Divina was finally killed. But then the weight of the house perched itself on her thoughts. Mierda. Todo en esta vida, a big mierda ride. She remembered God, or God talked to her and told her to stop being such a selfish puta and get the freaking vickvaporú. Alba crawled around the house, close to the floor, recoiling every time she saw men's shoes, plugging into the dirt, swimming deep into the soil, deeper into the soil, watching some of the horse's bones go by, skeletons of children, a lost shoe, emeralds gleaming cutting pieces from her arms that quickly regrew, she swayed from side to side with her mouth open, eating fresh dirt, swallowing fresh dirt, bathing in its misty coolness.

The Dandy Lawyer was the last man, the last man in that line. The only one who came back one, two, four times, ten times in awe that any woman would even think about not wanting him. Homeboy enjoyed a challenge, a little bump in the wedding road. Many women before had just thrown themselves like free bags of potatoes, secretly placing his hand on their crotches, licking fingers, letting him hump their culos. Pero Alba. Na-nais. The niña sat stone-cold hugging that radio like a doll, never softening to his touch or his words or his German horse. She only seemed to care about that stupid radio. El descaro. He saved himself for last precisely because he knew his blue blood was irresistible and Alba's blood was merely above average. But now his patience wore thin. Yes, the jeva's body curved like a dreamlike goddess; yes, he'd be able to brag about conquering the Juans' muñequita to all the other losers; yes, that somber aura attracted him, gave him a boner, that hot freaking weirdo in those naguas. To pound those naguas. Jesucristo. What else was there to do for a rich boy in the fifties but business meetings, whiskey, perfectly trimmed mustache, and pounding naguas? That's right, cachaco, nada.

But like I said, his patience wore thin. The thought of future bragging sent chills through the Dandy's hands, but Alba's head buried in the radio buttons killed his mojo. Otra vez Alba con la joda. The Dandy raised his eyebrows, opened and closed his hands brusquely in a *bueno what's up* gesture, suggesting Papi should say something. Alba knew what was happening pero se hizo la loca Papi knew what was happening pero se hizo el loco. The Dandy played with his mustache smiling thinly at Delsira, who now turned to him rocking the rag doll, asking him to nurse her. Annoyed, homeboy first rejected the extended arms clasping the saliva-soaked doll, but then Delsira's eyes watered—la animaleja, always manipulating people with tears—and the Dandy not only accepted the saliva-soaked doll but rocked the saliva-soaked doll, nursed the saliva-soaked doll with a fake bottle. The three of them— Alba, Papi, and Delsira—perplexed at the image. It was the first time our girl saw a man rocking a baby like a mama, there was even some *love* trapped in his brown eyes, and it all disgusted her. It reminded her of Octavio, a radionovela boy with half his face burned during a fire in Turbaco. A poor boy. A boy obligated to spend his life by his mama's side because she didn't let him out on the streets with that face, she couldn't take the chisme, the burlas, the pointing. So the boy stayed at home taking care of his siblings. He rocked the babies, nursed them, etc. Secretly. He was burned and poor. But *this*?

Y entonce Alba broke the silence: Bueno ya, this is stupid. Papi, I'm not marrying a man who acts like a—here she turned her hand, raised her pinky—y punto.

The Dandy threw the doll across the living room, broke a flower vase he'd brought that day, and stomped out of the house—not before calling Alba a buena para nada, your daughter is *not* a señorita, and adding Papi would never own a real car.

When Alba was twelve years old women pulled at her hair for two weeks straight. Sister Yamira, her mother, and two vecinas with their own hair wrapped in plastic bags, hunched over Alba's head in the kitchen. Puro piojo. The women were summoned to their lice-killing duty and in they came remangándose las mangas, with vinegar, scissors, filed nails ready to crush, and—you guessed it—vickvaporú. Cundía estaba la nena. When she stood still Alba could see brown spots jumping off her head, kamikazes diving into her notebook, dancing on her scalp, stealing all her blood. Let them steal my blood, she said. ¡Pero niña! Alba was all darks before darks was even a thing. She channeled all that Catholic fervor into her scalp and told the women the insects needed her blood to survive. Let them live inside me. No kidding pela'a. Our girl's real goal was to piss off her mama because she'd caught her mama wearing no underwear when the milkman knocked on the door, caught her bent over reaching for bottles of milk and smoking one underneath the mango tree. But Mama was not having it. They chased her around the house. Alba, por favor, how old are you?

Quarantined.

Every piece of cloth washed with boiling water, her sisters' hair braided at all times. Which of course didn't help her already outlaw status amid the sisterhood. But did she care?

Papi received a passive-aggressive letter from school suggesting the expulsion of Alba for being *unwashed and to some extent dirty and to some extent disgusting and to some extent a threat to school hygiene* and that was that. For three days straight the women tried smashing, boiling, slapping the lice but the little fuckers set up an entire city with malls and shit in there. The underground third world for lice.

Until one day, after praying to God for guidance, Sister Yamira chopped off all of Alba's hair.

Y fue por eso that Alba got a boy's haircut.

Y fue por eso that she got to play Joseph, Jesús, and all the men in the school plays.

Y fue por eso that when Joseph and Mary fall in love they kiss. It's somewhere in the Bible.

Y fue por eso that María Magdalena threw herself on top of her when she played Jesús.

Y fue por eso that she was darks before you were darks and the girls called her *la niña niño*.

Y fue por eso that sometimes to evade the stares, the pointing, giggling, grabbing of her breasts, she'd wear her father's shirts and buy holy water and sit by the park with her radio.

Y fue por eso that Papi confused her with the vecina's son one day and told her she'd actually look pretty good as a man, too bad she was a señorita.

But back to our girl's drama.

He's right, Alba, Papi said. You're *not* a señorita. Papi stared into his whiskey, some real sadness concentrated on his face. He played with his mustache in a way Alba knew could only mean Papi was about to do something he didn't want to do. A brush of fingers arched it perfectly around the invisible lips, a sip of whiskey, a brush of fingers arched it perfectly around the invisible lips, a sip of whiskey, and so on. Mama yelled from her room, but no one paid attention until they all saw her banging shit around the kitchen, until they all smelled the walking vickvaporú with smeared makeup and only one pink sock getting a glass of water. Jesú Cristo. Papi went up to her, kissed her hand, which only infuriated Mama even more.

I think we can all agree this has gone too far. Esto rebozó la copa, Alba. I think we can all agree that was our best chance at getting you a good, honest man to marry. Don't interrupt me, carajo. I think we can all agree you've crossed a line and that line was el Señor Veléz and since el Señor Veléz will not be coming back . . . Did you even know I was negotiating a discount on a car? I'm out of line? You know what's going to happen now? You're marrying the next huevón that walks through that door and that's that. The next huevón. That's it, mija. I'm done with this circo. Your mother is done with this circo.

Pero, ¡Papá!

Papá nada, Alba. Papá nada. And in the meantime no more radio. Preste pa'cá la radio.

Mama sighed, shut her door. Here they go again. Every time Papi wanted something out of Alba he'd hide her radio. She'd go for days without eating, without showering, without changing her clothes in protest, reeking of tigrillo plus accumulated sweat plus concentrated menstruation until she fainted over breakfast one day and the radio was quickly returned. In secrecy Papi would apologize, patting her back, leaving two cigarettes in her boudoir. That was his way of saying, I care for you, mamita, stop being such a pain in the ass.

But this time was different. This time there'd be no cigarettes, no paternal comfort for our girl, who was so over it, so over Papi behaving all look-at-me look-at-me, I can take your radio and make you miserable because I'm your father, I have a dick, you have to follow everything I say. So over it. And her mama. And her sisters. And the bwak

bwak bwak of chickens on the patio, right in the middle of the house poking at her lace dresses and her miserable body sweating profusely, thighs sticking together, rubbing each other. Over. It.

This time she didn't fight Papi, she didn't hide food in her room, she didn't mentally prepare to colonize the house with her dread, her longing, her frustration, her bad smells.

Está bien, Papá. Take it.

¿Está bien? I already did. You know what's *not* all right, Alba?

Her sisters giggled from their rooms, Papi shushed them but they wouldn't stop. Alba was a witch and this was the inquisition with a lowercase *i*. Papi's inquisition. What would they do with her if she didn't marry? Where else could she go? Papi was not about to house a solterona for the rest of his life, and Alba was not about to pluck feathers from chickens and join Mama's asthmatic fan club.

Anything else, Papi? She stood up firmly, with an air of pride and superiority, and dared gaze Papi in the eye. She left the Crown radio on the couch without even eyeing it one last time. It was all very dramatic. Of course. But this is how our girl wanted it. A gloomy background orchestra, black birds, and Albita starring in her own radionovela. Gliding past Papi with an irresistible elegance, asking to be excused, to be forgiven, feeling some sort of boiling energy running through her focused on her liver, lungs, her lower stomach beating with what can only be described as unequivocal desire. Desire for what—who knows. She felt hot and gorgeous and like a fucking boss even though the fifties in Cartagena had the misses all up in subjugation mode, but the jeva glided through that living room, through the patio, up the stairs with a pulsating confidence that began deep inside her pussy and radiated out to every bit of her.

Annoyed, Papi waited for a response. Say something, carajo, silence will not save you Alba, por favor. Pero Papi se quedó esperando. Then yelling: We need some holy water in this house! Alba please, we need you to go get some holy water for your mother.

Her sister Lurdes lay on top of her bed eating grapes, writing letters to her girlfriends. They eyed each other but said nothing. Lurdes knew Alba was not a mosquita muerta like everyone else thought, she knew Alba played la-la dumb sometimes to avoid dealing with Papi and Mama and Life, something Lurdes couldn't do. Lurdes always felt the need to stand up for herself, whereas Alba played oblivious, played dollhouse, and sometimes—like when Papi hid her radio—starved herself but never actually uttered a word, yelled. To the contrary, mi reina. She swallowed every bit of anger and then some.

Without her sister noticing, Albita grabbed the cigarettes hidden in the naguas drawer, some scissors, the new yellow skirt the Dandy sent as a gift long ago that was oh so gorgeous but could not be worn until the mancito was completely out of sight. Like now. Lurdes muttered something before Alba locked herself in the bathroom. Then yelled again.

Alba, just don't leave the bathroom full of hairs!

There was no eye-rolling for our girl in the fifties, but

if the expression existed her eyes would have circled back twice. She mocked Lurdes in the bathroom. She mocked her father. Everyone in that house—including her younger sister—controlling every bit of her and nothing she could do to stop it. It all felt natural, common sense.

Alba started trimming her pubic hair after she heard the women at church gossiping about stinking during their periods, one suggesting shaving the entire thing off, the other one gasping because that clearly had to be a sin. She'd never consciously stared at her pussy, didn't actually *see it* per se, but trimming soothed her. She hummed Los Panchos while chopping thick pieces of black hair. Then smoked a cigarette. It was the perfect procrastination combo.

She undressed to her underwear, lit up the cigarette, and felt sorry for herself. It really was a waste, this life. She could run away to her best friend's house, but then Marta's mother was so particular about table manners it drove Alba crazy. No, Marta's house was not an option. Alba touched the rolls of her belly, massaging them, they were few, thick, and well proportioned, just enough to give her the famous muñeca nickname. *So stupid*, she thought. *This body*. Cigarettes didn't calm her, didn't give her peace of mind, didn't make her look cool (although in my head she's a total rock star), but she wanted to damage herself in some way, wanted that energy roaring through her and her pain to coexist where she could see them. From below she could hear Papi still yelling at her to bring holy water to Mama. Dios mío. Papi, Alba knows and she's not listening.

~

Outside some other loser getting shot. She'd have to walk past the mass of gossipers and the mother yelling, past the men looking, always looking like they have eyes for nothing else, pretend not to see them, smile thinly with dignity, past more mothers with veils coming out of church, cross herself, showcase her golden rosary because the mothers knew Mama, and Buenas tardes Cleotilde, cómo está usted, past the rivers of red dust and heat pooling between her legs, her armpits, under her tongue. Her lips salty. And the women and the men and the children because Papi knew everyone and they called her *Albita, muñe, niña, pela'a, bombón, angelito caído, calladita, lotería, qué rico puerto rico, culo'e muje—everyone* guayándole la existencia. She'd have to walk past the rotting-tomato smell of the market mixed with fresh-baked bread, dogs chewing on dead pigeons, baskets full of papaya, mango, coco, plátano, aguacates slightly putrefied by the heat, and the gamines disgustingly eating the putrefied scraps with bare hands reminding Alba of the rotting Germanic pony and again of the Dandy and thus of Papi's frustration and Mama's anxiety with his frustration and the fact that she wouldn't get married and the fact that she would miss *La Salvadora* just when María and Jacinto were secretly hooking up. Muchacho.

Three kids next to the church begged for money. Alba handed them a few cents then bought a mango from the seño next to them in her square cart. A skeletal dog barked at the woman's feet. Inside the church was cool and dead quiet. Black-and-white pashminas on women's bowed heads. Christ forever bleeding, forever shining, forever openmouthed. Alba searched for the priest but couldn't find him. Papi knew him quite well and she'd been to the back of the church often. She recognized some of the señoras fanning themselves next to the baptismal font, they owed Mama money but no way was Alba walking up to demand cash. Alba hoped Mama didn't expect her to settle business. No way. I mean, Mama showed her the ropes, the ins and outs of the stuffed-animal business, but Alba never paid attention. One time she let Alba balance the books and three hundred pesos came out missing. No way. Mama probably didn't want her to walk up to these ladies although she'd been complaining about them for months and now they had seen Alba, nodded at her, and next time they saw Mama surely they would let her know they saw Alba, who did not care to approach them, and how was Mama raising her young girls? Malditas. The three women had no intention of chatting. She always did this, got riled up, then nothing happened. The three of them nodded at Alba, crossed themselves, then exited.

The back of the church empty except for the priest's robes on hangers, packs of long white candles, a gigantic Bible, a few chairs. María and all the other vírgenes. She crossed herself when passing La Virgen del Carmen, kissed her knuckles. Behind the vírgenes another door she'd never seen before. Alba hesitated for a second. She remembered verses of the Bible about conduct repeated many times by Sor Inés that ended with a *When in doubt always ask yourself, Will El Señor approve? Am I being a Martha or a Mary?* She didn't want to be either one. She needed the holy water to sprinkle around the house, make concoctions of ginger and honey for Mama. Dios mío, her mom. She needed to find the priest. She decided to be Martha if that meant finding holy water, and so Alba slowly turned the doorknob, the wood creaking against the wind crashing into the stained-glass windows.

The body on the other side of the door so unlike her own yet so familiar. Brown hips, brown ass, square shoulders with a small hunched back, and a thick scar traversing the back like a white river. Like homegirl was cut in two and a clumsy kid had glued her back together. There was something unusual about the way her back curved to the side reclining on the windowpane, an easiness, like she did this every day and it wasn't a big deal. Alba stood witnessing a routine that was far from what she'd imagined nuns did. Only a headpiece decorated the body. A backdrop that still kept the nun's body holy, hidden in some way, closer to God. Alba wanted to judge her, drop every Bible verse condemning the monja, but she couldn't stop staring at the body. She concentrated on the hands, roughed, manly, holding a cigarette with two fingers like she'd seen men do. Dios mío. Mi Dios. A naked nun smoking by the window, another fucker shot outside, and all you could hear was the cha-cha-cha son y ton of a loud vallenato. Y dice

Pasó volando y no ha cantao
Porque lleva el pico apretao
Pajarito resabio
Suelte ese beso robao

The nun shook her head in disapproval, crossed the air, then kept sucking on the cigarette. Alba stood in the back of the room, hidden by a movable wardrobe with different-colored robes thickly hung on it and then the life-size Jesucristo, Santo Tomás, and María surrounding the robes in a semicircle. It was a perfect hiding spot. She could see the nun from an opening between the incense-scented robes.

Alba felt a rush of shame for eyeing a naked nun even though nobody had explicitly told her not to stare at naked nuns, but nuns always covered their entire bodies and prayed, washed poor people's feet, and rubbed vick-vaporú like Sister Yamira did for her mama. Nuns didn't smoke naked by the window. And girls like her didn't stare at nuns smoking naked by the window. She knew better. And yet. Papi said she wasn't a señorita no more and either way Papi was not there so she could stare if she wanted to. And she did. Never in her fifteen-year existence had this cartagenera seen another grown naked body so close, not even her own. She was breaking the rules big-time, the unspoken rules. When she was little she used to remove the clothes of all her dolls searching for a body but found nothing. Silent, always silent and dumb. The closest she ever got to seeing a body was when María and Carlos hit it off in *La Salvadora*, even then the descriptions were awkwardly narrated as *they were passionately doing it*.

The nun coughed. Alba wanted to freeze that moment. Or at least take a picture. This naked body was a gift she wanted to inspect thoroughly. She wondered how the nun's pussy looked and her armpits and her anus and her right toe. She wanted to swim in the nun's body, inspecting every crevice, corner, every scar and mole. She wanted to smell her, remove the headdress, then smell her again. She wanted it all. She wanted it so much she could almost feel the texture of the nun's ass on her fingertips, the miniature cellulite potholes covered in tiny invisible hairs. She wanted to kiss the potholes.

Alba closed her eyes. Bible verses flew in and out, Sor Inés at school, her mama, the radionovelas—but the desire was bigger than all of that together. Bigger than the moral compass, the ethics class, the catechism class, the señoritas' class. A darkness swirled inside her, a darkness she knew from her loneliness, her radionovela longing, a darkness almost palpable now. The smooth holy body was certainly sent by God, the nun was holy and Diosito knew what he was doing. No need to question Him, the Lord works in mysterious ways. Amén.

That's when she noticed the shoes. The familiar black shoes.

Worn black shoes with a faded silver buckle on the nun's feet, the same freaking shoes visiting her house every week for the past, I don't know, forever. The shoes that asked for boiling water, kneeling at her mama's side, praying for her. The worn black shoes that just that morning had wiped their sweaty arms and neck with a kitchen towel Alba had yet to wash. Holy shit, mi reina. *Ay juemadre* is right. Sister Yamira in all her como-la-trajo-Diosito-al-mundo glory.

She could have yelled at the monja's indecency, the door was, after all, unlocked when Alba came in. She could have waited for Sister Yamira to dress, throw the habit at her, demand an explanation. None of that happened. Why. Alba didn't know she could feel like this. Why. The darkness still roaring.

Once she showed me the only picture anyone owned of Sister Yamira. It was Alba's sixteenth birthday party, right before she married Don Fabito, the next man to walk through the door; there are flowers and cake and pompous lace dresses. Sister Yamira at the corner of the table trying to look over the crowd at Alba's face as Alba blows out the candles. Sister Yamira's bare arms. Alba saved the photograph because it reminded her of that time her darkness ate her, a piñata explosion that left her exhausted and overwhelmed.

Alba left a note outside the church's door: *Sister Yamira, I came to get holy water but you were busy. I will come again tomorrow. Alba.*

CHAPTER CATORCE

Miracles are holy supernatural blessings dropping from the heavens into the chosen one's lap without prior warning. Bam, new legs. Bam, groceries. Bam, La Tata stands up from the couch. Bam, good hair day. Bam, your mother cooked something other than mustard chicken for dinner. *¡Milagro! ¡Arriba Cristo!* Sometimes miracles are predictable, like when Mami prayed during our flight from Bogotá mumbling shit nonstop until the customs guy stamped our passports with a *six-month stay* and aleluya the Lord responded to Mami's prayers. Milagro de Dios. Milagros, all around. A milagro is also God's way of saying something is right for you, it's God's ñapa, God's free supersized McCombo. Always good, God-intended, God-aligned. La Tata skipping el show de Don Francisco? A milagro. Mami getting extra flyer-delivering shifts? A milagro. Yours Truly receiving Jesucristo into her heart? You guessed it, cachaco. People feel extra special when receiving milagros, a stronger connection to the One Above, a nod from Papi Dios, a feeling that all is not lost, that there is some sense to this life beyond the materiality of our bodies. And yet. We always want more. Yes, hanging out with Wilson seemed like a milagro, but was it ephemeral? Mami wanted more from me, an assurance that this new four-week Wilson fling was solid, that there was commitment, possibly love, that she could breathe deeply and focus on getting lost in herself again.

She didn't say it to my face, but I heard Mami tell Tía Milagros on the phone that finally she could sleep in peace as I was with God and with boy. A true miracle. Mami let Wilson hang at the house all he wanted, when back in Bogotá the boys visiting me could only spend as much as an hour before being kicked out of the living room. Now we even closed my bedroom door without so much as a *watch your virginity* gesture from Mami, and no incessant questioning after he left. Even Lucía left us alone, which had me thinking this was all Mami's master plan—that she'd convinced Wilson to date me, paid him under the table, or begged Xiomara to manipulate her son into liking me. Mothers are capable of destroying worlds, the world, if they want to. Mine definitely knows this. ¿Y por qué no? I was a single sixteen-year-old after all, just barely united with Jesús, learning about my direct relationship with Him, etc. Plain looking, pale, hairy, with ingrown hairs where nobody should have them, but still I was young, so young, I was vulnerable, so vulnerable, still in jeans but now white T-shirts advertising my young love for the One Above and, yes, mami linda, this planicie was all Christian, all aleluya and no cigarettes, no eyeliner. I was testament that a life in Jesús truly turns you inside out. Look at this new wardrobe. Girls like me were fresh meat at church. Mamas hurried searching for boys to date us, church groups to join, leadership positions to fill, makeup to remove, pants to change, drinks to throw away, virginities to reattach, bodies to sew back together anew.

New were Wilson's skinny hands.

The way they pointed at me when he introduced me palm up, opened hands, this is Francisca. With both of my hands I grabbed his into a little cocoon and smelled them. They smelled stale but also like strong cologne and soil and I tried remembering this when the shekinas gave me the weird eye. I tried holding on to his hands, pushing Carmen way out of sight. I wondered if someone told Carmen. They must have, right? If Carmen found out Wilson and I now held hands. What would she do. Would she come back. Would she come back. Would she yell. Would she pick me. Would she?

I knew they whispered about us at church. Not only the girls but the boys and their parents. Everyone with their opinions stamped on their faces. The first day we appeared at the youth group holding hands the air almost snapped in two. Carmen and I used to hold those youth meetings together, remember? We drew up outlines of the prédica, the Jesucristo outings, the outreach efforts. I passed out the markers, the small Bibles. I brought her water and watched her preach. Now Wilson and I took on the leadership duet, only this time homeboy had to make sure everyone knew we were dating. As part of the Iglesia Cristiana Jesucristo Redentor congregation, all romantic relationships must be publicized immediately, especially teen relationships. It's stated in our workbook. Francisca es mi novia, he said to the nodding heads. Whatever. They were judging me, judging us, because two months ago Wilson was drooling all over Carmen and now look at the joven with the pálida lesser ungodly version of Carmen.

To be clear, some people at church still believed I was faking my conversion. "Some people" meaning Paula spreading gossip that she'd seen the satánica *me* smoking and that now I was a jezebel stealing someone's man. Some nodded, some looked askance, Paula freaking giggled, but I just passed around the Jesús Es Vida worksheet of the day. *Freaking Christian goody-two-shoes youth. Mi vida, you don't know what you're in for.* They distrusted me. Wilson? He was oblivious to the *zorrita, putica* name-calling. Boys can do whatever they want, even if they're Christian.

I cared. But I also wanted the weight of his arm around me all the time, the way he searched for me after the service was over, and how his eyes lit up. I never wanted to be alone again. I wanted Jesús and Wilson in the same bed with me spooning forever so that I'd have someone who touched me. Someone who asked if I wanted ketchup on my hamburger then stood up and got it with a smile. *Here's your salsa de tomate, belleza.* Wilson needed me now, called me in the afternoons, picked me up in his silver pickup truck to drive together to Iglesia Cristiana Jesucristo Redentor, his hand never leaving my left leg. Every time I saw the hand, Carmen's leg appeared like a mirage and I stared at Wilson's skinny hand, deep down wanting the body driving the car to be someone else's. Sometimes we'd stop by the 7-Eleven and he'd buy me Skittles and I let his hand get closer to my cunt. Just a little bit. I can't even tell you how much I loved Skittles. I used to buy the extra-large bags at Walmart and munch on them until my sugar levels were so high my fingers turned purple. I loved Skittles so much and Wilson was all clumsy, all lilt and good manners, and I was all about that touch. All about the extra attention and spooning his tight little butt. What can I say, the boy had a nice ass and from behind I could pretend it was anyone's. It was Wilson's one minute and then it wasn't. He'd moan a little, like a girl, and then we passed out on my bed for hours.

On one of those spooning rainy afternoons I felt the water coming again. Wilson passed out dormidito, his back to me. Dark neck similar to Carmen's with a few freckles and tiny black hairs spiraling. I smiled, overtaken by the memory of her. Wanting to call it back, call back her smell. Our late-night prayers. The sky above lit green by the tiny fluorescent crosses. Playing with the hairs, I leaned my head to smell the neck, kiss it. The rain outside drumming on the window. Fierce. The rain carrying a certain sadness. Or maybe it was just me. It felt like I was swallowing the rain, like I couldn't speak and was drowning. I was a vessel for the lluvia, a vessel for the fiebre tropical that wouldn't stop. Wilson smelled like him. There were no crosses above. I gently kissed the back of his neck, swallowing the ocean inside.

~

Mami woke us up with a glass of Milo and a grilled-cheese sandwich. Homegirl had kept it together all this time but ever since I started dating Wilson bits of her were falling apart, flying off like loose feathers, and it was painful to watch. I didn't want to see it. I pretended to not see her puffed-up eyes, greasy hair, and just thanked her and chewed on my sandwich.

A week before, I'd caught her crying alone with Cristina from *El show de Cristina* on the TV. Mami was not one to sob profusely or throw herself on the floor or yell when crying. Her crying was proud and silent, almost indistinguishable. She'd always cried like this, stoic without letting herself go too much and of course wiping her eyeliner, holding that Kleenex for dear life. If it weren't for the ball of Kleenex in her fist pointing me to her eyes I wouldn't have that image now stuck in my head: Mami on the stained flowery couch, tiny white balls of Kleenex around her. A sad flower garden. I didn't want to think about what could be wrong with her, did she want me to ask? I thought my Christianness plus Wilson would bring us bliss. What else did she want? Was it her hair? Three times she'd clogged the tub with chunks of hair but laughed the matter off. Maybe it was her hair, knowing the clock didn't stop for her, off it went with the brown chunks of hair. But I didn't want to know. I didn't ask what was wrong, I walked right past her into the kitchen and slammed a Pop-Tart into the toaster. And just like that day, I jammed the grilled cheese down my throat, chugged the Milo, and left with Wilson to drive around the neighborhood and to the lake.

What's wrong with your mom?

Nothing. She's losing hair, that's all.

Well, but did she pray about it?

I hated other people seeing what was happening inside our house. Not even Pablito knew about La Tata's Sprite cans or about Mami's new sadness or about Lucía who was just, well, being Lucía, which was enough of a problem. And now Wilson staring at our trapos sucios, what if that was a turnoff? What if he thought he was better off with a girl with no crying mother and a fully stocked fridge? I took his hand and placed it right where my thigh began.

We parked in front of the lake and watched cans of Coke and decapitated toys wobble on the surface. The car had no gas so we had to sit there with the windows down inhaling natural air, a rare occurrence in Miami. Unless you're at the beach, there's no reason for you to torture yourself breathing natural air when AC is perfectly capable of giving you the same oxygen quality with a cool, crispy swing. Mami said Carmen was coming back for our big Navidad en Jesucristo service. I imagined Carmen watching us from the other side of the lake and wasn't sure who she'd be mad at. Would she hate me or hate Wilson? I see Carmen swimming naked in the lake, her tits pointing to the sun and diving deep toward me. I braid her hair. She begs me to open the door so she can get in the truck with us, then she pushes Wilson out of the car and drives off with me. We go to South Beach, park the car near a warehouse. She sucks on my neck, leaves hickeys while she whispers she owns me. Of course we wake up full of bruises. Pero cachaco, Carmen'd probably go for Wilson. Forgive him, kick *me* out of the truck. Homeboy would not think twice. Don't get me wrong, I knew he liked me, he did, but I wasn't stupid. Whenever Carmen was mentioned his eyes wrestled and I felt like an old wife who knows her husband is cheating but still wants him to come home and kiss her good night. I stared at Wilson and he smiled. I let him put his hand right on the warmth of my crotch and unbutton my jeans. He seemed reluctant so I pulled my pants all the way down. We were silent for a few minutes while he stared ahead, then at my hairy thighs.

Wilson, por Dios, I'm not gonna say anything.

This is so wrong, Francisca. You know better.

She would totally pick him. The youth group would be delighted. Throw them a party with balloons and a rainbow love cake and not invite me because this love was meant to be.

It is so wrong, but I won't say anything. I promise. Carmen is coming back in a month, did you know?

I wanted a reaction. I wanted him to love me, desire me, fuck me.

There were two types of Christian boys at the church: the frigid pelaos who didn't even touch their dicks and genuinely prayed to God, and the machitos who jerked off to magazines, stared at the shekinas' tits, and prayed to Dios. God is merciful, God is forgiving. Wilson was the second kind. I knew this. That awkward swag plus I'd caught him staring at Carmen's boobs before. I let him kiss me because the machito was flexible and now here we were, my ugly boy underwear showing my unshaved legs and that one scar across my left thigh.

I held his hands while we both thought about Carmen.

Before he could answer I put my tongue inside his mouth, played around like a worm in a cave. I was a terrible kisser at sixteen and he was too. He squeezed my boobs hard like they were stress balls and I told myself I deserved it. I deserved having a clumsy boyfriend, I deserved his uncut fingernails clawing at my tits, and I deserved his love for Carmen. We both deserved not loving each other. His dick was hard against my leg. With his warm hand he slapped my pussy softly, slap, slap, over my boy underwear, slap, slap, and I moaned a little. We did this for twenty minutes until I forced two of his fingers inside.

On our way back home I kept wondering how much he thought about her. Carmen and I did not look alike but then again what did Wilson know about the diversity of women's bodies? Nada, mi reina, cero pollitos. He reminded me of a poodle all thirsty for sex, ready to hump any minute. Quickly he'd forgotten about *Thou shall not lie with an unmarried woman* and lay with the unmarried woman who passed for his biggest crush. *Our* biggest crush. An open can of worms, of fingers swimming around thighs and stomach.

We passed Publix, Pollo Tropical, the Pastores' house. We passed women in rocking chairs drinking beer, old men peeing on the street, four *¡Descuento! ¡Cirugía Plástica en Minutos!* billboards. The sky clear and blue like my veins. Not one cloud, not one drop of water. All that water now inside me, filling me up like a pool, refusing to leave. The beauty of the sky was so fucking depressing I felt like crying. I played with Wilson's curls, feeling the tiny bumps of acne on his neck until he pulled over suggesting we pray.

¿Ahora quieres orar? ¿Ahora?

I think we should ask Jesucristo to forgive us. It will only take one second, come on, amor. Let's do it together.

Only because he called me *amor*. Amor. Amorcito. I used to say *amor* in front of the mirror when I was twelve pretending it was my lover calling, *amorcito divino*, then make out with my arm until I left dark bruises.

¿Y tú crees que Dios nos va a perdonar?

He didn't say anything.

Wilson, so does that mean we're not doing this again?

I put my hand on his dick to reassure him. Ducks squeaked around the truck, poking at the tires with their beaks, some even slamming their heads on the side door.

These birds are so nasty, I said to him.

Pero mi amor, they are also creatures of God.

Come on, please tell me you don't find them disgusting.

He took my hand off his dick, kissed it, then asked when exactly Carmen was coming back. Neither of us knew.

There were rumors at church about her: Carmen married a peso pesado pastor and was going to move to the coast. Carmen had been found with her veins slit open, the devil's work, and was now locked up in a Christian rehab camp. Carmen, like every other girl at church, was getting surgery en Medellín: A new nose. New boobs. A new cuerpazo. Carmen was searching for her *real* parents and the Pastores were going, ay Papi Dios, loquitos. My favorite so far went something like *Carmencita, ay la pobre, they say the Pastora found her possessed one night with blank eyes dancing reggaetón and crying.* And, lastly, of course, Carmen was pregnant.

Mami had dropped the Carmen bomb without any explanation or specific dates and I could tell Wilson was anxious to know. Wilson said Xiomara didn't know either. Carmen transformed into a mystical underworld goddess, invisible yet always present, orange hair and thick legs kicking it with us in the truck. We both longed to know more but dared not say anything, only stared at the widening road, palm tree after palm tree exploding into the sun, waiting for any leads on her arrival. This horrible anxiety, like someone had latched on to my stomach with their teeth and hung there. Fuck Carmen and fuck that feeling. Que se joda esa nena, I was happy. I searched for Wilson's hand and told him okay, we should pray together. His thin hands on mine, Oh Jesús perdónanos. We prayed and prayed and then he put on the new CD from Art, that balding lead church singer who secretly took all the church girls' virginities but refused to marry them, those girls who came up to me after service, whispering in the bathroom, because I guess I looked like I'd done some shit and so I stole pregnancy tests from Publix for them. None of these girls ever used condoms because Arturo promised a golden townhouse and a new Honda Civic.

I sang loud and clear. I knew Wilson needed me to recite the right prayers, to showcase my righteous Christian girlhood. A part of him wanted that Christian jeva as much as he enjoyed my tits and pussy. I get it. And I needed him to spoon me, finger-fuck me, proudly parade me around during service like an expensive poodle, drive me to the lake and away from my house and say amor, amor, amor, over and over in my ear.

~

Y Francisca, ¿cómo está Wilson?

That's Mami for you. Not *How's your relationship, how do you feel about your new boyfriend*, no señor. How's Wilson.

He's fine, Ma.

Pass me the chicken, said La Tata pointing to the mustard chicken softly with her mouth.

Lucía and I forked our chicken, circled the white plate with it. She even tried stashing it in her panties but couldn't fit it all. She saw me eyeing her but la chiquitica couldn't care less—staining her purple cotton panties with mustard. Like Mami wasn't gonna know. Who washes your underwear, niña.

No playing with your food, Francisca, Mami said jamming another piece in her mouth, chewing mindlessly. In automatic mode Mami worked her usual magic on the dining table: praying before eating, eating while Art sang "Contigo Señor," no elbows on the table Lucía, no slurping your juguito de guayaba Francisca, no chewing with your mouth open. This shit had energized Mami before. That motherhood power of aquí mando yo hijueputas and bam bam bam. When we first got here homegirl pointed to things, demanded action, the household structured around Myriam's Principles. Mami was our dictator and leader. We relied on her for things to move. She was in everything and even when she wasn't around you could hear her behind you: *Francisca, nena, is that really what you're wearing for church?* Not now. Her automatic mode running on low batteries like that Duracell pink bunny commercial where the bunny slowly drums until he falls to one side.

First of all, she forgot to recite the entire food prayer and just mumbled something incoherent. I said, Mami do you want me to finish praying? She nodded.

La Tata already chewing on her food before I was done. Lucía wiping yellow from her belly.

Y Francisca, Mami continued, ¿cómo está Wilson?

Lucía chuckled. La Tata went around the table into the kitchen, opened the fridge, and poured herself more Sprite.

Mami, you already asked Francisca that question, Lucía said.

The guayaba juice was thick and pink like vomit. It tasted like vomit too, but I swallowed it with a delicious face.

El jugo está deli, Ma, I said.

Is it?

She was not there but none of us wanted to bring her back. We were all the way inside, our skins thick carcasses like little hamster balls that just took us places. We were tied together by this thin familial blood string that obligated us to share a pastel townhouse at the Heather Glen Apartment Complex but once inside we migrated from the surface of our skins deep into the mountain range of our stomachs.

Outside someone yelled, Alba, Albita, muñeca. La Tata eyed Mami with distaste and said that was her boyfriend. ¿Novio? Now Roberto was her novio. La Tata probably did it to upset Mami, give her something to complain about. Be up in her face because after sixty-seven years, what had she really accrued in life? A museum of old photos, endless Sprite cans, a vast collection of Christian CDs en español in a medium-sized room somewhere in Miami. Or maybe she truly felt butterflies for Mr. Roberto, our very own borracho cubano mamahuevo—what the venecos called him. La Tata's smirk wanted confrontation but Mami gave her none. Mami nodded then turned to me. Do you want more juice then?

I let her pour me more juice. Some weird sad energy clipped my rib cage from watching Mami. I wanted her to stop being the center of attention with her sadness. Lucía asked to be excused, La Tata grabbed her cane and stumbled outside while Mami watched me con esos ojos tristes, perdidos, she watched me drink the pink guayaba vomit.

I placed my hand on hers. This was all I could do.

She turned to me and said, The Pastores paid for rent this month.

I nodded.

Is there more juice, Ma?

Milagros has another job lined up for me at Gap. Glorita es la manager ahí and Milagros knows her.

I poured more juice. I will drink all the jugo de guayaba in this and the next life if only to shut her up about this.

We'll be fine, she said. Can you imagine, Francisca, your mamá working at Gap?

I couldn't. Luckily for me the phone rang. Mami picked it up.

Wilson! she said. Sí, acá está Francisca. I waved for her to continue talking to him.

¿Y cómo va la presentación de Jóvenes para Navidad? ¿Ah sí? You don't say.

She lit up a bit with Wilson. To Mami, Wilson was a good Christian boy with good Christian values, a good varón to have around. When she finally passed me the phone I told my boyfriend to spend the night at our place. Mami raised her eyebrows. I mouthed, Mami, he'll sleep on the couch. She mouthed back that she didn't like the idea of my boyfriend sharing a roof with me. I said, He's here all the time, duh. Sleeping is different, she said.

Grilled cheese plus juguito de guayaba is what Mami offered Wilson. He'd been playing soccer with the boys from church, they all wore jerseys with *Jesús es un golazo* written on the back and fake gold necklaces with a soccer ball pierced by a cross. He searched for me because, of course, like everyone with taste buds, Wilson hated guayaba juice. You don't have to drink it if you don't like it, said Mami. Solo dime. And he did. Mami was okay with that, Mami didn't disintegrate or crumble to pieces on the floor. She was better than I thought. She poured the juguito down the drain and sat with us watching MTV's *The Real World: Las Vegas* where blond chicks in Daisy Dukes jumped on a heart-shaped bed drunk out of their minds yelling, WE'RE IN VEGAS BITCHES. It was Wilson who asked to change the channel, he couldn't stand that stuff. Yeah, me neither. He changed the channel to a rerun of *Caso cerrado*. I was so done with *Caso cerrado* already—La Tata adored that show but La Doctora Polo never returned her letters. Now: two women in tight dresses, highlights, dangling shiny earrings, you know, the jeva Miami drill.

Here we go again, two women fighting over a dude. Boring, I said.

Mami wanted to keep watching because one of the women resembled a paisita she knew back home. Okay. After a few minutes it was evident the women were not fighting over a dude. La Doctora Polo kept yelling, *¡Descarada! ¡Descarada! ¡Descarada!* They both owned this apartment down in Brickell worth enough dough to appear on national TV yelling at each other, showing off tattoos of each other's names circling a rose right on their tits. I moved uncomfortably, trapped between Wilson and

Mami. The women were also *into* each other, or had been at least. Both of them looked like trashy porn stars. Even La Doctora Polo could not believe these two shared a romantic past, she demanded a commercial break. It was all too much for her. It was all too much for everyone. None of us said a word during the commercial break. A heavy gooey silence keeping us together. Years later someone told me the people on those shows were paid actors, but how could the women fake the tattoos? What about the blurred videos and photographs kissing? All fake, she said. But right then I told Wilson to change the channel. He didn't want to, Mami didn't want to either. But this satanic shit? Sometimes, Francisca, you gotta look evil in the eye. But I didn't want to look evil in the eye. The fuck. I was trying to be Christian, follow Baby Jesus, which meant moving as far away as possible from evil. Every time I sorta understood what Christianity was, some wiser Christian like my boyfriend or my mother introduced new ideas that fucked up all my goody rationality. I didn't want to look evil in the eye, period. I stood up and left. I am tired, need to sleep, good night to you both. Neither of them protested. Golden faces glowing in the TV light.

The ceiling fan annoyed me. Even when the heat was bearable Lucía had to sleep with the fan on. The sound soothes me, she said. Bullshit. And even after all those months I still woke up every day with a dry throat and it was all her fault.

I lay in bed listening to the whoosh whoosh, waiting for it to shatter. Tiny blades everywhere, little deadly airplanes. I could hear the TV from my room. La Doctora

Polo asked the women if they loved each other and only the tight purple dress responded she did, very much. The other one yelled, Tú no me amas, what you love is money concha'e-tu-madre. A looming sadness shone from the tight-purple-dress woman. I believed her. She was losing her amorcito on national TV and that had to suck. If I ever went on *Caso cerrado* I'd be the girl in a tight purple dress, although instead of a dress I'd wear skinny black jeans and a huge T-shirt. La Doctora Polo would make fun of me, *Por qué are you wearing such a stupid T-shirt?* I'd try to explain moving to Miami, detail Iglesia Cristiana Jesucristo Redentor, explain my new devotion for Jesús, but she'd just roll her eyes. I'd seen her do this to people. The audience always laughs and La Doctora Polo points with her long fingernails while her eyes pop out. *No puedo con esto, definitivamente esto es un chiste, señora.* She'd then introduce the person suing me. A video of Carmen in tight jeans with rhinestones will play as she walks from the back of the studio past the rows of people and stands on a podium next to me. She's here to fight me. She brought documents, pictures, she doesn't look at me but in her costeña accent says, *Ajá Doctora Polo muy buenos días.* I beg Carmen to stop this nonsense. I call her amor: *Amor, por favor, stop this nonsense.*

Do you know why you're here, Señorita Francisca? La Doctora Polo asks.

I don't.

And I really don't know. But I have a feeling combing through me that it's because Carmen wants me out of her life or wants me to join another church or wants me to return Wilson to her fan club. But that's not why we're here. We're here because Carmen loves me so much. Pictures of us kissing appear on screen and she tells La Doctora Polo she has a huge crush on me but that can't be and La Doctora Polo has no idea what to do because I don't want to fight Carmen but Carmen is here to fight me.

Lucía mumbled in her sleep. Sometimes she would scream and I had to shake her awake. Lucía, estás soñando. Tonight she giggled like someone was tickling her, what could she possibly be dreaming about? I wanted some of her dreams.

The townhouse was pitch-black except for the blue TV light shining from the living room. As I walked out of my room I closed my eyes, I knew the place so well. Over here what I called the Hallway of Fame, joyous pictures of Bogotá, black-and-white pictures from Mami's youth, her long shiny mane taking over half the frame. La Tata's snores reverberating from her door, like a tennis ball back and forth. She was her own sound system, her own orchestra, her own maracas, tamborcito, acordeón. And that particular smell even meters away from her room: vickvaporú, ron, Johnson's talcum powder. Pictures of Jesús nailed on the cross and one with Roberto were taped on her door. I giggled. Mami's door ajar, the small television passed down from Milagros that angered me whenever I saw it, her room looked so poor. Her bed still made. As I walked past Mami's room and into the kitchen I saw them still sitting on the couch, Mami's head resting on Wilson's shoulder. His arm around her, grabbing her shoulder. A clipping dread pumped through my veins—What. Are. They. I didn't want them to see me, but as I moved closer I realized they were both asleep. Did he put his hand around her before falling asleep or after? Mami would never ask Wilson to put his arm around her. Na-ah, esa no es Mami. But then again homegirl was all disconnected, all la-la land, all droopy eyes, all not like her. But she didn't. She couldn't. I tiptoed until I could hear Mami's heavy breathing, her mouth slightly open. A chunk of Mami's hair fell on Wilson's chest so that the brown hair seemed fused into his jersey, part of him. There was an undeniable harmony in their sleep, a horrible peace that I wanted to disrupt so badly but couldn't. I poured myself some water and went to sleep.

~

That next week Wilson nagged me constantly but I didn't want to see him. I need some time, I said. For what? he said. I think Jesús wants me to take a week from my church duties, you know, a week for myself. Just a week.

Jesús hadn't said nada about a week off. To be honest holy homeboy never clearly spoke to me, but I sometimes felt a sudden lucidity during church while praying, like when you exercise a lot and your head clears up and you swear never to drink again. I did that a few times. Back in Colombia when my girls and I got wasted en la Charcutería de la 93 puking all over the park, hiding amid the bushes with boys. The next morning sipping on caldo I swore over MSN to the world, Jamás me vuelvo a emborrachar. Until the next weekend—and there we were with Tequimón, our bell-bottoms, and black eyeliner puking in public. Here I didn't have to swear about not drinking, that was past. I prayed and elevated my voice to the drumbeats. So did Mami.

Only a week? he said. We still need to finish the Christmas manger plus I can't find a good Joseph costume.

You check Party City?

Duh, amor.

I thought, *Why couldn't he just wear sandals, white pants, and a brown shirt? Also, why was his arm around Mami?*

Amor, Francisca. Is this because, you know, of what happened at the lake the other day?

What do you mean?

I told you we needed to pray about it afterward, qué no. But I can pray more for you.

You mean how I touched your cock?

He fell silent. I knew he hated real genital words. I wonder if Mami had known about me grabbing his cock, if she had known about his two fingers in my pussy, would she have fallen comfortably asleep with her hair hanging on his chest?

I think a week off is fine. I'll let the Pastores know we're taking a week off.

Wilson, por favor. You don't have to tell them.

Are you asking me to break my contract with Jesucristo and my church?

Sometimes, cachaco, sometimes this cute kid and his crown of curls drove me insane. La Estupidez con *E* mayúscula.

Yes, that's what I'm asking. Por qué qué. Did you also tell Jesucristo and your church that I grabbed your dick? Do you want me to stop grabbing your dick? Ah, Wilson? Whatever.

It's also *your* church, Francisca.

Immediately I dialed Pablito. I needed some non-church interactions, I needed to know non-church people existed. Just in case. And my best non-churchy bet was the Argentinian loser in his Star Trek shirt.

Buenos días, casa Marinelli, how may I direct your call?

That's how he answered the phone. Every. Time. Ay Pablito.

¿Qué haces, huevón?

¿Y con quién tengo el gusto?

Pablo, deja la maricada. Let's meet by the pool.

I'm busy right now, Francisca.

No you're not. What are you doing? Slaying real-life dragons in your room? Getting a blow job?

I do not appreciate your jokes.

Yes, you do. Come on, meet me at the pool.

He dragged that awkward body of his up the stairs, around the pool, then sat in a white plastic chair next to me wearing new dad sunglasses.

What's with the sunglasses?

He made a gesture toward the sun.

Dude. But *those*?

Do not even get me started, he said. I've seen you at Publix with your *I* ♥ *Jesucristo* shirts and all. Helena saw you at Sedano's passing out flyers last month. Every time I see you it is worse. I did not think you would take it so seriously.

Pablito lecturing me about not taking shit seriously. The same dude playing marathons of *World of Warcraft* and bidding on miniature Batman figurines on eBay.

Are you going to try and convert me? he said. I want to see you try.

The fucker teased me. Who did he think he was? I

couldn't get bullied by the ultimate loser, what did that make me?

You're just jealous, Pablo. Shut up.

He glanced at me with a *why am I here* face, raising his palms in a *this is unbelievable* gesture. I didn't want him to leave. I had no idea exactly what I expected of Pablito, just for him to be there and not question me. For him to change something about this swimming darkness. For him to say, *It's okay, let's both bounce.* I looked around at the swaying palm trees, the green edges of the pool, the garbage around the trash cans like a little homeless altar. He noticed. The boy had magical intuition for a dude.

I stole some cigarettes from my mom, you want some? he said with this dumb smile.

But you don't smoke, remember?

I can always learn, right?

The thin Marlboro Light urged me to smoke it. My lungs inflating, my hands relaxing. I still didn't understand what was so satanic about smoking. In her kitchen back in Bogotá, Tía Milagros hung a small wooden plaque that read *No me diga que no fume porque es con mi plata y con mi pulmón.* I agree. It's my money and my lungs.

Well I don't smoke anymore, I said.

I felt Mami's approval nodding somewhere in the back of my head.

He seemed disappointed. The cigarette rolled on his fingers, he placed it between his lips. How do I look?

Like a loser who doesn't know how to smoke. It's backward.

He asked me how Mami was doing. Real talk. How *was* Mami? I didn't want the Pastores to keep paying our rent, is that why Mami rested her head on Wilson's shoulder? Did my boyfriend feel bad for her? He didn't have to. That's not his business. That's low, Mami, getting a seventeen-year-old to feel sorry because your ass can't pay rent. We never did talk about it, Mami and I. When I woke up the next day Wilson was gone and she was doing laundry acting como si nada.

But I said, She's fine, how's yours? ¿Sabes qué, Pablo? Give me that cigarette.

If Mami can rest her head on Wilson, if the Pastores can pay our rent, I can smoke a cigarillo, papá.

Uuuuy Miss Rebelión, here you go. He laughed. Let me light that for you, señorita. Will they excommunicate you from your church because of this? Will Satanás rise and party with us now?

The group of venecos plus two new Puerto Rican kids entered the pool without even noticing us, blasting la reina Ivy Queen a lo que da, colonizing half of the seating area, popping cans of beer and chugging them down immediately. Pablito hated reggaetón and non-Christian reggaetón was prohibited at church even though all the youth were dying for some perreo. The two jevitas who yelled ¡Vaca! at Pablito followed behind in bikinis barely covering their nipples, one of them had a book and I tried reading the title but couldn't. Probably some trashy self-helpy thing like Paulo Coelho. So stupid. Tanning lotion dripped from the girls' shoulders and the boys asked them to rub each other's backs and they did. ¡Así! ¡Qué rico! they yelled. Brown bodies glistening in the sun. The girl with the book walked toward us asking for a lighter. You could tell she was barely twenty-one or twenty-two but seemed much older. I couldn't take my eyes off the silver dangling belly-button piercing, she noticed and to my surprise smiled. ¿Te gusta mi pircin, pela'a? It doesn't hurt, she said. You should totally get one.

Not Venezuelan, but costeña, mi amor. I lit the girl's cigarette.

She stood in front of me blowing smelly beer smoke in my face. When I coughed she laughed. Nombe, you got to close your eyes, you've never had smoke blown in your face? Carmen's full chapped lips didn't blow smoke but danced as she preached. What would Carmen say if she saw esta otra costeñita blowing smoke at me? Pero acá Carmen no tiene voz ni voto, she left, she's not here, a la mierda con esa nena.

No, nunca, I said.

Pablito sat awestruck, brown eyes peeled blinking repeatedly. The girl's friends splashed or yelled or something in the pool. No sé. I only saw lips. A weird desire to hold her ran through me, to bite her belly button and mouth.

Why don't you do it to me? she said. Blow on my face.

Mi reina, please tell me why my arms reached out and held this girl's shoulders in place so tight while a stream of white smoke flew out of my lungs into her.

Sexy, she said. You want a beer?

Before I could mutter a response Pablito To The Rescue interrupted, Perdone señorita but Francisca is under-age and cannot ingest alcohol.

A boy yelled from the pool, Andrea ya, métete a la piscina, mi amor.

Pablito whispered to me, She's so drunk.

Gracias, pela'a, she said and walked away into the pool, kissing the boy with the Che Guevara tattoo on his chest.

~

I tried crying that week but couldn't. I considered piercing my belly button just to show Andrea, just to piss off Mami, plus maybe Andrea would want to hang out with me by the pool again or drive me around or blow white stinky smoke in my face again. Maybe I'd be her pela'a. Andrea and I up late shit-talking, chain-smoking, driving Mami crazy, and when Carmen returned she'd have to search for another right hand, another Sedano's outreach partner, another girl to hold hands with while sleeping.

The door slammed.

Franciscaaaaaaa, Lucíaaaaaaa, bajen ya a comer.

Mami arrived home from her first day of work at Gap at four p.m. She'd left before sunrise. I didn't want to see her face.

I *hate* Pollo Tropical, can we eat something else que no sea pollo? We're all gonna grow wings.

Lucía chuckled. I'd love some feathered wings.

She made chicken sounds just to annoy me. Mami didn't respond. Mami opened and closed drawers reaching for paper plates. Mami poured Tropicana juice in four Styrofoam cups and asked Lucía to help her. La Tata called dibs on the plátano con bocadillo.

Again, I prayed:

Gracias, Señor, por esta comida que nos das, por favor bendícela y bendice a todos los miembros de esta familia. Dale de comer a los que no tienen alimento. Amén.

Amén.

I stood up and searched the fridge for a Hot Pocket. La Tata interrupted me, Francisca mija, your madre brought this food and this is what you're eating. A ver mimi, siéntate.

Dry chicken, tasteless fríjoles, a mazacote of white rice. Lucía asked Mami about her day and Mami nodded and said it went great. She said she saw an alligator swimming in the lake by the mall this morning. No way! Lucía demanded all the details. I knew she was making it up. Mami sat folding Gap T-shirts for seven hours at a warehouse in Plantation after she'd made sure everyone in this shithole of a town knew she'd been the gerente general of a multinational insurance company and blah blah. Cachaco, por *favor* who was she kidding with that alligator story. Myriam por Dios, dónde está la clase, dónde está el tumbao, dónde está la berraquera. Mami was nowhere to be found. I stared at my plate following Mami's voice detailing the rough green scales, piercing black eyes of the alligator. Was Lucía that stupid? Maybe Lucía also figured out Mami lied, maybe we all did but looked the other way, wanting her sadness and lying to disappear on their own. Wanting our good ole holy homeboy Jesús to deal with it, not us.

Pollo Tropical on the dinner table the entire week minus Thursday, when La Tata cooked some carne deshilachada and coconut rice to save our palates.

A pink house of Colombian chicken ghosts. Roaming in and out as we pleased, sometimes not even a *Buenos días*, not even a *Did you eat, mimi?* La Tata off drunk laughing it up with Roberto, playing dominó with the dominó she bought at the Dollar Tree until late at night porque, ¿por qué no? Mami passed out by seven p.m. so nobody kept La Tata away from the Sprite cans, from Roberto, from being loved. Girlfriend fell asleep borracha pero feliz, murmuring, Never get married, mimi. And, also, Si te contara las tristezas de mi vida.

When La Tata returned I undid her bra. Poured her water and gave her two ibuprofen, kissed her forehead wishing we were back in Bogotá, wishing this were all a dream, that we were inside someone's head and soon the dream would pop and we'd be sitting around La Tata's house in Belmira playing Pictionary. *Jesús, please pop the dream bubble.* But Jesucito said it didn't matter. Even if we went back, none of my friends from Bogotá emailed me anymore. I didn't even sign in to MSN because, aló mi reina, pointless.

CHAPTER QUINCE

La mujer que quise me dejó y se fue,
y ahora ella quisiera volver.

Qué hiciste, abusadora.

—WILFRIDO VARGAS

When I was eight, Mami and I danced in front of the hall-way mirror to Wilfrido. We danced together because she was my mami and I her daughter and we gyrated our hips to "Abusadora" by Wilfrido Vargas, right hand in the air, left hand on hip, y vueltica vueltica vueltica.

Y uno y dos y un, dos, tres.

Y ahora, nena, your left foot out, left foot in, right foot out, right foot in, y vueltica vueltica vueltica.

Marching in front of the mirror, tirando paso to the best merengue de moda *qué hiciste abusadora, qué hiciste*, sometimes Mami would even grab two hairbrushes and we'd use them as microphones: *Ahora sí, te mata la pena, mientras yo gozo con una mujer buena.* Pa' delante, pa'trás, y vueltica vueltica vueltica. Esaaaaaaa. She'd grab my hand and spin me then clap clap clap and, Esaaaaaaaaa es mi hija. That's my daughter, carajo. Hands in the air, sending kisses to the fake audience. Ay gracias, gracias, thankyouverymuch. She'd hold both of my hands and then we'd both spin together laughing uncontrollably, flying round and round until I begged her to stop and she said, Qué, I can't hear you. Mami I'm going to throw up! She showed me the cover of Wilfrido's CD, Look at that leather jacket, she said. And those sunglasses.

I remember Wilfrido's curly hair *tupido tupido*, gelled in that papi look, and I remember wanting those glasses just because Mami thought they were cool. Isn't he such a churrera of a man?

Sometimes back in Bogotá on the weekends she woke me up, right hand on stomach, left hand in the air, eyes shut, merengue-marching right on the wooden floor—A levantarse, Francisca! I'd hide beneath my dinosaur sheets and just groan waiting for Mami to pull me out of bed and onto the wooden floor until we'd both be dancing bien pegao, sa sa sa, sacúdelo que tiene arena. Pa' un lado, pal otro. During family reunions after the whiskey and the aguardiente bottles were empty, Mami'd announce to everyone, Pere pere pere you haven't seen dancing if you haven't seen Francisca. We were a dúo dinámico, getting down after sundown meneándolo al son del perrito. Lucía awkwardly joining us, but everyone knew it was a Mami and Francisca duet. We were Donato y Estéfano, Marc Anthony y La India. I never felt happier than when I saw Mami winking at me from the stage, calling me with her index finger.

Mami said that Mariana, the girl who worked at La Tata's house when they moved from Cartagena to Bogotá, taught her all that hip shaking. She'd make Mami stand erect against a wall and shake her shoulders until they could tremble on their own. I practiced standing against a wall but could only shoulder shake for ten seconds whereas Mami's shoulders were a walking vibrator. It's because you're cachaca, nena. Cachacos don't know one thing about dancing. For a while I wanted to be costeña. I wanted to be like Mami, shake those shoulders down the street until I dislocated them just to show Mami I could. So I'd stand in front of the mirror hand-gesturing dramatically saying all the costeña words I knew: ajá, nombe, picao, bololó, animaleja, ajúa, full bacano. I'd drop the words in front of Mami like nothing, Ajá Mami what we doing today? Ay sí Mami, full bacano full bacano. She acted like it was normal and just followed my lead, nombe pela'a. I remember mujeres de bien staring at us with distaste at Unicentro as we stood in line to get Mimo's ice cream, hand-gesturing like I'd seen men in vallenato videos do. But Mami didn't care. She let me fall into the costeña persona and encouraged it. Even when La Tata asked her if she'd taken me to a developmental psychologist because that wasn't normal, Where's she picking that up? Did you call the school?

It wasn't until a girl from school teased me, called me low-class, guisa, ñera, india guajira maluca, and it wasn't until I yelled at her in the middle of the schoolyard, HIJA DE LA GRAN PUTA GONORREA TE VAS A MORIR, and the nuns dragged me by the ear, that Mami finally said I had to stop. She chuckled when she heard I'd yelled such curse words. She's a kid, Mami said to the nuns. It won't happen again. But I wanted to be so much like her.

I dreamed Mami shook it to Ace of Base in the town-house kitchen and I joined her. Before Jesucristo gentrified her heart, she loved "I Saw the Sign" and "All That She Wants" so much she had me print out the lyrics and write their Spanish phonetic pronunciation below each verse. In the kitchen her arms reach for the ceiling then drop abruptly, up and down, up and down, then both hands stretch over her heart, *I saw the sign and it opened up my eyes, I saw the sign*, Mami extends a hand, I reach for it. She pulls me onto the white kitchen tiles where chicken burns on the stove until the smoke alarm goes off but we don't care, instead we do the Egyptian, we do the Macarena, then Mami spins spins spins and pulls out chunks of her hair and yells, and yells, and I can't hear her because *No one's gonna drag you up to get into the light where you belong, but where do you belong?* is blaring and I'm digging it and Mami's frustrated, throwing things into the stove, bills stack up in the pan, CDs, La Tata's cans, until it's like we're at a club next to a smoke machine and I dance with my eyes closed, humming, *I've wondered who you are, how could a person like you bring me joy?* But Mami doesn't stop screaming, doesn't stop throwing things, and when I woke up she was by the kitchen counter popping two white happy pills from the new fuchsia pillbox Milagros gifted her.

Mami's eyes yellow from the sunlight hitting the windows.

Why hasn't Wilsoncito visited you? She slowly lifted her eyes, stared at me.

She chugged more water, then smiled thinly. None of us had known Mami popped those happy pills until that week. She explained to us over dinner the pills helped with migraines. None of us said anything, but I knew Mami took Excedrin for migraines. Apparently, according to La Tata, Milagros suggested Mami needed a joyful boost and provided Mami with some of her own stash of happy pills prescribed by a Cuban doctor out of a garage because nobody here had health insurance (this I will learn many years later). Pastillas de la felicidad.

I don't know, Ma.

Bueno pues, I invited him for dinner.

Of course she did.

Okay, I said picturing *this* new Mami moviéndolo al son de Wilfrido, but couldn't. She'd thrown away all her merengue collection. The Ace of Base CD I'd hidden inside one of our Samsonite bags.

He's going to be helping me glue crosses on hats for the women's Christmas presentación. Además I still need to pick up a few things from Walmart.

Maybe if I just played that song she'd remember the steps, maybe if "I Saw the Sign" just randomly played and Mami just randomly happened to hear it she'd drop everything and throw her hands in the air and call me with her index finger.

Buenísimo, I continued. But I'm not going to Walmart.

~

A Che Guevara poster was taped on the street window of Pablito's house. Pablito hated that poster and told me so every time I mentioned it, but his parents had their convictions, which is why the entire neighborhood hated them. Don't go posting some leftist shit amid Venezuelans and

Colombians, mi reina. The sun took no vacation. Orange, balling on the sky, completely overdoing it, shining as if no night came after her. We were stuck at the Heather Glen Apartment Complex with an eternal beating sun. I rang the doorbell then realized I had no idea what I was doing there. Pablito wasn't expecting me.

He answered wearing only his boxers, you could still see cigarette burns on his hairy belly.

Buenas tardes, Francisca, did we schedule a meeting?

I looked around inside his dingy apartment, the light coming from the other window tinted everything yellow.

I wanted to tell Pablito my dreams. I wanted somebody to hear what was happening with Mami. So that this wasn't only mine. I wanted this sick feeling inside to be outside, be someone else's responsibility.

Do you have an extra cigarette? The only thing I could mutter.

He grunted. Am I your cigarette dispensary now?

Ay Pablito. I didn't know how to tell you.

We lingered there in the doorway for a second.

Is there anything else, Señorita Francisca? He tried joking with me but my heart was so gone.

I needed a perfect place to smoke the cigarette in peace. I walked past the pool, chasing the disgusting ducks with red balls on their beaks. Patos desgraciados, inmundos, asquerosos. What the fuck happened there, Nature? After a few blocks my back was wet and slimy. I searched for Andrea and the venecos, but the pool was empty except for a happy raccoon feasting on trash. Wilson would probably enjoy a pierced belly button, lick my jewel, or maybe both Andrea and Wilson could lick my jewel. In front of

Carmen. Ay cómo gozo yo, Mami would *die*. She probably invited Wilson after the service on Sunday when I'd run to the bathroom to evade him. We'd said hi in the parking lot and I faint-kissed him on the cheek mostly so Paula wouldn't suspect and go shit-talking with the shekinas. I expected him to go all papi macho on me so I could roll my eyes and feel hurt and dramatic, but he just whispered he really liked me and he missed driving around the lake with me, which I understood as missing his hand inside my pants. I missed his hand inside my pants too, but what about Mami?

Nada. Nada about Mami. This was about the cigarette I was about to smoke, this was about me strolling perdida around the neighborhood with its broken Fisher-Price toys and old people in front yards with oxygen masks like Darth Vader taking in the sun. Buenas tardes. Buenas tardes, mija, they say back and wave. Y uno que otro gringo that also waves, that also carries their oxygen tanks like a humongous green purse next to them. La Tata used oxygen back in Bogotá, por la altura claro, but now at sea level her lungs tienen un volador por el culo.

Palm tree, palm tree, lake, dirty pool, highway. I walked and walked and walked one foot in front of the other, not giving one single fuck where I was going, not giving one single fuck about the old man asking por un pesito, mi niña, que no tengo nada, hombre, walking by him and the lady with the mangoes and why would anyone ever move to this place?

Porque sí. Porque les toca. Porque Mami packed two bags. Porque Jesús died for you. Porque Bogotá is dead and tan-tan you have a new life.

Y como todo en la vida. La hijueputada, at the stop sign there it was: Carmen's house.

Pendeja que soy, I probably just walked in circles.

I stood behind a tree across the street and lit the cigarette. So strong, I stared at it. Marlboro Red, of course. Pablito's mom was literally killing herself with this stuff.

On the door hung a huge gold Christian fish and a small banner that I couldn't see but remembered exactly what it said: *In this house we praise the Lord.* Inside: Carmen's room. The Pastora's fake grin as she offered me Chocolisto, without Carmen noticing La Pastora wanted me out of her life while the Pastor, oblivious to life, snapped his fingers, Francisquita! So good to see you again, Dios te bendiga, jovencita. I could knock and tell them I left a sweater in her room, I could walk up the stairs and smell the Fabuloso and beg the Pastores to let me sleep in her bed. I'll keep this side of the bed warm for her until she gets here.

Halfway through the cigarette and already lightheaded, floating in a pool of smoke and relaxation and a sudden *We used to cut flyers inside that house.* Flip-flops, no bra, greasy hair. I received Jesús in that house because I wanted so much for her to drive me back and forth every day, because I wanted to see the ugly white van parked outside my apartment and get those chills and swim inside them until she turned to me chuckling and murmured: pela'a. Whispered: pela'a. Yelled: pela'a. Goodbye, pela'a. Hasta mañana, Francisca.

~

One week later and Wilson still hung at my house without me because, por qué no, si in that house nobody respected me. Sometimes I'd come back from Pablito's house and he'd be there on the couch folding red and green pieces of cloth with Mami.

Should we open up space for you in our closets? I said to him.

Francisca! Wilson is our guest. Mami wore a red leather jacket, red skirt, red pantyhose, red heels, red lipstick while Wilson stickered gold crosses on pamphlets with La Tata's help.

Who are you supposed to be, Mami?

As a woman leader Mami organized the women's presentación and had a lead role in the Christmas play.

Wilson responded, She's Temptation.

No shit, I wanted to say to him.

Temptation? I asked Wilson. Tentación? I asked Mami.

¡Que sí, Francisca, Tentación! she said, turning around for me to see her entire sinful costume. ¿Cómo te quedó el ojo, ah?

In the Christmas play Mami tempted the good men who were following Jesús but were derailed into sin by a luscious woman, in this case Mami. That was her role in the play. She rushed through the living room pointing at red things, marinating chicken, calling the Pastores, Glorita, Zutanita, Fulanita so they wouldn't forget to pick up the Styrofoam hut for Jesús's birth. Now, at times, it was impossible to shut Mami up—she ran around like there was a cocaine rocket in her ass then sadly crashed on the couch. Boom. The entire week: Electrified Mami, Depressed Mami. Electrified Mami, Depressed Mami.

Sometimes Depressed Mami lasted a bit longer than Electrified Mami but then she doubled her happy-pill dose y estuvo.

We were two weeks away from our Navidad en Jesucristo and I'd decided to help fix the shekinas' makeup and the little girls' dresses because that way I didn't have to rehearse, I didn't have to dress in red clothes, I only showed up and painted their faces. Done.

Una muchachita vino a buscarte, said Mami over her glasses looking at me suspicious, ¿Andrea? Sí, Andrea was her name, creo. She left her phone number, acá mira.

Mami handed me a crumpled piece of lined paper. Who is this Andrea? Both Mami and Wilson eyed me in judgment like they were my parents.

Una chica ahí, Mami. I met her the other day with Pablito by the pool. She goes to another church over there by the movie theaters. I put the crumpled paper inside my jeans.

Iglesia Sobre la Roca?

Yes, Mami, that one.

I've heard terrible things about that church, she said.

They're all sons of Jesús, mimi, La Tata said tratando de soften the situation. Everyone at Iglesia Cristiana Jesucristo Redentor prided themselves on belonging to that specific congregation and frowned upon any other church. Didn't matter they were Christian.

We're better Christians, people whispered during cafecito.

All churches differed in little things. For instance, at *our* church kids couldn't read *Harry Potter* or play with Barbies because they were satanic, whereas other churches didn't have Christian salsa. For example.

Mami popped another pill and I said, Wilson let's go get some soda para el almuerzo.

Once inside his truck I put his warm skinny hand on my thigh. Let's go to the lake, I said.

But the soda? And your mom?

I caressed his curls, pulled on them.

Está bien, está bien. Let's go.

When I was una carajita chiquita chiquitica Mami used to tell me my tesorito was precious and nobody ever could see it or touch it until you get married nena, ¿entiendes? It made me feel like we had some secret between us, a treasure buried between my legs that I was bound to protect and that only Mami and I knew existed. Boys may ask to touch your tesorito but only las cualquieras, fufurufas, desvergonzadas let boys touch their tesorito, she repeated when I was eleven and by then I responded, Mami you mean mi cuca? Francisca! Where did you learn that word? We don't say that word in this house.

Cuca cuca cuca.

Everyone wanted to protect my tesorito: Mami, the nuns at school, the woman from the Kotex commercial, the doctor.

But by age thirteen I wanted my tesorito to run off freely, away from the nuns, away from Mami, and into someone's touch. Whoever's. An open beating heart waiting to be loved, but mostly, caressed. Mostly, fucked. Or finger-fucked. Like Wilson did. Although this time his nails were long and when he pulled out, his fingers were bloody red.

Don't freak out, I said.

Okay, he said freaking out.

Nobody ever told me you could put fingers inside your tesorito, even during "sex" class at Catholic school we were shown two anatomical drawings of a uterus and a penis and then told one went inside the other. My tesorito longed for something else, but I told Wilson that day he definitely needed to trim his fingernails.

I don't think we should be doing this. He cleaned his fingers with Kleenex.

Here we go again.

Why did I have to end up with the biggest pussy in this shithole. How many boys out there wanted to finger-fuck my tesorito? Many. Probably. If they knew.

Okay, I said.

Are you mad?

I'd been playing this test in my head every time we went to the lake: if I still felt something when he touched me then it meant I did like boys even if I thought of Carmen. And if I didn't even think of Carmen when he touched me then I was golden.

I eyed him up and down, then laid my head on his shoulder. I grabbed his hand and put it on my hair.

Consiénteme, Wilson, I said.

He clumsily stroked my head, running his fingers through my hair, murmuring prayers, kissing my forehead. We did this for fifteen minutes until I thought, *Yes, okay, I like Wilson.* Let's go get that soda, I said.

As he started the car he said, Your mom told me Carmen is coming a week early. Next week, actually. Is that true?

It *was* true.

AQUÍ VA HABER CANDELA.
AQUÍ VA HABER CANDELA.
AQUÍ VA HABER CANDELA.

Carmen was coming back and I looked like a mosquito con patas. Like a zombie who'd been run over by a bus. My skin gray. I was skinnier than ever with black bags under my eyes even when I applied Mami's foundation. Plus my curls were dry as fuck and I only wore them in a bun. This horrible rash had appeared on my arms a few days before because the fucking heat never ceased to be. Mátame, Jesús. How was I supposed to get it together in a week?

¿Por qué no me dijiste that Carmen was coming back a week early, Mami?

Se me debió haber olvidado, but now you know.

Olvidado. One forgets to flush the toilet, to buy toilet paper. One does NOT FORGET CARMEN IS COMING BACK, MAMI.

What else did Mami know? Had Carmen dyed her hair? Was she chubbier? Had she mentioned she wanted to see me?

Then Mami said something like, I thought you two were fighting or you weren't speaking, but all I could hear was: *Pela'a, pela'a, pela'a.*

Y después Lucía yelling.

Lucía fighting with Mami because Lucía is not a biblical name and she wanted to change her name to Safira.

Safira? yelled Mami. SAFIRA?! Over my dead body will you change your name to Safira. Eso es puro nombre de puta, Lucía. I am not, óyeme bien, I am *not* working este culo todo el día so you can go around changing your name to Safira.

But then Lucía started asking everyone to call her Safira, even La Tata called her Safira, because she did not respond to her real name, and Mami suffered like only she knew how to suffer but then remembered she was depressed, popped a few pills, and let Lucía be Safira even though Mami wasn't dead yet.

I took the money I'd been stealing and went over to Pablito's to ask him to drive me to the mall. How could Mami tell Wilson and not me? Lo que necesito is something cute, no joda. Some outfit that didn't say *I've been waiting for you all this time and I look the same, maybe a bit grayer.* Which I hadn't, didn't.

Before I could ring Pablito's bell, Andrea drove past and offered me a ride. The Strokes blasted from her car. I hadn't heard them in months. She wore aviator sunglasses and a black choker.

¿Segura? I said. My friend is waiting for me though.

Ven nena, I'm going that way too. Súbete que I don't bite.

Unlike Carmen's, Andrea's car was spotless. A tiny pine tree hung from the rearview mirror, it smelled great. Not one crumb or tampon or Bible falling to pieces on the floor. But leather seats that gently hugged my back. She offered a cigarette that I of course accepted wondering if she was going to blow on my face, cursing Mami for the garlic mustard smell in my mouth. *If she asks me to blow on her face I won't.*

Do you have any gum? I asked.

It's in my purse between your feet.

Andrea. Perfectly tanned, perfectly smooth brown skin with gold bracelets on each wrist clinking as she turned the steering wheel. Black bold eyelashes and I could tell she wore colored contacts because of the sudden greenish relief in her eyes. She caught me fake drumming on my legs. Do you like The Strokes?

I used to, I blurted.

¿Y qué pasó?

She blew smoke out the window. I thought, *I can't get into it with you. I love The Strokes but you'd probably laugh if I told you I now listen to Christian soft rock and to someone named Art.*

I just grew out of it, I said. But I still like it.

She turned it up, all the way up. A dreadful shame perched in the back of my head because I had lost The Strokes, because Carmen was coming back, and there I was in Andrea's car in awe of her smooth skin.

Yeah, it hurts to say, but I want you to stay
Sometimes, sometimes

We drove over the bridge, onto the highway as the blurry orange sun cascaded on the Everglades to our right. Shadows cut Andrea in two. Her full lips half-pink, half-magenta singing "Someday" in a terrible accent, worse than mine.

Promises, they break before they're made
Sometimes, sometimes

I could watch her without her noticing and I did. I didn't understand why she picked me up, for all she knew I was just another teenage Christian dumbass aleluya girl. She glanced at me, smiling, showing off her big white teeth. Carmen's teeth were uneven but I thought that made her unique. But the way Andrea chuckled and her thighs, Dios mío, like Carmen's. I tried not to look at her boobs but it was impossible, the shade of her bra barely hiding underneath a threadbare tank top. A pulse hit my pussy and I searched for the sun.

I've seen you around, she said checking for my reaction. Driving in a white van with the same person. ¿Ella es tu novia?

The sky purpled at the edges. I felt the hologram of Carmen settle over me and wondered if Andrea saw it too. Was it the way I held my cigarette? Was it the skinny jeans? Why would she think I had a girlfriend? And Carmen of all people who would never look like a—I moved uncomfortably on my seat, blowing the smoke so hard I spat on myself.

Nena, it's just a question. She chuckled. Tranquila, she's not your girlfriend, got it.

A gaping feeling banged in my stomach like someone knocking from the inside of my rib cage. I was overwhelmed with shame. I couldn't believe it was so obvious. Not that Carmen was my girlfriend because for all I knew she didn't even remember my name.

She's not, I said wanting to fucking cry.

Andrea said, Let's change the subject. But, cachaco, the subject refused to change, to leave, the subject was a pink cannibal flower growing from my crotch to every extremity in my body blowing me up like a balloon, and I felt it too, I felt the flower eat my feet, my hands, the belly button I so wanted to get pierced. I felt the pink cannibal flower reach for my throat and I floated away out of her impeccable car with no throat, no hands, no belly button, no feet, and I ballooned out of her black Toyota up and up until all I could see were the gray roads, patches of green land, green water, a film of grief permeating everything, y por allá a lo lejos our townhouse y al lado del townhouse La Tata and Roberto sharing a beer, playing dominó, tongue-kissing, y detrás del townhouse Lucía evangelizing to a small crowd of ducks with a microphone and a loudspeaker y al lado de ella Mami depressed gluing crosses, popping pills, resting her head on Wilson's shoulder, y más adentro la Iglesia Cristiana Jesucristo Redentor y diagonal a la iglesia Carmen's house with a *Welcome Home* sign y entre las palmeras Jesús giving me the finger.

Before dropping me off Andrea stopped the car in front of the pool and said she didn't mean to assume anything about me. I know. She'd picked me up because I looked like I had some brains.

Whataboutyourstupidboyfriendwith theCheGuevaratattoo, I wanted to say but didn't.

This place is a shithole, she said.

I nodded.

Then she got all nervous and admitted she once had a girlfriend in Santa Marta that looked just like me, Tú sabe all skinny and lost but she knew her shit. Y tú me acuerdas tanto a ella. I looked straight ahead, the ducks fought over a bag of Doritos. The winner duck was missing an eye. Then Andrea touched my arm, left her hand there for a few seconds, and said, Pero no quiero que pienses that I'm coming on to you I'm not. Podemos ser amigas And there it was: my pussy pulsing like a freaking tambor again.

~

The Pastores had been back for two weeks already when they announced Carmen's return to everyone that Sunday. *¡Gloria a Dios!* Cheers swelled. The shekinas stood up shooting their arms to the ceiling and a *¡Gloria a Dios! ¡El Señor es vida!* in unison. Art dedicated the alabanza to the child of Jesús coming back to her flock of sheep. *¡Gloria a Dios!* As the youth leader Wilson elevated the Jóvenes en Cristo in prayer because our leader was coming back, sana y salva, to bring more holy wisdom to our congregation.

She's a new woman, the Pastora said with pride. A woman with a newfound love for God and life.

Amén, hermano. Amén, hermana. Y todo el mundo batiendo palmas y La Tata shaking it with her cane y Mami a ojo cerrado one hand on heart, one hand reaching for the sky, y Lucía explaining she now went by Safira, handing out flyers at the entrance with all the information for our Navidad en Jesucristo y Yours Truly walking out and into the bathroom, locking myself in a stall.

Paula was washing her hands when I opened the door. She eyed me through the mirror but said nothing, then chuckled.

¿De qué te ríes? I said.

Nothing, nothing.

There was this swelling energy beating through me. A gaping relief in not caring about shit. *Bring it on, perrita. A ver.*

I want to know. Is it my hair? Do I have mocos? A ver.

It's just—you know, la dichita esa with Wilson is about to be over.

¿Ah sí? And why do you think that is?

Francisca, por favor, she said placing hand on hip in a

duh way. You and I both know Wilson se muere for Carmen. You're his segundo plato, in the meantime, until Carmen returns.

Esta perra de mierda.

She didn't wait for me to say anything but just turned around and left. ¡Vamos a ver! I yelled after she'd closed the door. *Laremilputaquteparió.*

Wilson rode back with us in the van to our house. I didn't even care anymore. He was finger-fucking me, wrapping his arm around Mami's head, plus, according to Paula, Carmen could not wait to jump on his dick. Or whatever. The pimp. Who would have thought, such a clumsy boy. Un papi completo after all. Congratulations.

Mami asked him how excited he was that Carmen was coming back. Very, he said not looking at me. She's a great youth leader, Mami continued. You guys must miss her.

I MISS HER, MAMI, ME. Pero tú ni siquiera fuiste able to tell me first she was arriving one week early. Mami knew I missed Carmen pero se hizo la loca. Why Mami. Before Wilson could elaborate I surprised myself saying out loud, I miss her.

Everyone nodded in silence.

La Tata and I watched *El show de Cristina* while Mami and Wilson prepared the paper flowers for the kids' dance. A few months ago Mami would have complained, plopped on a chair with a martyr look stamped on her face, and created an entire spectacle because none of us helped her. Que cómo era posible, que ella no había venido hasta Miami para esto, que aquí nadie ayuda.

Not now, mamita, not now. She tuned in to some weird monotone rhythm in her body that had her hitting only one note over and over. Like someone hit the same piano chord, tan-tan, over and over. This is Mami cooking mustard chicken: TAN. This is Mami searching for gum in her Walmart purse: TAN. This is Mami cutting flyers: TAN. This is Mami after peeing: TAN. This is Mami putting groceries in the fridge: TAN. Same Mami. One-note Mami.

After a few hours Wilson and Mami left to go get something or other at Wilson's house. Xiomara is expecting us, Mami said, and I locked myself in my room. I watched them get in the van from my window. Wilson carried a box of the famous crosses over to the trunk, Mami pointed to the trunk, smiled at him. Before they each went to their respective doors she got close to him, stroked his hair. Like a kid? Like a pet? Like a lover? Wilson said something I couldn't decipher and Mami's smile reached a different note.

I shut the blinds. Turned on the ceiling fan. Then La Tata yelled, Mimi, que la televisión me está hablando en inglés. Ayúdame.

~

My father was not the first man to kiss Mami. A few years ago while Mami demonstrated how to do my nails properly, how to stand properly, how to, overall *Francisca, comportarse como una dama*, she showed me a Polaroid picture of a mustached man (that looked a lot like Wilfrido, in a good way) jamming his mostacho in her mouth.

There were other pictures too.

A few Polaroids and other photographs with curved edges and soft warm colors. Mami in bell-bottoms. Mami in a mini-bikini. Mami looking happy. Even though her teeth had braces and she was trying to keep her flowing hair out of her eyes. The mustached dude hugged her and her smile was so pure, so untouched by sadness. You would never guess she had a fuchsia pillbox or fainted when the Pastor prayed over her.

He was almost your father, she said blowing on her nails.

La Tata always repeated that padre puede ser cualquier pero madre solo una. Which means anyone could have been my father but only Mami could have been Mami.

I thought about the mustached man as my father and the three of us (in my dream Lucía wasn't born yet) driving to Melgar and the mustached man diving in the pool, wetting his mustache while Mami and I properly coated our nails beige. Red is for fufurufas, nena.

She hadn't dated anyone since my father and whenever someone in the family brought it up she told them to look around, *Does it look like I have time for huevonadas?*

But Wilson was not a huevonada.

Wilson was a man without a mustache. A man that could appear in one of Mami's Polaroids but now Mami had no braces and her smile was thin, almost invisible, and instead of a hug Wilson would wrap his arm around her and they'd watch TV and Mami would feel the moment returning, the moment when any one dude could be my father but only Mami could be Mami, the moment Wilson, Mami, and I drove to Melgar, and when Wilson dove into the pool Mami and I braided our hair properly, in tight braids.

CHAPTER DIECISÉIS

Can you spare an extra cigarette? I said a little desperate.

Carmen was going to land tomorrow night via Avianca, via the Caribbean, via exile, via corazón de sancochito, aguapanelita, arrocito'e fríjol negro, via Jesucristo.

I'd found Andrea's number that night burrowed in my pants and after much consideration, which is to say walking in circles, which is to say biting my lip till it bled, which is to say would she think I'm into her, which is to say what else am I gonna do for the next twenty-four hours—after much consideration I decided to dial.

Sorry. Es Francisca.

Francisca! So good to hear from you, pela'a. Pero claro. I'm going down to the pool in an hour. Meet me there?

A white plastic lounge chair with a ferocious mama raccoon that wouldn't leave displaying her tiny teeth like an angry kid at the dentist. ¡Shu shu shu! The mama raccoon hated me, I hated her back. Fuck these stinky animals.

When we first moved to Heather Glen Apartment Complex, Mami was all excited because, Nenas, this is our first house (apartment, I corrected her. Townhouse, Mami corrected me) in the U S of A. The guy in the Hawaiian shirt at the *New Renters This Way!* office promised outstanding, one-of-a-kind facilities with crystalline lakes, beautiful ducks, and unforgettable sunsets by the pool. That's exactly what he said and what was written on the *Welcome to your new home!* flyer. Didn't say nothing about pissed-off raccoons unwilling to move out of the plastic lounge chair with the cigarette burns.

A few venecos smoked a joint on the other side of the pool by the Jacuzzi and when Andrea stepped in she waved at them.

You know them? I asked.

That one in the red cap es mi primo. Es un burro completo.

I nodded. I hoped they wouldn't wanna hang out with us. I don't know why but I really wanted to see Andrea or maybe I really wanted to bum a cigarette from her.

She offered a cigarette.

Gracias, I said. No quiero que pienses that I'm only using you for cigarettes.

I hope not, she said with this gorgeous grin showcasing perfect white teeth. Dios mío, were her teeth *white*.

I tried coming up with ways of explaining Andrea to Carmen. I tried coming up with excuses explaining the white van coming to my house again next week to Andrea, once Carmen was here and we went back to our routine. *Pendeja pendeja pendeja. Pedazo de estúpida. Pedazo'e mierda.* That's such a stupid thought. ¿Qué crees tú? Carmen y yo are not going back to outreach at Sedano's. Let's get that straight. She's coming back to jump on Wilson's dick, she's coming back to her Christian throne where Paula et al. feed her holy grapes while she dances around the pulpit.

Carmen is not coming back to me.

Carmen is not coming back to me.

Carmen is not coming back to me.

I repeated that over and over in my head.

That girl from the van is coming back tomorrow, I said not wanting to say it. So the white van may be here next week.

The girl who is not your girlfriend? Andrea said teasing me.

Right.

My body was so tense. I kept on wanting to tell Andrea about Wilson but not really doing it. Why. I kept wanting to say, *I have a boyfriend, you see, Carmen is not my girlfriend but I have a boyfriend so it's impossible for me to have a girlfriend when I have a boyfriend named Wilson watching* Caso cerrado *with Mami every afternoon, gluing crosses.*

The venecos waved at us as they left. We both waved back. Mama raccoon and us alone by the pool.

Solo janguiemos, she said and reached for my fingers.

I followed the tip of her fingernails trusting my fingers. So easy. I gently grabbed the tip of each of her fingers then caressed each one in circles, like I was braiding her fingers. It was so comfortable to play with her fingers, like we'd been doing this every day. Perfect soft (red) fingernails. I chuckled at the thought of Mami seeing Andrea's red nails. We smoked cigarettes and listened to The Strokes from her iPod. We watched the ducks cornering mama raccoon, Andrea rooting for the raccoon and I, sadly, rooting for the ducks. The ducks won. I gently pulled her arm. We smoked more cigarettes. She played with my fingers, smoked more cigarettes. For a second I pretended I stroked Carmen's palm, Carmen's hairy arms. I'd been thinking so much about her and now I couldn't even make out the details of her face but only pieces, fragments of her body.

We smoked and smoked and smoked so many cigarettes that by eight p.m. I was made entirely of smoke, bones of smoke, skin of smoke, curls of smoke, if someone had blown on me I could have disappeared.

I asked Andrea for some perfumed cream so Mami wouldn't notice I'd been smoking. She squeezed some Victoria's Secret fruity cream on my hands and I rubbed it on my neck and hair. Here, she said spraying perfume, now you smell like me.

Then her boyfriend called.

Then I remembered Wilson was dining with us.

Andrea handed me an extra cigarette. Just let me know cuando quieras volver a fumar again, she said before walking off.

~

I can see her handing her passport to la señorita at the airport who then asks, ¿Usted tiene residencia de los Estados Unidos? And Carmen proudly hands Patricia or Zoraida her green card. And Patricia or Zoraida then asks Carmen if she packed her own bags, is she taking any encarguitos, does she reside in Miami, and what does she do in Miami? Alabar a Dios, Carmen responds. When she walks outside and up the stairs into the airplane, Carmen waves at the congregation that, crying from the inside of the airport, holds signs that read *CARMEN ES UN ÁNGEL, DIOS TE BENDIGA HIJITA, y GLORIA A DIOS.* The congregation causes such commotion the police have to escort them out with their fake guns and batons, until someone hands the Policía Bachiller a roll of bills and the congregation runs back inside sending kisses, kneeling in prayer. Carmen's hair is a mess, but there's still a stupid guy with a stupid *Colombia* mochila sitting next to her that no se calla about her beauty, qué churra, so she asks the azafata to change her seat. *Sí buenas tardes, the flight to Miami is three and a half hours exactly and the temperature right now in Miami is thirty degrees Celsius,* says the woman over the intercom. Carmen eats chicken instead of veggie pasta. She drinks cafecito Juan Valdez papá, while la señora de enfrente doesn't shut up about lo horrible que está Bogotá, yo ni sé para qué vuelvo, sí sí. Carmen tries to sleep but can't. Wears a *Jesucristo Es Mi Parcero* hoodie with pride as she walks to the bathroom. Carmen pees and for the first time thinks about me and remembers she didn't bring me anything. That's fine. Remembers she could give me one of those colorful manillas she bought at Usaquén, because I'm easy to please. And then Miami. And then it's time. And the Pastores blow up two hundred balloons that arch around the entrance and there's a long line of people waiting to hug her. I stand in line. I'm right behind Wilson, right before Paula who doesn't stop murmuring *Satanás Satanás* all the way until Wilson and Carmen hug, his hands up and down Carmen's back, he gives her a flower and doesn't look at me. Then it's my turn. Then I feel my skin moving. My skin moves, it opens to receive her, it's been saving that space between my bones for her, and I'm ready. She only shakes my hand, gently pats my back. Hola, Francisca. Y ni un besito y ni un te extraño y ni un let's talk later when all these motherfuckers leave. And so I'm screaming, cachaco. I'm screaming at her que cómo es posible that you didn't even send me un puto email, que cómo es posible, Carmen, that you didn't even say adiós, carajo, and the women all whisper ay qué vergüenza la hija de Myriam and the men carry me out but what I really want is for her to run her fingers through my hair, what I really want is for her to lie next to me with one hand on my stomach while I breathe in her neck, and I tell her this and before they throw me out into the streets she remembers—it was just a matter of time, a matter of refreshing her memory—and Carmen runs toward the door and the balloons explode and I feel her tongue inside me and the warmth of her body. She smells like strawberry and I trace her bushy eyebrows with my fingers. The Pastores explode. And Mami explodes. And Carmen leans in: I also missed you, pela'a.

~

La Tata called me to get into the car because we were late for service. I was wearing the greenish-blue plaid shirt I bought at the mall over my best black T-shirt and my skinny black jeans with the tiny hole but they looked so good, no extra loose fabric, and my butt looked firm. I'd never found anything else like them. Casual, you know, like I didn't care that I hadn't seen her in months.

Is *that* what you're wearing to church? asked Lucía, and I just walked right past her. Mami didn't even check my outfit. She almost left without me, but La Tata held the door open.

Dicho y hecho, mi reina. What did I see when we arrived at church? Balloons. And what color were the balloons? Gold (gold is joy, joy in Jesucristo, gold is celebration, celebration in the Espíritu Santo) and silver (because why not). La Tata all excited because that meant it was a special service and there would probably be food at the end from Mi Pequeña Colombia and La Tata loves their empanadas de carne.

Mami said, Oh that's today? But we don't even hear her, the three of us already out of the van embracing this hermano, that hermana, y yo buscando a Carmen. I didn't want her to sneak up on me, I wanted to know where she was so I could gauge my feelings. Wilson was there helping with the microphone setup. He winked at me from the stage and I looked around making sure nobody else saw it. Did Carmen know about us by now? Xiomara in a gold sequined shirt calling me with her fingers, Panchita mi niña come give me a kiss. The Pastora also came up to me, ¡Dios te bendiga, Francisca! Then hugged me in a weird way. She never just walked up to me and hugged me, not since I converted. I asked her about Carmen. Oh she's getting ready with all the shekinas backstage. Xiomara interjecting, Oh Carmencita is such an angel! And how she's grown in the past few months. Then the Pastor intervened and said, She's excited to see you!

Okay.

Grown? I didn't feel anything. I had felt everything already and now I was numb to all the excitement.

The service went as usual: the mingling, the one-hour

alabanza, the prédica about returning to Jesucristo, the testimonios, the absoluciones (Mami, as usual, fainted), the diezmo. This time the youth were not asked to leave. This is a celebration because our daughter has come home! the Pastora announced.

Mami dozed on and off next to me, her eyes watery after the absolución, her Bible open to the wrong Evangelio. I touched her hand and it was freezing. The last thing I wanted to do was take care of her in this moment. Damn, Mami. I looked at her sad face and wanted to blame her for something. Everything. Then her eyes flickered and I got scared.

Mami, I poked her. Mami, despiértate.

I am, she said. But she was already dreaming.

I asked La Tata for some water, she didn't have any. But I got some rum, she whispered. Quietly I snuck into the back of the room, past the hallway where the water fountain was, next to the shekinas' dressing room. Dark shadows moved in there, one of those bodies was Carmen. A dark fish swimming to me. I found a few Hershey's kisses, a banana, and grabbed them along with the glass of water. A song came on, thank God, and everyone rose to sing.

Mami slumped in the chair like a rag doll.

I had to be quick before anyone noticed, before they started whispering horrible things about her, making up stories, if anyone asked me I'd say she stayed up all night praying and gluing crosses, I wouldn't mention the pills, I wouldn't mention her crying on the sofa, I wouldn't mention her head resting on Wilson.

Mami, ven, tómate esto.

Gently I gave her the water, the chocolate, she wouldn't eat the banana. I knew her heart was crying but I refused to see it. Ven, I said, and placed her head on my shoulder, wrapped my arm tight around her.

I stroked her head.

She'd lost so much hair, I could feel bald spots. I'd found chunks of hair in different wastebaskets around the house but I hadn't known it was this bad. Weak light came through the windows. A hazy yellow colored the swaying heads, the singing bodies enclosing us that I couldn't hear, silent chants to Jesús that I couldn't make out, yelling so much it was invisible. Only Mami's paced breathing on my ear was audible. Her dark ocean roaring. I kissed the spots on her head.

Carmen looked at me looking at her.

She stood in between her parents onstage, holding hands with both as El Pastor elevated a prayer asking Dios to bless the congregation, bless his hija who was a servant of Papi Dios. I looked away not before a faint smile appeared on Carmen's face as she shut her eyes and yelled, ¡Amén! Cheers, alabanza, aleluya al Señor.

I barely recognized her.

I wanted to leave and pretend this had never happened.

The gaping feeling in my bones didn't know how to adjust. Her hair was long, ironed straight with golden highlights. She wore pearls? Yes, pearls in her ears. Even underneath her shekina dress I could tell her boobs were much bigger and I wondered if she'd gotten a boob job in Medellín. Carmen wasn't there. She wasn't inside that polished body, that smooth brown skin with plucked eyebrows and that perfected flipping of hair that didn't belong to my Carmen. My skin had opened up waiting for her and she didn't show up. Who is this. How do we zip Carmen out of that costume. She'd never mentioned surgery and I wondered if the Pastora forced her and I wondered if she turned into a beauty queen to move further from me and closer to God. And now a boycott was taking place, an alarm blaring inside me: *Get away. Get away.* Her face was a face and not Carmen. I wanted to leave. The service was almost over and Mami was already sitting up straight at least. She wanted more water. I got her more water and she popped two pills.

Mami, I said, are you okay?

Que sí, nena. Your mamá is always okay.

I had no time for this, I wanted to leave. Mami, I said, can we please leave now? La Tata already on her way to the empanada line, Lucía hugging Carmen. Mami, I repeated, I can drive. I didn't know how to drive. She chuckled, Por Dios nena. At least she smiled. I knew we weren't going to leave for a while. I tried making small talk with a few people as far away from Carmen as possible, then I noticed I still had the cigarette Andrea gave me. I stepped outside into the parking lot and walked behind the dumpster.

Part of me wanted to stare at Carmen, make sure there wasn't a zipper on her body where I could unzip this costume and have my costeña back. I smoked praying the cigarette wouldn't end, gazing at the darkened, half-dead palm trees. Cars raced beyond this slab of cement. The air as crisp and cool as it'd get that year. I saw a trail of ants around my feet carrying tiny pieces of leaves on their backs, trabajando como hormigas, Mami used to say. Working like ants. When I blinked again she was there.

¿Y es que you aren't gonna say hi to me o qué, pela'a? There it was: pela'a. Pela'a. But I didn't feel anything.

Hola Carmen, I said and gave her a distant hug. She smelled like an old woman, like a tía.

Up close I also noticed something was off with her nose. She talked with so much ownership, like pretty Colombian girls do. It bored me. *Aquí estás*, I thought, *toda una reina. Reinita de Dios*. I didn't want to be there, piecing her together or apart. I wished she'd never come back so I could still have her.

We chatted for a bit. Stupid small talk. She talked about the congregation in Colombia, congratulated me on my relationship with Wilson, and then mentioned something or other about helping her with outreach.

I don't think I want to be part of the Jóvenes anymore, I said without thinking. I may take a break from church.

You can't take a break from Jesús, she said in a *duh* way. He's already *here*, and she touched the space between my boobs.

I could tell she was waiting for my reaction. I stood erect against the wall still smoking. I let her hand stay on my skin for a few seconds, red fingernails on my green plaid shirt. I blew smoke away from her. When I took her hand she said, I have a new boyfriend, un rolito más lindo who's moving here next week—but by then I wasn't even listening. I knew Carmen wasn't there. And yet. I gently caressed her hand, kissed the top of it, and told her I was glad. You look very happy, I said and left.

~

That night Wilson ate dinner with us. Mustard chicken, habichuelas, and, luckily, platanitos. That was La Tata's touch and I thanked her for that. Mami and Wilson were finishing the Nativity scene costumes while watching Joel Osteen on the TV.

Mami, you can't even understand what he's saying, I said.

That's the point, Mami responded with a threaded needle between her lips. I'm learning inglés.

Wilson cut pieces of brown, blue, red textile and arranged the finished holy dresses in a Walmart box by the door. They did this all night. I went into my room. A vast relief in not being up for anything—nothing—combed through me. No Mami. No Wilson. No iglesia. No Carmen. No Francisca.

Carmen left so much space in my skin.

I looked for the rest of the money and rolled it inside my hoodie, Lucía sound asleep on her bed murmuring the entire Eclesiastés. I flipped on the ceiling fan. Mami and Wilson sleeping on the couch, snuggling together, her mouth slightly open, her right hand on his chest. Styrofoam crosses around them. I grabbed a packet of Pop-Tarts from the kitchen. Outside, the night was chilly but warm enough to walk. At the corner La Tata and Roberto exchanged murmurs and Sprite cans. I walked and walked until I saw the Heather Glen Apartment Complex sign. *Welcome Home!* it said underneath. This is a stupid idea. I didn't even know where to catch a bus out of Florida. I walked to the pool and saw someone lighting a cigarette. Andrea, of course.

What are you doing here? I said.

She handed me a cigarette. What are *you* doing here?

Looking for you, I lied.

Mentirosa, Francisca. I could see her teeth smiling in the darkness.

Ven acá, she said and I rolled another lounge chair next to hers.

We lay there smoking and eating Pop-Tarts side by side while a pair of raccoons ransacked the garbage. I pressed my hand into hers. We stayed like that for what seemed like hours, then she rolled toward me, pulling me to her, letting all her warmth cover me like a blanket. She kissed the back of my neck and I pretended that I wasn't crying.

ACKNOWLEDGMENTS

Mil gracias to my family—birth and chosen—for all the love, encouragement, and support. Thank you Ma, María Estella Lopera Juan, for answering every church question with an incredibly kind and open heart. To Michelle Tea for championing this novel and being an all-around generous badass. To my editor Lauren Rosemary Hook for believing in Francisca, her Spanglish, and the world that swallows her. To the rest of the Feminist Press crew—Jamia Wilson, Jisu Kim, Drew Stevens, Nick Whitney, Lucia Brown, and Dorsa Djalilzadeh—thank you. Hearty thanks to all the people who read parts of this novel and provided feedback: Nona Caspers, Miah Jeffra, Carson Becker, Chad Koch, Ploy Pirapokin, Luke Dani Blue, and Lauren O'Neal. Auntie Truong Tran, thank you for the writing space and kiki. To my grandmother, Alba Corina de Jesús Juan, for raising me a punta de telenovelas and stories. Gracias, Brush Creek Foundation for the Arts and the San Francisco Arts Commission, for taking a chance on this story. To Daniela Delgado Lopera, porque ajá. Rebeka Rodriguez, my heart, thank you.

Amethyst Editions
at the Feminist Press

Amethyst Editions is a modern, queer
imprint founded by Michelle Tea

**Against Memoir: Complaints,
Confessions & Criticisms**
by Michelle Tea

Black Wave by Michelle Tea

The Not Wives by Carley Moore

**Original Plumbing: The Best of Ten Years
of Trans Male Culture**
edited by Amos Mac and Rocco Kayiatos

Since I Laid My Burden Down by Brontez Purnell

The Summer of Dead Birds by Ali Liebegott

Tabitha and Magoo Dress Up Too by Michelle Tea,
illustrated by Ellis van der Does

We Were Witches by Ariel Gore

amethyst editions

The Feminist Press publishes books that
ignite movements and social transformation.
Celebrating our legacy, we lift up insurgent
and marginalized voices from around the
world to build a more just future.

See our complete list of books at
feministpress.org

THE FEMINIST PRESS
AT THE CITY UNIVERSITY OF NEW YORK
FEMINISTPRESS.ORG